NEW YORK RE
CLASSICS

MW01199784

MEMORIES OF THE FUTURE

SIGIZMUND KRZHIZHANOVSKY (1887–1950), the Ukrainian-born son of Catholic Poles, studied law and classical philology at Kiev University. After graduation and two summers spent exploring Europe, he was obliged to clerk for an attorney. A sinecure, the job allowed him to devote the bulk of his time to the study of literature and his own writing. In 1920, after a brief stint in the Red Army, Krzhizhanovsky began lecturing intensively in Kiev on the theater and music. The lectures continued in Moscow, where he moved in 1922, by then well known in literary circles. Lodged in a cell-like room on the Arbat, Krzhizhanovsky wrote steadily for close to two decades. His philosophical and satirical stories with fantastical plots ignored official injunctions to portray the new Soviet state in a positive light. Three separate efforts to print different collections were quashed by the censors, a fourth by World War II. Not until 1989 could these surreal fictions begin to be published. Like Poe, Krzhizhanovsky takes us to the edge of the abyss and forces us to look into it. "I am interested," he said, "not in the arithmetic, but in the algebra of life."

JOANNE TURNBULL has translated a number of books from Russian—including Andrei Sinyavsky's *Soviet Civilization* and *Ivan the Fool*, Asar Eppel's *The Grassy Street*, and Andrei Sergeyev's *Stamp Album*, and Sigizmund Krzhizhanovsky's Seven Stories, winner of the 2007 Rossica Translation Prize—all in collaboration with Nikolai Formozov. She lives in Moscow.

MEMORIES OF THE FUTURE

SIGIZMUND KRZHIZHANOVSKY

Translated by
JOANNE TURNBULL
with Nikolai Formozov

NEW YORK REVIEW BOOKS

New York

THIS IS A NEW YORK REVIEW BOOK
PUBLISHED BY THE NEW YORK REVIEW OF BOOKS
435 Hudson Street, New York, NY 10014
www.nyrb.com

Stories copyright © by Éditions Verdier
Translation copyright © 2006, 2009 by Joanne Turnbull and Nikolai Formozov

Published by arrangement with Editions Verdier, which publishes these stories
under the following titles: "Quadraturin," "Le Marque-page," "Le Thème
étranger," "L'Embranchement," "La Treizeième Catégorie de la raison," and
"Mémoires du futur."

Library of Congress Cataloging-in-Publication Data

Krzhizhanovskii, Sigizmund, 1887–1950.
  [Short stories. English. Selections]
  Memories of the future / by Sigizmund Krzhizhanovsky ; translated and with
an introduction by Joanne Turnbull.
      p. cm. — (New York Review Books classics)
  ISBN 978-1-59017-319-0 (alk. paper)
  1. Krzhizhanovskii, Sigizmund, 1887–1950—Translations into English.
  2. Short stories, Russian—Translations into English. I. Turnbull, Joanne.
  II. Title.
  PG3476.K782A6 2009
  891.7342—dc22

                                    2009009752

ISBN 978-1-59017-319-0

Printed in the United States of America on acid-free paper.
10 9 8 7 6 5 4 3 2 1

CONTENTS

INTRODUCTION

> "I live in such a distant future that my future
> seems to me past, spent, and turned to dust."
> SIGIZMUND KRZHIZHANOVSKY

IN 1959, in his now-famous essay denouncing Soviet socialist realism, Andrei Sinyavsky wished for "a phantasmagoric art with hypotheses instead of a purpose and grotesque instead of descriptions of everyday life." One must learn, he said, "how to be truthful with the help of absurd fantasy." Sinyavsky could not have known then that Sigizmund Krzhizhanovsky (1887–1950) had done just that. Krzhizhanovsky—whose experimental realism features hyperbole, irony, paradox, and phantasms—was long dead and his writings (novels, stories, plays, essays, almost all unpublished) buried in the State Archives. Among them, "Memories of the Future."

Born in Kiev to Catholic Poles, Krzhizhanovsky was the youngest of five children, the only son, highly musical. As an adolescent, he secretly read Kant's *Critique of Pure Reason*, a deeply unsettling experience: "Before it had all seemed so simple: things cast shadows. But now it turned out that shadows cast things, or perhaps things didn't exist at all." Kant, as he put it, had "erased the fine line between 'I' and 'not I.'" Soon after that, he came across Shakespeare. In the mail. Unbeknownst to him, his father, an accountant at a sugar refinery, had ordered a volume in translation: "The translation was rough and inexact, but I began to read the book—and suddenly I felt that I had a friend who could protect me from the metaphysical delusion."

Krzhizhanovsky took a degree in law at Kiev University while mastering half a dozen languages and exploring Europe. After the Revolution of 1917 and a brief stint in the Red Army (manning his guard post he would recite Virgil to himself in the original), he lectured intensively in Kiev on the theater and music. He abandoned the poetry he had been publishing in journals ("I'm enough of a poet not to pen verses") and began writing stories. One of his first, a Gogolesque adventure called "The Runaway Fingers" (1922), follows the rebellious hand of a world-famous pianist as it flees the stage in mid-performance. But it was his move to Moscow—a quasi-character in many of Krzhizhanovsky's stories—that would galvanize his fiction: philosophical "novellas," as he called them, with fantastical plots.

The heroes of these fictions are often "former people"—as those for whom the Bolshevik regime had no use came to be known. Former people included members of the nobility, the clergy, the merchant class, and, most important for Krzhizhanovsky, doubting intellectuals. Under Soviet rule, these ostensibly unreliable citizens—damned by their origins and/or by their vocations—were in perennial danger of exile or imprisonment or worse. If they weren't forced out of their apartments, they were forced to share them with some of the thousands upon thousands of newcomers descending on Moscow and other cities in the wake of the Russian Civil War.

A newcomer himself, Krzhizhanovsky arrived at the Bryansk Station in the spring of 1922 armed with several letters of introduction. With their help, he hoped to find a room. Not an easy task. "People who had been to Moscow scared you," a character in one of his stories frets, "the buildings are all packed to the rafters. You have to camp: in vestibules, on backstairs, boulevard benches, in asphalt cauldrons and dustbins." One letter, to Nikolai Berdyaev, the religious philosopher, led nowhere: Berdyaev, a former person, would be sent into foreign exile that summer. But another letter, to Ludmila Severtsova, wife of the noted evolutionist, produced lodgings on the old Arbat, a long, crooked street in the heart of the city. An elderly count who resided at number 44 allowed Krzhizhanovsky (very tall, thin, slightly stooped, with a pale nervous face and a pince-nez) to occupy a small, dark room at the back of his apartment.

Into that unfurnished space, as cramped as Sutulin's "matchbox" in "Quadraturin," Krzhizhanovsky insinuated a wooden bed with a horsehair mattress, a desk with two drawers, an armchair with a hard seat, and a set of hanging bookshelves. Rather than take money for the room, the count suggested that Krzhizhanovsky take paid English lessons from him. The lessons did not last long. The count soon died, the countess moved out, and far less sympathetic neighbors moved in to what would now become a communal apartment. "The crowdedness in Moscow is dreadful," the children's poet Kornei Chukovsky wrote in his journal in 1923. "In apartments a particular *Moscow* smell has set in—from the accumulation of human bodies. In every apartment every minute one hears the flushing of the water in the WC, the WC toils without respite. And on the front door there's a note: one ring for so-and-so, two rings for someone else, three rings for a third person, and so on."

Krzhizhanovsky was more circumspect about the closeness of his quarters: "I've discovered a new way of successfully stretching out my legs while sitting at my desk," he exulted to a friend. The year was 1924. He was teaching drama theory in the experimental studios at the Kamerny Theater and had begun a lifelong love affair with his adopted city. The following year the literary journal *Rossiya* would print his story "Shtempel: Moskva" (Postmark: Moscow): thirteen letters to a friend in the provinces about the meanings of Moscow. Like Krzhizhanovsky, the fictional letter-writer is a newcomer whose affection for the city is fostered in part by the smallness of his room. In order to think a thought through, he likes to pace from corner to corner, but the corners of his cubbyhole are too close together to permit pacing. So out onto the

Arbat he strides, up to Arbat Square, and along the boulevards, and on and on—across the river, perhaps, or into an old cemetery or up to his favorite Krutitsky Tower. He looks and he listens to "the timid peals of church bells...reminding us of *what is most nonexistent* in this country of nonexistences: God."

Krzhizhanovsky's characters, like Krzhizhanovsky himself, tend to be walkers and thinkers for whom prosperity is measured in meals taken daily ("I have lunch every day—and that's already a lot," he confided to a friend in 1925) and decent pairs of shoes ("The toes of my new shoes have a proud and perky look: they're evidently hoping to shuffle off to a better future"). Like the theme catcher in "The Bookmark," these heroes live "outside of things, surrounded by formulas and phantasms." They strike up conversations on boulevard benches with whoever happens to be sitting at the other end or in the cheap canteens where they eat, when they do.

"I am a crossed-out person," Krzhizhanovsky said of himself. Many of his characters, too, have been crossed out by the Revolution ("the lifequake"). They have lost their moorings in an illogical world whose margins they inhabit: "I don't understand," says a man in "The Branch Line." "Understanding," comes the reply, "is strictly forbidden."

In a marvelously titled essay, "Strany, kotorykh nyet" (Countries That Don't Exist), on man's imaginative attempts to expand "the walls of the world," Krzhizhanovsky refers at one point to *Gulliver's Travels*: "Interestingly, in both the first and second parts, Swift, as a true artist, allows himself to violate the proper dimensions only once—to shrink or to enlarge the bodies of the people among whom his hero lives. Otherwise, he is exceedingly precise and nowhere does he deviate from a realistic manner of writing." Here, in essence, is Krzhizhanovsky's own creative method, what he calls "experimental realism."

Over the next five years (1925–30), while working as an editor for the *Great Soviet Encyclopedia*, he would compose many of his most outstanding novellas, including the seven in this collection, samples all of his boundless imagination, black humor, and breathtaking irony: a man loses his way in the vast black waste of his own small room; the Eiffel Tower runs amok; a kind soul dreams of selling "everything you need for suicide"; an absent-minded passenger boards the wrong train, winding up in a place where night is day, nightmares are the reality, and the backs of all facts have been broken; a man out looking for work comes across a line for logic but doesn't join it as there's no guarantee the logic will last; a sociable corpse misses his own funeral; an inventor gets a glimpse of the far-from-radiant communist future.

(Krzhizhanovsky may have something in common with Kafka, but as the critic John Bayley has noted, "the flavor and personality of his writing is all his own." In point of fact, Krzhizhanovsky first read Kafka only in 1939—near the end of his writing career—and was very surprised.)

Written in 1929, "Memories of the Future" is the tale of inventor Max Shterer and his "timecutter," a machine that allows him to travel backward and forward in time. Fascinated by time as a child, Max has no use for H. G. Wells's *The Time Machine*. Krzhizhanovsky's short novel is not that. It takes place in a real country (Russia), in real time (beginning when Max—the author's rough contemporary—is four, skipping ahead to 1957, then dropping back to 1928), against a backdrop of real events (the 1905 and 1917 revolutions, the World War, and Lenin's New Economic Policy).

Expelled from university on the eve of the war, Max is sent to fight and promptly taken prisoner by the Germans. By the time he returns to Moscow, his father has died, the Bolsheviks have seized power, and his inheritance (more than enough to fund his timecutter) has been inherited by "the people." Reduced to a hand-to-mouth existence, he eventually meets an anxious group of former people willing to pawn what possessions they have left to get out of the Soviet present.

Krzhizhanovsky, whom one Russian critic has termed "a spy for European culture in the Bolshevik night," took a dim and dispirited view of the Soviet present, especially the literature—"all that mousing about with pens" ("Someone Else's Theme"), those "empty literary boxcars" ("The Bookmark"). Indeed, the literature train kept passing him by. "I have a platform ticket to literature," he lamented in a notebook. "I see other people seeing people off and going away. But I'm not meeting anyone and not seeing anyone off." Not only were the novellas in this collection never published in his lifetime, they were never so much as shown to a publisher. When Max Shterer submits his own, autobiographical "Memories of the Future" to a publisher, the latter is appalled:

"Listen here, what is this?!" he sputters. "Have you given any thought to what you've written?"

"I had hoped that other people might do that," says Shterer. "My concern is the facts."

"Facts, facts! Who's seen them, these facts of yours? Where, I ask you, is the witness who will come forward and corroborate them?"

"He's coming. Or don't you hear him? I mean the actual future."

Krzhizhanovsky's stories, the ones he did make public, had not so much their readers as their listeners. He gave readings, formal and informal, in Kiev, then in Moscow, and later on in Koktebel, on the Black Sea, where he was a guest some summers of the poet and painter M. A. Voloshin. Another admirer was E. F. Nikitina. She regularly hosted a distinguished literary circle at her Moscow flat on Tverskoi Boulevard and, during the temporary return to capitalist trade (New Economic Policy or NEP), ran a publishing cooperative, Nikitinskie Subbotniki.

In 1931, Krzhizhanovsky left his job working on the *Great Soviet Encyclopedia*, having fallen out with its acting director, P. N. Lebedev-Polyansky, who doubled as the head of Glavlit, the top Soviet censor. Unemployed and unpublished (since 1925), Krzhizhanovsky now found himself—like Shushashin in "Red Snow" —in danger of being banished from Moscow as a "nonworking element." The resourceful Nikitina came to his rescue by quickly printing the only book of his ever to appear in his lifetime: *Poetika zaglavii* (A Poetics of Titles). It was a booklet, in fact, a thirty-four-page monograph on a neutral subject that Krzhizhanovsky cared deeply about: the art of composing titles. In it, he chides writers for clamping titles on texts "pell-mell and in haste, like the hats on their heads." Just as a book is a distillation of "life's phraseology," so its title should be a distillation of the book. "If the title is right," says a character in "The Bookmark," who also happens to feel strongly about titles, "the whole text will hang on it, like a coat on a peg."

Be that as it may, Soviet editors in the throes of promoting proletarian culture did not look kindly on Krzhizhanovsky's compositions: they were "untimely," they said, "not contemporary." The steady rejections of those stories Krzhizhanovsky did venture to submit and their later dismissal by the great Gorky himself (socialist realism's main architect) forced him to resort to other forms in order to eat: dramatizations of Chesterton's *The Man Who Was Thursday* (which was performed) and Pushkin's *Eugene Onegin* (which was banned); articles on laconism and the psychological novel for a dictionary of literary terms; essays on the dramaturgy of the chessboard and the art of the epigraph, on Shaw and Shakespeare.

Why did Shakespeare need the image of the dream that runs through all his plays? "The answer is plain," says Krzhizhanovsky. "A dream is the only instance *when we apprehend our thoughts as external facts.*" (The italics are his.) Krzhizhanovsky's fictions, too, take place in a false-bottomed world: a world where dreams have the weight of reality and nightmares come true, where characters get away from their authors, locomotives outrun logic, and people walk on the sunny side, but only at night. "In revolutions, events attain a speed approaching that of scene changes in a play," Krzhizhanovsky wrote in 1934. "Thought winds up in the position of the Shakespearean 'fool,' who comes too late by only one scene, but always and invariably comes too late."

Krzhizhanovsky's belated acceptance into the Soviet Writers Union in 1939 did nothing to help his lyrical, satirical phantasmagorias past the censors, but it did afford them a lower berth in the State Archive of Literature and Arts. There they were delivered after his death in 1950 by the former actress Anna Bovshek, his longtime companion and eventual wife. There all but one of the works in this collection would be unearthed by scholars a quarter of a century later and first published some fifteen years after that. All but "Red Snow"—perhaps the most unorthodox of all of Krzhizhanovsky's unorthodox stories. Long thought lost, it was found by chance in Kiev in 2005. Bovshek, as it turned out, had taken the story with her when she left Moscow in 1967 for her native Odessa. She had evidently been afraid, says Vadim Perelmuter, Krzhizhanovsky's Schliemann, that the presence of "Red Snow" among the writer's manuscripts would threaten the survival of the rest.

At the end of "Shtempel: Moskva," the letter-writer learns—to his consternation and horror—that his correspondent in the provinces has taken the liberty of typing all his letters and sending them back to Moscow. To a publisher! Frantic, he races off to retrieve them. Rushing along the boulevard, his heart starts to pound so hard he has to sit down on a bench to catch his breath: calm people are going calmly by; children are digging busily in the sand. Now his thoughts take a different tack. "Perhaps it's all for the best," he reasons. "Words, once they've broken away from your pen, might as well go, like orphan urchins, where they will—they have *their own fate.*"

—JOANNE TURNBULL

For facts about Krzhizhanovsky's life that could not be gleaned from his own writings or from the published reminiscences of friends, I am indebted to Vadim Perelmuter, compiler and editor of Krzhizhanovsky's *Collected Works* in five volumes in Russian (St. Petersburg: Symposium, 2001–2010).

MEMORIES OF THE FUTURE

QUADRATURIN

FROM OUTSIDE there came a soft knock at the door: once.
Pause. And again—a bit louder and bonier: twice.

Sutulin, without rising from his bed, extended—as was his
wont—a foot toward the knock, threaded a toe through the door
handle, and pulled. The door swung open. On the threshold,
head grazing the lintel, stood a tall, gray man the color of the
dusk seeping in at the window.

Before Sutulin could set his feet on the floor the visitor stepped
inside, wedged the door quietly back into its frame, and jabbing
first one wall, then another, with a briefcase dangling from an
apishly long arm, said, "Yes: a matchbox."

"What?"

"Your room, I say: it's a matchbox. How many square feet?"

"Eighty-six and a bit."

"Precisely. May I?"

And before Sutulin could open his mouth, the visitor sat
down on the edge of the bed and hurriedly unbuckled his bulging
briefcase. Lowering his voice almost to a whisper, he went on.
"I'm here on business. You see, I, that is, we, are conducting, how
shall I put it . . . well, experiments, I suppose. Under wraps for now.
I won't hide the fact: a well-known foreign firm has an interest in
our concern. You want the electric-light switch? No, don't bother:
I'll only be a minute. So then: we have discovered—this is a secret
now—an agent for biggerizing rooms. Well, won't you try it?"

The stranger's hand popped out of the briefcase and proffered Sutulin a narrow dark tube, not unlike a tube of paint, with a tightly screwed cap and a leaden seal. Sutulin fidgeted bewilderedly with the slippery tube and, though it was nearly dark in the room, made out on the label the clearly printed word: QUADRATURIN. When he raised his eyes, they came up against the fixed, unblinking stare of his interlocutor.

"So then, you'll take it? The price? Goodness, it's gratis. Just for advertising. Now if you'll"—the guest began quickly leafing through a sort of ledger he had produced from the same briefcase—"just sign this book (a short testimonial, so to say). A pencil? Have mine. Where? Here: column three. That's it."

His ledger clapped shut, the guest straightened up, wheeled around, stepped to the door... and a minute later Sutulin, having snapped on the light, was considering with puzzledly raised eyebrows the clearly embossed letters: QUADRATURIN.

On closer inspection it turned out that this zinc packet was tightly fitted—as is often done by the makers of patented agents—with a thin transparent paper whose ends were expertly glued together. Sutulin removed the paper sheath from the Quadraturin, unfurled the rolled-up text, which showed through the paper's transparent gloss, and read:

DIRECTIONS

Dissolve one teaspoon of the QUADRATURIN essence in one cup of water. Wet a piece of cotton wool or simply a clean rag with the solution; apply this to those of the room's internal walls designated for proliferspansion. This mixture leaves no stains, will not damage wallpaper, and even contributes—incidentally—to the extermination of bedbugs.

Thus far Sutulin had been only puzzled. Now his puzzlement was gradually overtaken by another feeling, strong and disturbing. He stood up and tried to pace from corner to corner, but the corners of this living cage were too close together: a walk amounted to almost nothing but turns, from toe to heel and back again. Sutulin stopped short, sat down, and closing his eyes, gave himself up to thoughts, which began: Why not...? What if...? Suppose...? To his left, not three feet away from his ear, someone was driving an iron spike into the wall. The hammer kept slipping, banging, and aiming, it seemed, at Sutulin's head. Rubbing his temples, he opened his eyes: the black tube lay in the middle of the narrow table, which had managed somehow to insinuate itself between the bed, the windowsill, and the wall. Sutulin tore away the leaden seal, and the cap spun off in a spiral. From out of the round aperture came a bitterish gingery smell. The smell made his nostrils flare pleasantly.

"Hmm...Let's try it. Although..."

And, having removed his jacket, the possessor of Quadraturin proceeded to the experiment. Stool up against door, bed into middle of room, table on top of bed. Nudging across the floor a saucer of transparent liquid, its glassy surface gleaming with a slightly yellowish tinge, Sutulin crawled along after it, systematically dipping a handkerchief wound around a pencil into the Quadraturin and daubing the floorboards and patterned wallpaper. The room really was, as that man today had said, a matchbox. But Sutulin worked slowly and carefully, trying not to miss a single corner. This was rather difficult since the liquid really did evaporate in an instant or was absorbed (he couldn't tell which) without leaving even the slightest film; there was only its smell, increasingly pungent and spicy, making his head spin, confounding his fingers, and causing his knees, pinned to the floor, to tremble slightly. When he had finished with the floorboards and the bottom of the walls, Sutulin rose to his strangely weak and heavy feet and continued to work standing up. Now and then he had to add a little more of the essence. The tube was gradually emptying. It was already night outside. In the kitchen, to the right, a bolt came crashing down. The apartment was readying for bed. Trying not to make any noise, the experimenter, clutching the last of the essence, climbed up onto the bed and from the bed up onto the tottering table: only the ceiling remained to be Quadraturin-ized. But just then someone banged on the wall with his fist. "What's going on? People are trying to sleep, but he's..."

Turning around at the sound, Sutulin fumbled: the slippery tube spurted out of his hand and landed on the floor. Balancing carefully, Sutulin got down with his already drying brush, but it was too late. The tube was empty, and the rapidly fading spot around it smelled stupefyingly sweet. Grasping at the wall in his exhaustion (to fresh sounds of discontent from the left), he summoned his last bit of strength, put the furniture back where it belonged, and without undressing, fell into bed. A black sleep instantly descended on him from above: both tube and man were empty.

2

Two voices began in a whisper. Then by degrees of sonority—from piano to *mf*, from *mf* to *fff*—they cut into Sutulin's sleep.

"Outrageous. I don't want any new tenants popping out from under that skirt of yours... Put up with all that racket?!"

"Can't just dump it in the garbage..."

"I don't want to hear about it. You were told: no dogs, no cats, no children..." At which point there ensued such *fff* that Sutulin was ripped once and for all from his sleep; unable to part eyelids stitched together with exhaustion, he reached—as was his wont—for the edge of the table on which stood the clock. Then it began. His hand groped for a long time, grappling air: there was no clock and no table. Sutulin opened his eyes at once. In an instant he was sitting up, looking dazedly around the room. The table that usually stood right here, at the head of the bed, had moved off into the middle of a faintly familiar, large, but ungainly room.

Everything was the same: the skimpy, threadbare rug that had trailed after the table somewhere up ahead of him, and the photographs, and the stool, and the yellow patterns on the wallpaper. But they were all strangely spread out inside the expanded room cube.

"Quadraturin," thought Sutulin, "is terrific!"

And he immediately set about rearranging the furniture to fit the new space. But nothing worked: the abbreviated rug, when moved back beside the bed, exposed worn, bare floorboards; the table and the stool, pushed by habit against the head of the bed, had disencumbered an empty corner latticed with cobwebs and littered with shreds and tatters, once artfully masked by the corner's own crowdedness and the shadow of the table. With a triumphant but slightly frightened smile, Sutulin went all around his new, practically squared square, scrutinizing every detail. He noted with displeasure that the room had grown more in some places than in others: an external corner, the angle of which was now obtuse, had made the wall askew; Quadraturin, apparently, did not work as well on internal corners; carefully as Sutulin had applied the essence, the experiment had produced somewhat uneven results.

The apartment was beginning to stir. Out in the corridor, occupants shuffled to and fro. The bathroom door kept banging. Sutulin walked up to the threshold and turned the key to the right. Then, hands clasped behind his back, he tried pacing from corner to corner: it worked. Sutulin laughed with joy. How about that! At last! But then he thought: they may hear my footsteps—through the walls—on the right, on the left, at the back. For a minute he stood stock-still. Then he quickly bent down—his temples had suddenly begun to ache with yesterday's sharp thin pain—and, having removed his boots, gave himself up to the pleasure of a stroll, moving soundlessly about in only his socks.

"May I come in?"

The voice of the landlady. He was on the point of going to the door and unlocking it when he suddenly remembered: he mustn't. "I'm getting dressed. Wait a minute. I'll be right out."

"It's all very well, but it complicates things. Say I lock the door and take the key with me. What about the keyhole? And then there's the window: I'll have to get curtains. Today." The pain in his temples had become thinner and more nagging. Sutulin gathered up his papers in haste. It was time to go to the office. He dressed. Pushed the pain under his cap. And listened at the door: no one there. He quickly opened it. Quickly slipped out. Quickly turned the key. Now.

Waiting patiently in the entrance hall was the landlady.

"I wanted to talk to you about that girl, what's her name. Can you believe it, she's submitted an application to the House Committee saying she's—"

"I've heard. Go on."

"It's nothing to you. No one's going to take your eighty-six square feet away. But put yourself in my—"

"I'm in a hurry," he nodded, put on his cap, and flew down the stairs.

3

On his way home from the office, Sutulin paused in front of the window of a furniture dealer: the long curve of a couch, an extendable round table . . . it would be nice—but how could he carry them in past the eyes and the questions? They would guess, they couldn't help but guess . . .

He had to limit himself to the purchase of a yard of canary-yellow material (he did, after all, need a curtain). He didn't stop by the cafe: he had no appetite. He needed to get home—it would be easier there: he could reflect, look around, and make adjustments at leisure. Having unlocked the door to his room, Sutulin gazed about to see if anyone was looking: they weren't. He walked in. Then he switched on the light and stood there for a long time, his arms spread flat against the wall, his heart beating wildly: *this he had not expected*—not at all.

The Quadraturin was *still* working. During the eight or nine hours Sutulin had been out, it had pushed the walls at least another seven feet apart; the floorboards, stretched by invisible rods, rang out at his first step—like organ pipes. The entire room, distended and monstrously misshapen, was beginning to frighten and torment him. Without taking off his coat, Sutulin sat down on the stool and surveyed his spacious and at the same time oppressive coffin-shaped living box, trying to understand what had caused this unexpected effect. Then he remembered: he hadn't done the ceiling—the essence had run out. His living box was spreading only sideways, without rising even an inch upward.

"Stop. I have to stop this Quadraturinizing thing. Or I'll..." He pressed his palms to his temples and listened: the corrosive pain, lodged under his skull since morning, was still drilling away. Though the windows in the house opposite were dark, Sutulin took cover behind the yellow length of curtain. His head would not stop aching. He quietly undressed, snapped out the light, and got into bed. At first he slept, then he was awoken by a feeling of awkwardness. Wrapping the covers more tightly about him, Sutulin again dropped off, and once more an unpleasant sense of mooringlessness interfered with his sleep. He raised himself up on one palm and felt all around him with his free hand: the wall was gone. He struck a match. Um-hmm: he blew out the flame and hugged his knees till his elbows cracked. "It's growing, damn it, it's still growing." Clenching his teeth, Sutulin crawled out of bed and, trying not to make any noise, gently edged first the front legs, then the back legs of the bed toward the receding wall. He felt a little shivery. Without turning the light on again, he went to look for his coat on that nail in the corner so as to wrap himself up more warmly. But there was no hook on the wall where it had been yesterday, and he had to feel around for several seconds before his hands chanced upon fur. Twice more during a night that was long and as nagging as the pain in his temples, Sutulin pressed his head and knees to the wall as he was falling asleep and, when he awoke, fiddled about with the legs of the bed again. In doing this—mechanically, meekly, lifelessly—he tried, though it was still dark outside, not to open his eyes: it was better that way.

4

Toward dusk the next evening, having served out his day, Sutulin was approaching the door to his room: he did not quicken his step and, upon entering, felt neither consternation nor horror. When the dim, sixteen-candle-power bulb lit up somewhere in the distance beneath the long low vault, its yellow rays struggling to reach the dark, ever-receding corners of the vast and dead, yet empty barrack, which only recently, before Quadraturin, had been a cramped but cozy, warm, and lived-in cubbyhole, he walked resignedly toward the yellow square of the window, now diminished by perspective; he tried to count his steps. From there, from a bed squeezed pitifully and fearfully in the corner by the window, he stared dully and wearily through deep-boring pain at the swaying shadows nestled against the floorboards, and at the smooth low overhang of the ceiling. "So, something forces its way out of a tube and can't stop squaring: a square squared, a square of squares squared. I've got to think faster than it: if I don't out-think it, it will outgrow me and..." And suddenly someone was hammering on the door, "Citizen Sutulin, are you in there?"

From the same faraway place came the muffled and barely audible voice of the landlady. "He's in there. Must be asleep."

Sutulin broke into a sweat: "What if I don't get there in time, and they go ahead and..." And, trying not to make a sound (let them think he was asleep), he slowly made his way through the darkness to the door. There.

"Who is it?"

"Oh, open up! Why's the door locked? Remeasuring Commission. We'll remeasure and leave."

Sutulin stood with his ear pressed to the door. Through the thin panel he could hear the clump of heavy boots. Figures were being mentioned, and room numbers.

"This room next. Open up!"

With one hand Sutulin gripped the knob of the electric-light switch and tried to twist it, as one might twist the head of a bird: the switch spattered light, then crackled, spun feebly around, and drooped down. Again someone hammered on the door: "Well!"

Sutulin turned the key to the left. A broad black shape squeezed itself into the doorway.

"Turn on the light."

"It's burned out."

Clutching at the door handle with his left hand and the bundle of wire with his right, he tried to hide the extended space from view. The black mass took a step back.

"Who's got a match? Give me that box. We'll have a look anyway. Do things right."

Suddenly the landlady began whining, "Oh, what is there to look at? Eighty-six square feet for the eighty-sixth time. Measuring the room won't make it any bigger. He's a quiet man, home from a long day at the office—and you won't let him rest: have to measure and remeasure. Whereas other people, who have no right to the space, but—"

"Ain't that the truth," the black mass muttered and, rocking from boot to boot, gently and even almost affectionately drew the door to the light. Sutulin was left alone on wobbling, cottony legs in the middle of the four-cornered, inexorably growing, and proliferating darkness.

5

He waited until their steps had died away, then quickly dressed and went out. They'd be back, to remeasure or check they hadn't under-measured or whatever. He could finish thinking better here—from crossroad to crossroad. Toward night a wind came up: it rattled the bare frozen branches on the trees, shook the shadows loose, droned in the wires, and beat against walls, as if trying to knock them down. Hiding the needlelike pain in his temples from the wind's buffets, Sutulin went on, now diving into the shadows, now plunging into the lamplight. Suddenly, through the wind's rough thrusts, something softly and tenderly brushed against his elbow. He turned around. Beneath feathers batting against a black brim, a familiar face with provocatively half-closed eyes. And barely audible through the moaning air: "You know you know me. And you look right past me. You ought to bow. That's it."

Her slight figure, tossed back by the wind, perched on tenacious stiletto heels, was all insubordination and readiness for battle.

Sutulin tipped his hat. "But you were supposed to be going away. And you're still here? Then something must have prevented—"

"That's right—this."

And he felt a chamois finger touch his chest then dart back into the muff. He sought out the narrow pupils of her eyes beneath the dancing black feathers, and it seemed that one more look, one more touch, one more shock to his hot temples, and it would all come unthought, undone, and fall away. Meanwhile she, her face nearing his, said, "Let's go to your place. Like last time. Remember?"

With that, everything stopped.

"That's impossible."

She sought out the arm that had been pulled back and clung to it with tenacious chamois fingers.

"My place...isn't fit." He looked away, having again withdrawn both his arms and the pupils of his eyes.

"You mean to say it's cramped. My God, how silly you are. The more cramped it is..." The wind tore away the end of her phrase. Sutulin did not reply. "Or, perhaps you don't..."

When he reached the turning, he looked back: the woman was still standing there, pressing her muff to her bosom, like a shield; her narrow shoulders were shivering with cold; the wind cynically flicked her skirt and lifted up the lapels of her coat.

"Tomorrow. Everything tomorrow. But now…" And, quickening his pace, Sutulin turned resolutely back.

"Right now: while everyone's asleep. Collect my things (only the necessaries) and go. Run away. Leave the door wide open: let *them*. Why should I be the only one? Why not let *them*?"

The apartment was indeed sleepy and dark. Sutulin walked down the corridor, straight and to the right, opened the door with resolve, and as always, wanted to turn the light switch, but it spun feebly in his fingers, reminding him that the circuit had been broken. This was an annoying obstacle. But it couldn't be helped. Sutulin rummaged in his pockets and found a box of matches: it was almost empty. Good for three or four flares—that's all. He would have to husband both light and time. When he reached the coat pegs, he struck the first match: light crept in yellow radiuses through the black air. Sutulin purposely, overcoming temptation, concentrated on the illuminated scrap of wall and the coats and jackets hanging from hooks. He knew that there, behind his back, the dead, Quadraturinized space with its black corners was still spreading. He knew and did not look around. The match smoldered in his left hand, his right pulled things off hooks and flung them on the floor. He needed another flare; looking at the floor, he started toward the corner—if it was still a corner and if it was still there—where, by his calculations, the bed should have fetched up, but he accidentally held the flame under his breath—and again the black wilderness closed in. One last match remained: he struck it over and over: it would not light. One more time—and its crackling head fell off and slipped through his fingers. Then, having turned around, afraid to go any farther into the depths, he started back toward the bundle he had abandoned under the hooks. But he had made the turn, apparently, inexactly. He walked—heel to toe, heel to toe—holding his fingers out in front of him, and found nothing: neither the bundle, nor the hooks, nor even the walls. "I'll get there in the end. I must get there." His body was sticky with cold and sweat. His legs wobbled oddly. He squatted down, palms on the floorboards: "I shouldn't have come back. Now here I am alone, nowhere to turn." And suddenly it struck him: "I'm waiting here, but it's growing, I'm waiting, but it's ..."

In their sleep and in their fear, the occupants of the quadratures adjacent to citizen Sutulin's eighty-six square feet couldn't make head or tail of the timbre and intonation of the cry that woke them in the middle of the night and compelled them to rush to the threshold of the Sutulin cell: for a man who is lost and dying in the wilderness to cry out is both futile and belated: but if even so—against all sense—he does cry out, then, most likely, *thus*.

1926

THE BOOKMARK

I

THE OTHER day, as I was looking through my old books and manuscripts tied tight with twine, it again slipped under my fingers: a flat body of faded blue silk and needlepoint designs trailing a swallowtail train. We hadn't seen each other in a long time: my bookmark and I. Events of recent years had been too unbookish and had taken me far from those cabinets crammed with herbariumized meanings. I abandoned the bookmark between lines as yet unread and soon forgot the feel of its slippery silk and the delicate scent of printing ink emanating from its soft and pliant body wafered between the pages. I even forgot... where I had forgotten it. Thus do long sea voyages part sailors from their wives.

True, books had crossed my path here and there: rarely at first, then more and more often; but they did not need bookmarks. These were unraveling signatures glued pell-mell into crookedly cut covers; along the rough and dirty paper, breaking ranks with the lines, brown-gray letters—the color of military broadcloth—rushed; these reeked of rancid oil and glue. With these crudely produced bareheaded bundles, one did not stand on ceremony: shoving a finger in between the sloppily pasted signatures, one tore the pages apart the better to leaf through them, tugging impatiently at the raggedy, tooth-edged margins. One consumed these texts posthaste, without reflecting or delectating: both books and two-wheeled carts were needed then strictly to supply words and ammunition. The one with the silk train had no business here.

And now again: the ship was in port, its gangway down. Library ladders scanning the spines of books. The statics of frontispieces. Silence and green reading-room lampshades. Pages rubbing against pages. And, finally, the bookmark: just as it had been, all that time ago—except that now the silk was even more faded, and its needlepoint design covered in dust.

I pulled it out from under a paper mound and placed it in front of me—on the edge of the desk: the bookmark looked affronted and slightly grumpy. But I smiled at it with warmth and affection: to think of all the voyages we had taken together—from meanings to meanings, from this set of signatures to that. Now, for instance, I recalled our difficult ascent from ledge to ledge of Spinoza's *Ethics*—after almost every page I had left my bookmark alone, squeezed between the metaphysical layers; then the breathlessness of *Vita nuova* where, at passages linking one poem to the next, my patient bookmark had often had to wait until the emotion that had taken the book out of my hands subsided, allowing me to return to the words. And I couldn't help remembering . . . But all of this concerns only the two of us, me and my bookmark: I'll stop.

Especially as it is important in practice—since any encounter obligates—to repay the past given us with some bit of the future. In other words, rather than tucking the bookmark away at the back of a drawer, I should include my old friend in my next reading; instead of a series of memories, I should offer my guest another bundle of books.

I looked through what I had. No, none of these would do: they lacked the logical caesuras and dramatic shifts that force one to look back and to pause, that call for the help of a bookmark. I ran my eye over the freshly printed titles: in that jumble of meager contrivances there was nowhere to stop. No corner to be found for my four-cornered guest.

I looked away from the bookshelf and tried to remember: empty literary boxcars of the last few years clattered through my mind. Here too I could see no place for my bookmark. Somewhat irritated, I first paced—from wall to wall—and then, arms thrust into the sleeves of my overcoat, went out for my usual late-afternoon walk.

2

I am billeted at the bend in the Arbat, catercorner to the church of St. Nicholas, so the boulevards are only a few hundred paces away: first I pass the window of the secondhand store walled off by the backs of gawkers, then I follow the sidewalk—past doors and signs—straight to the square. This time too an absurd habit, left over from the long-forgotten hungry years, made me stop to peer in the window of a food shop: through the cloudy glass, those same defenseless, pimply chicken legs sticking out of greasy paper peered back with dead pomp.

I tore my eyes away and proceeded along the pavement through the polygon of Arbat Square to Nikitsky Boulevard; through another square, more packed boulevard sand—and I began to look for a free place on some bench or other. One bench, with a slumped back and squat, bent-iron legs, had room at one end. I sat down, shoulder to someone's shoulder, intending to finish thinking about what I'd begun at home, among my books and bookmark. But on this bench someone was already thinking—what's more, out loud: he was second on my right; turned toward the man seated between us, the stranger went on talking. Squinting in the speaker's direction, I glimpsed only fingers fidgeting with an unbuttoned coat breast, as with the neck of a cello (the rest was hidden by the tall and stout figure of the man being addressed).

"Or take this. I call it 'The Tower Gone Mad.' The gigantic four-footed Eiffel Tower, its steel head high over the human hub-bubs of Paris, was fed up, you see, fed up with having to listen to that hurly-burly street-entangled life strewn with clangs, lights, and clamor. As for the muddleheaded creatures swarming at its feet, they had equipped the inside of its pointed crown poking through the clouds with global vibrations and radio signals. The space inside the tower's needlelike brain now began to vibrate, began to seep down through its muscular steel interlacements into the ground, whereupon the tower wrenched its iron soles free of the foundation, rocked back, and lunged off. This happened before dawn, let's say, when people were asleep under their roofs, and the Place des Invalides, the Champs de Mars, adjacent streets and quays were deserted. The thousand-foot colossus, barely able to lift its heavy swollen feet, crashes across the cast-iron arc of a bridge, circumvents the sad stones of the Trocadéro and lumbers up the rue d'Iéna toward the Bois de Boulogne: in that narrow defile of houses, the tower feels ill at ease, once or twice it knocks into sleeping walls, houses crack and crumble, spilling bricks and waking neighbors. Less frightened than embarrassed by its clumsiness, the tower lurches into the next street. But in this still-narrower defile, it has no room at all. Meanwhile, Paris the light sleeper is waking: projector lights striate the night fog, anxious sirens blare, and high overhead engines are already droning. The tower now lifts its flat elephantine feet and jumps up onto the rooftops; roof beams crackle under the Eiffel monster's leaden tread; multiplying catastrophes as it goes, it soon reaches the edge of the Bois and, cutting a wide swath with steel blows, continues on its way.

"Daylight is beginning to glimmer. Thrown into a panic, Paris's three million have jammed all the train stations; news of the tower gone mad is pounding off the presses, skimming over the wires, skipping from ear to ear. The sun climbs above the horizon and gives Parisians the chance, when they turn their heads at the usual angle toward the usual place where the tip of the tower always usually loomed, to see unusually empty air—and nothing else. Initially, this only adds to the uproar. Now these eyes, now those, seem to have seen the gigantic latticework, now wading toward them around bends in the Seine, now threatening to jump down on the city from Montmartre. But soon both the morning fog and the false alarms have dissipated, and millions of sanguine souls, who had reacted to the disaster by beating their shirtfronts and combing the papers, are indignant and demanding revenge: Catch the runaway! Americans from hotels on the Place Monceau are out clicking their Kodaks, photographing the steel giant's tracks imprinted on bodies and wreckage, while a poet from Saint-Célestin, come on foot (so as to save ten sous) to the smashed bare base, chews a meditative pencil and debates what would best suit the situation: Alexandrine rhymes or zigzags of free verse?

"Swaying and droning in the wind, shimmering with the brilliance of its metal battens, the tower forges ahead; only the soft friable ground slows its steps. Though the runaway knows clearly *whence* it comes, it scarcely knows *where* it is going: chance propels it northwest, straight into the sea. The steel behemoth wants to turn back—but what's this? Cannons ranged in a semicircle ready to fire. High-explosive shells attempt to bar its way; humming beneath their hits, the steel breaks through the first ring and, scattering cannons, storms north: to the formidable fortification walls of Antwerp. Batteries thunder: steel clashes against steel. Reeling from the hits, rocking on its lacerated joints, the tower screams out in an iron voice and staggers around to the southeast. Like a wild beast driven back into its cage with whips, the tower is ready to return and dig its feet back into the square people have assigned it. But just then it hears, from faraway in the east, a barely audible radio call: 'This way, this way!'

"You'd like me to move over? Certainly..."

Someone had sat down to the speaker's right, nearly flattening him: for a second his fingers stopped fiddling with his coat breast which jutted forward; now I could see an angular profile, a scraggy beard, and a mouth twitching from words as from a tic.

"You and I, of course, know who was calling the lost tower and from where. And now it knows where to go: due east. The revolutionary will join the revolutionaries. From capital to capital the wires hum with fright: 'The mad rogue has been Bolshevized.' 'Stop the tower!' 'What a disgrace!' 'Spare no effort.' 'Join forces.'

Ranged cannons again try to bar the fugitive's way: once more the clanking colossus, battered by blows of steel against steel, breaks into its savage and terrible hymn. Riddled with shell bursts and shaking its needlelike crown, it trudges onward in the direction of the summons. In its dreams, the tower can already see flags like red poppies flying over a vast—stalk to stalk—human field; it imagines a resounding square surrounded by ancient gap-toothed walls: there it will sink its iron soles into the ground while . . . while scattered armies retreat and clear the way. Diplomatic heads, meanwhile, are frantic: 'The tower is escaping!—We let it go.—Emergency measures.—What to do?'

"The steel giant's pursuers, half trampled beneath its heels, decide to attack its spire; having lost the battle on the ground, they move to the airwaves: antennas in Paris, New York, Berlin, Chicago, London, and Rome falsify their frequencies and plead from all sides: 'This way, this way!' They promise and lure, beckon and lie, jam voices from the east and discombobulate the tower. It wavers, unable to get its bearings, its steel head spinning. It pushes a little farther east, then swings south, then changes direction again, and finally, worn out by the conflicting signals, not knowing where to go or why, follows where its invisible traces are leading. People everywhere are gloating with joy. Residents of towns and villages in the returning tower's path are temporarily evacuated while in Paris the smashed square by the Cathédrale des Invalides is quickly smoothed out and a proper ceremonial planned. But along the way, at the point where three mountainous borders meet, the tower encounters a waste of water: the stillness and depth of Lake Constance. Passing over that blue mirror, the vanquished giant catches sight of its reflection, inverted and sun-shot, with its spire pointing down. The sonorous steel shivers with disgust and, in a last paroxysm of rage, severs the invisible traces. Then it lifts its leaden paws, stands erect, and plunges (can you imagine?) crown-first from the alpine ledges. Comes the clatter of tumbling rocks and crags torn away, then, echoing from gorge to gorge, the plash of crushed waters: towering above the overflowing lake are the rigid limbs of the steel suicide. I wanted just to give you an outline, but it seems I got carried away and..."

His fingers, as if they'd finished playing the story, ran down his coat breast and disappeared into his pocket. His eyes, too, seemed to be looking for cover. The stout man's shoulder stirred against mine.

"Well, if you tinkered with the plot, perhaps...Only you've got something wrong: the diameter of Lake Constance is fifty-five miles, so a thousand-foot-high wedge couldn't possibly cause it to overflow. And then..."

"And then: towers aren't in the habit of walking. Isn't that so?" the sharp-featured man laughed and slumped back; now even his coat breast was eclipsed by the cumbrous figure separating us, and his voice, when he piped up again, seemed soft and indistinct.

"Look. Another theme. Up there. Do you see?"

"Where?"

"Right opposite you. Fourth floor. Last cornice on the left. A foot and a half below the window, below those smudges of white-wash. Well?"

"A ledge...I see."

"Now I'll show you a theme as well. Keep your eyes on the ledge: there it is, confined to those three feet. Can't jump, can't escape. My little theme is stuck."

Drawn into this strange game—the man being addressed and I, and even a pair of eyeglasses that popped out suddenly from behind a newspaper at the other end of the bench—we immediately located the crosspiece that had caught the sharp-featured man's eye. Above the boulevard trees, between windows piled high in the façade of a building under reconstruction, rows of short narrow ledges jutted.

"There we have our first item; the second is—well, makes no difference to me—a tomcat, say, an ordinary vagabond tom. The result is this: driven by something—by a couple of stones thrown at it, or by hunger, suppose—our cat hustles up the zigzag stairs and through a half-open door into someone's apartment or perhaps an office where people are expected any minute...yes, an office, that will do better. Feet stamp at the tom, give chase—then fear catapults him up onto the windowsill (the window stands wide), and down onto that ledge: our exhibit is ready. Still, it wouldn't hurt, it wouldn't cost us anything, to stretch the building up past the chimney tops—from four stories to thirty—to narrow the streets, cobweb the air with wires, and set whirling below, along the tire-polished asphalt of the city-giant, hundreds and thousands of automobile wheels and seas of hurrying, eyes to the ground, businessmen.

"So: the cat vanishes out the window, two or three pairs of eyes follow it then go back to their numbers and calculations; the window slams shut; soon the workday is done and the doors too have clicked shut: the cat is alone—on a narrow strip of brick wedged into the building's stone face. The window above is quite close, but for a jump there's no room, no support: mustn't try: death. To jump down, from ledge to ledge, would be hopeless: it's too far and claws can't grip stone: death. Slowly straightening up, the tom inches along the wall: precipice. Fur bristling, green cracks of pupils hanging over the edge, he sees through the smoky air creeping blurs below; cocking an ear, he hears the incessant rumble of the streets: better wait. We are dealing, as I've said, with a cat averse to sentimental purrings, a homeless vagabond with fight-torn ears, hunger-sunken sides, and a heart well insulated against life: our hero is not afraid and does not lose his self-possession—he has been robbed of all possibilities, save that of sleep. Very well—hugging the wall still closer, he closes his eyes. Here one might recount the tom's dreams, poised at a height of thirty stories, two inches from death. But let's go on. The chill evening air and perhaps hunger as well force him awake: below he sees tangles of lights, stationary and moving. He wants to stretch, to arch his back: but there's no room. His dusk-widened pupils scan the walls scored with yellow windows. Our tom, of course, doesn't realize that in one window people are arguing about the political system Europe will have a hundred years hence, in an-

other they're listening to a lecture on a fashionable Boston religion, in a third they're poring over a chessboard, in a fourth...
but to the tom, all of this (even were I to reveal it to him with the aid of some fictional device or other), all of this, I repeat, is of no use: beneath his paws is a narrow stone step, and either way, up or down: death. The sly tom again tries to hide behind his eyelids, in his dreams, but the cold seeps under his bedraggled fur, tugs at his skin, and prods him awake. One by one, the windows go dark. Raindrops spatter and presently a downpour is lashing the ledge: the wet stone wants to slip out from under the tom's paws. He clings to the wall with his shivering body and cries, but the rain is banging on the canted rooftops and pounding down the downspouts: the poor tom's cries barely reach his own ears. Soon both fall silent: the rain and the cat. The last windows on the bottom floors go dark. Glistening roofs mirror the rose-colored dawn.

"Once again the sun bowls into the blue, dragging the day after it. Blinds go up. From the stone chasm below come the honks, clanks, clangs, and clamor of the crowd. A passerby looks up by chance and sees a black dot far above, almost under the eaves; he squints through his eyeglasses: 'What could that be?'—but the minute hand on his watch propels him onward. Midday. Two small children, flanking a governess, whose stiff fingers they clutch, have come out for a walk. Mouths agape, they look all about them—at the wires, the walls, and the cornices: 'What's that, missus?' 'Watch your step.' Thus do little people learn from big people to watch their step. The sun has dried and matted the tom's fur. A fierce hunger is knotting his intestines. He tries again to cry, but from his parched mouth comes only a rasp. The hot sun makes his eyelids droop, but nightmares instantly wake him: hanging his head over the edge of the cornice, the tom sees the floor of streets begin to sway and dance toward him—closer and closer; contracting his muscles, the tom is ready to jump when... he wakes up: the asphalt floor goes tumbling back down thirty stories—like an elevator cut loose—straight down.

"Again evening. Again yellow squares of windows. And in

each one of them, long lines of words, problems, and bookmarks, patiently awaiting their pair of eyes. Once more the dead of night—the city subsides and the pavement lies bare. Pressing an ear to the stone, the solitary cat hears the hollow hum of the wires suspended between him and the asphalt.

"Another dawn. On the next ledge—not three yards from the cat's mouth—sparrows are chirping. The cat swallows his saliva and regards the twitterers with turbid eyes. The sparrows cut loose from the ledge and dive into the air.

"A fresh morning. From three floors down, from a window flung wide to the sun, comes a confused rendition of one of Metner's *Fairy Tales* or, better yet, a chorale prelude by Bach: such an august and gracious contrapuntal combination. The tom cares not a whit: he knows only the music of tin cans tied to his tail— Bach leaves him cold—and so, I regret to say, no catharsis takes place. Especially as a sudden wind slams the window shut, and the harmony with it. I must tell you that this wind, which blows in some mornings from the sea, begins as a breath but often turns into a cyclone. Now, too, it first caresses the tom's crusted fur, and then, having built, tries to wrest him from the ledge. The tom has no fight left in him: filmy eyes wide, he clings to the stone with claws weak as water. The wind takes a swing and sweeps him off his paws: with a single toss, the tom goes tumbling down. His fall is briefly broken by the swaying wires below: they catch and cradle the vagabond, rocking him till the steel loops give way and let him drop, down onto the asphalt. Automobile wheels run over the body, and then a street-cleaner's cart comes by—our theme is scooped up with a metal spade and thrown onto the rubbish heap. The place where nearly all themes are thrown today, if indeed they are ... *themes*."

The man to whom this story was addressed uncrossed his right leg from his left then crossed his left leg over his right. This hardly resembled a reaction. At the other end of the bench, the eyeglasses engrossed in the story of the cat jerked back. And soon their place was taken by a pair of eyes that quickly hid behind the varicolored cover of a book.

Absorbed in listening, I hadn't noticed the gathering dusk. The air, now cool, rocked between the buildings: leaves twitched, dust swirled along the paths, and from somewhere—from the building site, most likely—a wood shaving skittered toward our bench: swiftly twirling, it cavorted across the boulevard and came to rest a few steps away. I noticed the intent look on the theme catcher's face as he turned the feathery, loosely curled shaving over in his hand. He gazed at it, affectionately squinting.

"Well now, and this too. Why if you straighten out its curls and look hard, there's substance enough for a short story, some ten pages. And no need to hunt for a title: 'The Shaving.' There. Then ever so carefully—spiral by spiral—something like this: a carpenter, a young fellow by the name of, say, Vaska Tyankov. He knows and loves his trade. With his ax and his plane, he will do wonders—and gladly. But the countryside is poor and work hard to come by, so Vaska Tyankov goes to the city from time to time to earn his bread. With Vaska, in his beveled wooden chest, go his chisels, ax and planes, while from there, hidden under his tools, come stowaway bundles of leaflets and proclamations. Meetings in the city take up more and more of his leisure. Events follow events. February—July—October. The Party comes out from underground, seizes power. Carpenter Vaska, long known as comrade Vasily, swaps his padlocked box of tools for a bulging briefcase fitted with a steel clasp. He's up to his ears in work: automobiles convey comrade Vasily from conference to conference, typewriters tap, telephones yap: 'Rush'—'Priority'—'Urgent.' Comrade Vasily's eyelids are puffy with sleeplessness, a pencil permanently attached to one hand: reports, resolutions, congresses, official missions, urgent summonses. Only rarely—and timidly, dimly at that—do his dreams evoke the smoke rising over low log houses, the ripe rustling rye—and again the click-click open and shut of his briefcase, 'have heard . . . have decreed,' and the pencil in hand.

"Then one day—the most ordinary 'one day' imaginable—yet another telephone call forces Tyankov out of bed and into his boots. Shoving his briefcase under his elbow, he dashes down the stairs. Outside the car is hooting. He kicks open the front door—and what does he see coming toward him, buffeted by puffs of wind, but this light shaving, curly as a ringlet and fragrant with resin. Tyankov glances about: no one (the driver is fussing with the tire cover). Then he quickly bends down and slips the feathery whorl into his briefcase. The tire cover is pulled on, the door slams shut, and the automobile cuts through his meetings, from entrance to entrance. Report, dissenting opinion. Another report. Someone with a slew of numbers. Tyankov wants to trump those numbers with his own. He opens his briefcase and scrabbles for the folders, but here—again—is that soft lock of a shaving. The joints of his fingers sing with a familiar sensation: between thumb and index—the plane's oblique projection, and slowly curling over his hand—the rustling ringlets, fragrant with wood and resin. Comrade Vasily is about to pull his hand back, but too late: a stippling of warm shots ripples along the nerves from his fingers to his brain, in his ear an invisible workbench creaks, under his elbow a rough board rocks, his hand is suddenly alive with the old carpenter's reflex. Government official Tyankov tries—you understand—to pick up his pencil, but his hand refuses and demands its due. The tenacious shaving is already wrapped around his index finger like a wedding ring; now not just his hand, but his entire arm, shoulder, body, tightening and tensing, are calling for the old work that was in their blood and muscles and from which they were forcibly parted. In short, the peasant in Vaska is reasserting his right to exist; he was silent for years, and might have gone on being silent if not for an insignificant shaving—and . . . Look at that, it's . . ."

We all (the whole bench) looked where his finger was pointing: as though tired of listening, the shaving, gently pushed by the wind, caracoled away down the path. The wind seemed to have whisked the story away with it. But the silence lasted no more than a minute.

"Never mind. I once," the voice went on musingly, as if to itself, "stumbled over a cartridge clip. An ordinary, rain-rusted cartridge clip—from a rifle, that is. Not far from here—on the boulevard. Ground into the sand, no doubt, in the days when we talked to each other with gunshots. And here it had turned up again. Well, I understood it right away. Right away. After all, what can a cartridge clip say: five bullets—one after another—along five trajectories and into five targets. I invented a plot along the lines of Andersen's 'Five Out of One Pod' or our Russian tale about the czarevitch and his three arrows... It's not my fault if bullets are more current than those idyllic peas. So then, I took five lives, five stories in a cartridge clip, and tried... but you don't care."

His glum companion made no reply. A minute later, a passenger tram, sighing and grinding sparks, came rattling along the rails behind us.

"Or, if one were to write about one of the city's suicides—an old, but inexhaustible theme—your title would be right over there, twenty steps away, in black and white. Just turn around and copy it down."

The man being spoken to did not stir, but I glanced over my shoulder and immediately saw the title, indeed in black and white, under three red lights, on a ruled board hanging in air.

"Ye-e-s," said the sharp-featured man, leaning forward with his elbows on his knees, "if I ever wanted to write about someone who put his neck in a noose or slit his throat, I would give my story a humdrum, urban title: 'Flag Stop.' Yes. And if the title is right, the whole text will hang on it, like a coat on a peg. The title, for me, is the first word (or words) of a story: it must pull all the other words after it, right down to the last. That's my feeling anyway. To think that people say," he went on, suddenly raising his voice and scanning the window squares blazing up to meet the night, "that there are no themes, that we are living in a time of themelessness. They hunt for themes—practically need hounds to do it—and scare up each new series of images with a battue, a throng, when those accursed themes, the devil take them, are everywhere you look. They're like the motes in a sunbeam or the mosquitoes over a swamp—that would be more exact. Themes?! You say there aren't any. My brain is bristling with them. Asleep, or awake, from every window, from all eyes, events, things, words: they swarm: and every one, no matter how tiny, wants to sting me. Sting me! And you say—"

"I, in fact, have said nothing. And I think what you say is nonsense. We have authors—"

"*Authors?*" his scraggly beard twitched nervously. "We have no authors: we have only second-raters. Imitators. And outright thieves. How do they go about finding themes? Some scramble up sliding library ladders in pursuit—and pluck them out from under book covers. They're not so bad. But others grab them right out of each other's hands; cadge them from State commissioning editors; or from underground—on the literary black market. They look everywhere they can think of for themes—everywhere but inside their own heads, it doesn't enter their heads . . . to look there. Ah, if only they'd announce on that pillar in red letters three feet high: *Lecture in the Hall of Columns. On the Nonexistence of Literature.* Oh, I'd show them . . ."

The speaker's voice rose to a dominant. Two or three passersby glanced in our direction and slowed their step. The cumbrous listener shifted his knees and sat up. His face (the streetlamps were now spattering bright electric bile) wore an expression of disgust, or perhaps confusion. Oblivious, the theme catcher gripped his listener's shoulder and elbow with the fingers of both hands, as though he were a theme in need of molding. The theme tried to jerk his arm away and grumbled something into his collar, but the theme catcher's voice, skipping from a high falsetto to a low apologetic whisper, restrained the recalcitrant elbow.

"You say this is 'nonsense.' Not at all: we writers write our stories, but literary historians in whose power it is to admit us or not to admit us into history, to open or slam the door, also want, you see, *to tell stories about stories.* Otherwise, they're stuck. And so the story that can be retold in ten words or less, the one easily summarized, squeezes in the door, while writings, which cannot produce that *something*, remain ... nothing. Now, my friend, why don't you try?"

"I'm in a hurry."

"That's just what I need. Try, hurriedly, in a word or two, to annotate the meaning, to exgistolate the gist, if you will, of any popular modern work about this or that, or neither this nor that: as you please. Well, go ahead. Your choice, and in a nutshell. I'm waiting. Aha, so you can't? Well then, put yourself in the future historian's place: he, poor soul, won't be able to either."

Having lost interest in his listener, the theme catcher turned abruptly to his right. At that end of the bench, a finger stuck inside his half-read book, an ear attentively cocked, sat a second silent witness to the discussion. He had long since given up reading so as to listen. The lower half of his face was muffled in a scarf, the upper half obscured by the long shadow of a visor.

Now the varicolored book cover resting on his knees caught the theme catcher's restless eye.

"Aha. I see you're reading that translation of Woodward's *Bunk.* Amusing. Isn't it?"

The visor nodded its shadow in the affirmative.

"You see," the sharp-featured man burst out. "It hooked you. How? You haven't read it?" he glanced back over his shoulder. "No? Well then. The idea: to debunk all the bunk of which life is made. The plot: a writer, at work on a novel, discovers a character missing. The character has slipped out from under his pen. Work comes to a halt. One day, the writer happens to look in on a literary reading and is stunned to find himself face-to-face with his character. The character tries to run out the door. But the writer— I think this is how it goes—grabs him by the shoulder and elbow, like this, and says: 'Listen, just between us, you're not a person, you're a ...' They end by agreeing not to spoil things for each other anymore and to devote themselves wholeheartedly to their common cause: the novel. The author introduces his character to an individual essential to the plot's development. This individual then introduces the character to a charming woman with whom he falls head over heels in love. The remaining chapters of this novel within a novel quickly begin to go awry and askew, like lines typed on a sheet that has popped out from under the bar. The author, upon receiving no new material from his love-besotted character, insists he break with the woman. The character tries to dodge, to play for time. At his wits' end, the author demands (this over the telephone) immediate submission to his pen or else... But the character simply hangs up. The End."

For some ten seconds the theme catcher regarded us all with a mischievous, almost childlike smile. Then a wrinkle appeared across his brow and his beard snagged on his fingers.

"No, that's not the end. The denouement is wrong. Misses the mark. I would...Hmm...Let me just think. Now I've got it: they don't talk on the telephone, they meet face-to-face. The author demands—the character refuses. Before you know it, one has challenged the other. They duel. The character kills the author. That's it, can't be otherwise. When the woman, whom the pseudo-man has been vainly trying to win, discovers that she was the cause of the duel, she goes to him herself. But now the man-character cannot love, cannot not love, he can't do anything: without the author, he is nothing, nil. *Punctum.** An ending like that would—I think—give a better approximation. Although..."

The speaker stopped short, shut himself up inside himself, and suddenly, without looking at anyone, got to his feet and walked off. What happened next was even less expected: his listener, who had seemed to be waiting for the chance to get rid of this fanciful inventor, jerked up, as though attached by a string, and trudged resignedly after him.

The middle of the bench was now empty. The man at the end

*Period (*Lat.*).

was absorbed in skimming the last pages of his book, evidently checking what he had just heard. Then he glanced over at me. We might have spoken. But just then a woman appeared and established herself between us. She powdered her nose then asked for a cigarette. Both I and the man with the scarf-muffled mouth remembered that the hour was approaching when to speak of literature on Tverskoi Boulevard was not the custom. We nodded to each other, and went our separate ways: I to the left, he to the right.

3

My second encounter with the theme catcher came about just as unexpectedly. Two steps from where I live, elbow to elbow. Lost in thought, he looked up abstractedly at the purposeful touch of my hand.

"You must be mistaken or—"

"No. I stopped you in order to propose myself as a character. Or don't you take ones like me? In that case, I beg your pardon."

Smiling sheepishly, he regarded me, only half remembering. I reminded him: the bench on the boulevard, the novel's double ending, the series of themes. He nodded with sudden delight and, taking my hand, shook it warmly. I've noticed this before: people who live outside of things, surrounded by formulas and phantasms, are averse to the usual gradualnesses, they befriend one and reject one immediately and completely.

"What interests me," I said, turning serious as, like old acquaintances, we set off side by side I can't remember where, or rather, set off nowhere, "is your accusation of themelessness. Who or what is on the defendants' bench: a day in the life of contemporary literature or..."

He smiled. "Sitting on that bench, which, as I recall, was just an ordinary boulevard bench, were you and I: I talked—you listened. And it all came down to a statement of fact, not an accusation.

Moreover, 'a day in the life of contemporary literature,' as you call it, is not or almost not to blame."

"But then I don't understand—"

"Not to blame," my companion insisted, "because . . . Incidentally, this reminds me of a caricature I once saw in an old English magazine: a girl and a stagecoach. In the first picture, the girl (she's carrying a basket) has caught up with the receding stagecoach; but to climb up onto the high footboard, she must put her basket down; having scrambled up onto the step, the girl turns around to collect her basket, but the stagecoach has already driven off; in the second picture, the poor girl jumps down, dashes back for her basket then runs after the lumbering stagecoach. She again reaches the step and this time settles her basket on it first; but while she is doing this, the stagecoach picks up speed, and the girl—in the third, and last, picture—exhausted and out of breath, plumps down in the middle of the road and bursts into bitter tears. By this I mean: the literary stagecoach will not wait, which is why the poet with poetry in hand, given conditions today, cannot possibly gain the elusive step: if the poet jumps into literature—then poetry is left behind, left out of literature; if poetry manages to attain the step, to attain an artistic level—then the poet, excluded and rejected, is left completely *out*. You, of course, disagree."

"I can hardly do otherwise. Still, my point in stopping you was not to refute your argument but to ask you a question. Tell me, what do you think of the time when the stagecoach hadn't yet been hitched to horses? In other words, of poetry in the past, before the Revolution?"

He shrugged. "I never think backward, only forward. But if for some reason you need me to . . . Though I'll probably say something absurd and beside the point."

"Please go on."

"You see, once upon a time, before the lifequake, so to speak, I made the acquaintance of a provincial attorney-at-law: crumpled collar, wife, children, greasy tailcoat—but attached to the top of his tattered briefcase with little metal screws was a chain of silver-plated letters: *Fire the hearts of men with the Word.* There. Now if that isn't clear, I'll try—"

"It's clear."

"Of course," my companion went on more quickly, "of course, the attorney disappeared long ago, along with all his effects, but the briefcase with its silver-plated 'Fire the hearts' survived. At least, I seem to have come across it once or twice. Though I can't say for certain: both times piles of papers and files were lying on top of it, but something in the expression of the tattered corners struck me . . . Right away I thought: that's it."

"What a strange man you are." I couldn't help smiling. "But please go on. Where did those mysterious meetings with the old briefcase take place?"

"The last one, if you'll believe it, was just the other day. In the office of a distinguished editor. Next to a red pencil and notepad. Why are you laughing?"

But in a second he too was chuckling, contorting his mouth like a child and twitching his eyebrows. Morose passersby gave us a wide berth. I looked about: a half-familiar crossroad; intent stone rumors of a church tower; faded grass sticking up between the cobbles; and off to one side, behind low ranks of houses, muffled by a mute: the dull vibration of the city's strings.

We hadn't planned this. The conversation itself had led us to these silent and lonely purlieus.

I was the first to return to words. "So you've been in those offices with red pencils. And your themes too?"

"Yes."

"What was the result?"

"Rejs."

"Meaning?"

"Well . . . The corners of my manuscripts were all marked: No and Rej. I have a whole collection of *Rej.*"

"You make it sound as if you'd collected them on purpose—"

"At first, of course, I didn't. But then I very nearly did. I no longer wondered whether my manuscript would be rejected, I only wondered *how*. Those people now in possession of the poor provincial solicitor's briefcase—with their manner of speaking, setting and resetting terms, arguing, penciling notes in the margins, pompously philosophizing, bowing and scraping before the telephone while eyeing their visitor with scorn, adjusting their pince-nez through which they see, *without* changing lenses, now close up, now far away, in accordance with the importance or insignificance of said visitor—these people gradually became, for me, a *theme*. Thereafter, my purpose in meeting with them was purely practical. For until I have fully elucidated a theme, until I have determined its source and uncovered every detail, I cannot rest. Ever. Yes, editors will have to go on dealing with my manuscripts and also with my eyes: until I hide them under my eyelashes.

"I ought to tell you that when I first arrived in Moscow (this was six years ago), I knocked right into the gigantic and unforgiving back of the Revolution. Walls minus many of their bricks were scrawled with shell bursts and drooling poster paints... Entrances were boarded up. On my way to my first editorial office, on an outlying boulevard, I passed such an expressive bench (I shall never forget it): its back collapsed as if in a faint, and one spasmodic leg sticking obscenely up in the air. I had a collection of stories to propose. The title? Very simple: *Stories for the Crossed-Out*."

"What did the editor say?"

"'Won't do,' he said, and pushed it away having read only the title. In another place my bundle disappeared into the incoming mail and returned via the outgoing. In a third... but this is dull. On one manuscript I remember finding the penciled comment: *Psychologizing*. Only once did I encounter anything like scrutiny. Having leafed through my manuscript, the man behind the editor's desk inspected me with his sharp graphite pupils and, tapping his pencil, said, 'And you? Are you one of the crossed-out or one of the crossers-out?' I have to admit I hadn't expected a question like that. 'I don't know,' I said stupidly. The man pushed the manuscript toward me: 'Well, you ought to find out, and without delay, don't you think?' Blushing profusely, I rose to leave, but the editor stopped me with a gesture: 'Just a minute. You have talent. But you must put it into a pen, and the pen into your hand. Your stories are, well, how shall I put it? Untimely. Put them away—let them wait. In the meantime, a person able to cross things out would, most likely, suit us. Have you ever tried writing criticism? A reappraisal, say, of reappraisals? You know what I mean. Do try. I'll look forward to reading.'

"I walked out feeling troubled and confused. There was something muddling about the man I'd left behind, behind that door. I remember I tossed all night, my elbows bumping against the hard theme that layers our entire life. My pen, as soon as I dipped it in ink, wrote: *Animal Disputans.** That was the title. Next came ... Perhaps this doesn't interest you?"

"Please go on."

"I took the title and the first verses of my song, if you will, from an old and long-forgotten book by the Danish humorist Holberg. This book—*Nicolai Klimmi Her subterraneum*, I believe it's called—describes the fantastic adventures of a traveler who winds up, I can't remember how, inside the Earth. The traveler is astonished to find that inside the planet, as inside a hermetically sealed vessel, lives a race with its own hermetically sealed State system, way of life, culture, everything that is customary in such cases. Over time the life of these undergroundlings—once rife with wars and conflict, cut off, hidden away beneath miles of crust—sorted itself out and settled into a harmonious routine. The problems of the hermetically sealed were all solved, everything ironed out and agreed upon. But in memory of those long-ago wars, Nicolai Klimmi tells us—no, please listen, it's rather touching—the land's noblest and richest magnates raised *animals disputans*. There isn't anything to argue about in an isolated country where everything has been determined and predetermined *in*

*Argumentative animal (*Lat.*).

*saecula saeculorum** but these disputants were trained for the purpose, fed a special diet that irritated the liver and sublingual nerve, then pitted against one another and forced to argue till they were hoarse and foaming at the mouth—to unanimous laughter and merry halloos from the lovers of old traditions... I did not draw any clear parallels. But that squinty man behind the editor's desk understood right away, from the first lines."

"I'm sure he did. And I suppose you never saw him again."

"No. On the contrary. He even praised my writing: he called it 'forceful' and 'sharp-edged.' But then, softly tapping his pencil, he began to blame himself: as a seasoned editor, he should have guessed...'You,' he went on slyly tapping, 'are no prosecutor. Why not try writing for the defense, so to speak, instead? Take some idea, social formula or class type, and defend it? I can't promise anything, but...' 'You think,' I burst out, 'that I would defend just anything?' 'Not at all,' he replied, sliding 'Animal Disputans' slowly back across the desk toward me: 'The choice of subject is entirely up to you. Needless to say. Good day.' What could I do? I left—and returned a week later with a new manuscript: 'In Defense of Rosinante.'"

"What a strange title."

"Well now he, my editor with the squint, didn't think so. The idea couldn't have been simpler. History, I wrote, had divided people into two classes: those who are on top (in the saddle) and those who are underneath (under the saddle): the Don Quixotes and the Rosinantes. The Don Quixotes sally forth on their fantastically marvelous and distant quests, straight to the idea, the ideal and the *Zukunftstaat*[†]; all eyes, beginning with Cervantes's own, are on them and on them alone. No one cares about the winded and mercilessly lashed Rosinante: steel stars of spurs slash his bloodied flanks while his ribs dance beneath the squeeze of knees and cinch. It's time, high time this jade, bearing history on its

*Forevermore (*Lat.*).

[†]State of the future (*Ger.*).

back, heard something besides goadings. Gradually unfurling my theme, I then switched to—"

"What did your editor do?" I interrupted.

"Well, what else could he do? He gave me back my manuscript and said, 'I won't be seeing you again soon. Or ever, I'm afraid.' As I stepped toward the door, I heard him rise from his chair. I turned around: he was standing with his palm outstretched. We gave each other a warm handshake and, do you know, I felt that this man—even across the abyss between us—was close...closer than some of my close friends. Of course, we'll never meet again. And I imagine he's seen many more like me since."

For a minute the story stopped. Wasteland and kitchen gardens stretched all about us. Along a distant embankment, shavings of white locomotive smoke curled up into the air in elongated rings.

"There is a custom," he began again. "A very naïve one. To help the soul, when it is passing through its trials, one places a saucer of clear water in the window: so that the soul may cleanse itself and endure further. But I was not given to see either the window or the saucer again. Over the next two years I asked nothing more of the briefcases. Yet I didn't give up writing. I was like one of those wild bees described by Fabre: even if you poke holes in their honeycombs, they will go on making honey; the honey drools through the holes, yet they, the sillies, go on making more.

"My situation was becoming direr every day. Dried fish and raw onions are cheap, I can tell you, but hardly nourishing. My pursuit of those elusive kopecks eventually led me inside a building where the many doors were numbered, the stairs steep as life. One of the literary bosses to whom I had applied for work turned out to be amiable and obliging. 'Sensitive topics,' he said, 'had best be put off, for the time being; as for great men, you may help yourself.' With that he pulled a sheet of paper out of a folder: a column of names—almost all of them crossed out ('for the crossed-out' flashed through my mind). The boss scratched his nose in annoyance: 'Those fellows grabbed the whole lot. But just a moment, just a moment, here's one that got away. Perhaps you'll have him: Bacon. He's yours. Ten thousand words. For a mass audience. Now I'll just—' The boss was about to take his pencil to Bacon, but I stopped him: 'Which one shall I write about?' 'What do you mean—which one?' The good man looked amazed. 'There's only one Bacon—write about him.' 'There are two.' 'You must be mistaken.' 'I'm not mistaken: Roger and Francis.' The editor's face darkened, but only for a minute. 'All right,' he gave up. 'So there are two. Write: "The Brothers Bacon." Fifteen thousand words.' 'But just a moment,' I persisted. 'How can they be brothers when one is three hundred years older?' The boss's face was no longer kind; he leaped to his feet and spat: 'You're all of you alike! I want to help, but you...Well, guess what! You can't have one, can't have two, can't have either!' Crossing the great empiricist out in his fury, he clapped the folder shut—and disappeared through one of the doors. I could only disappear through the other.

"I won't bore you with the whole forty days. One more of my trials will suffice. Friends, you see, had written a letter commending me to a top newspaper editor. I imagined that in that swift current I might set myself afloat more easily. The newspaper to which this editor belonged was, of course, red, though he himself had, in my opinion, his yellow spots. He agreed to a series of articles on pithy—or 'burning,' as he put it—topics. 'Be good to have a unifying title,' he said. I thought a minute, and suggested: 'At Home.' He liked it. Advance in hand, I set immediately to work. My first article—on what I considered a burning topic— was called 'Thirteen Ways to Recant.' Intended as a short guide, this piece listed all the ways to recant, from an open letter in a newspaper to... But when his eyes slid down to that *to*, my editor shook his head in grave reproach. His tone of exceeding solicitude turned to one of exceeding mistrust. I couldn't return the advance, so I had to settle my debt in words. In the end my signature appeared under a column of brevier, of which only the first third was mine, the rest was some sort of...I stormed into the editor's office brandishing the article. He heard me out, then snapped, 'You don't know journalism. I do. The only way we can work together is if you bring us facts and material (you have an eye, I won't deny it) and let us draw any conclusions ourselves.' I was too indignant to speak. He understood. We nodded to each other and parted ways...Why look, here's the cemetery."

Indeed, the string of reminiscences had led us to a vast and silent settlement of the dead, its crosses scattered about knolls.

"Are you tired?"

"A little."

We entered the enclosure through a gate. The path wound first to the right, then in zigzags among the stooped and decrepit crosses.

"We could sit for a moment."

"Let's do. Right here."

We sank down onto the prickly greensward. The theme catcher stretched out his long legs and cast an eye over the tops of the crosses.

"Um-hmm. If you've come into this busy world, live your life and leave."

I looked at him in silence. Weariness had made his chiseled features even sharper. As if to turn a tight screw tighter, he added: "I'd like a sleeping-car berth. For all eternity. And on the very lowest bunk. But that's nonsense."

His left hand began its mechanical dance up and down his coat breast.

"I've been led here, to the dead, any number of times before. By my thoughts. I always think on my feet, on the move: sometimes I walk and walk, and there aren't enough streets, so then I wander in here, to this place of silence. The old watchman in the watch box—over there by the gate, on the right—is an acquaintance of mine. He once told me a very curious story. He couldn't have made it up. He heard a noise, you see. This was before dawn. He listened: a crowbar striking stone. A call to the police, a squad arrives—and together they steal between the graves toward the sound. In one of the vaults they see a light. They creep up. Stick their heads in the door, and see—hunched over an open coffin, a dark lantern in hand—a back and moving elbows. They fall on the grave robber, drag him out—and what do you know! He's clutching a forceps, and in the forceps, trailing an extravagant root, is a gold tooth. He's a dentist (of sorts). 'The whole way to the station,' the watchman finished, 'the tooth-drawer cursed. Cursed and cursed. "Why take a working man from his work? Wore myself out with that corpse, and now I'll go to prison for my pains."'

"Well, I couldn't resist: I tried turning the incident into a story. I must still have it somewhere at home. It's about a burglar, no longer young but respectable (in his circle, of course). I've forgotten his name—it was a good name, but I've forgotten it. Well, anyway—call him Fedos Shpyn. Shpyn's work is clean, conscientious, unerring. But he is increasingly hindered by that greatest of afflictions for a thief: deafness. A man past his prime can't easily change professions. Shpyn continues to do what he has always done. His hands never fail him, but his hearing...One day he's caught red-handed: prison. He has time to consider the theme: 'Life is no joke.' Then he's released. Without means. He tries to find 'an honest job.' At his age, he doesn't need much. But thousands of young men are also out of work; who needs a deaf one with no skills? Shpyn goes back to his old trade. And back to prison. He's a recidivist. They take him to the dactyloscopy room and press his fingers to a board coated with wax. When they toss the old man back into life, he feels that something has been pulled out of the ends of his fingers, stolen, and that without that something, numbered and stashed away in the files, it's even harder. The ancient burglar doesn't like (and never has) people with sharp ears. He shuns even his fellows: he thinks they're laughing at him behind his back, making fun of that deaf duffer Fedos Shpyn. No longer able to rob the living, he must practice among the dead. 'They,' Shpyn muses, a smile spreading across his face, 'are even harder of hearing than I am.' But corpses, too, are a problem. Once upon a time people dressed the dead in their best, their cold fingers in rings and precious stones, their stiff feet in polished boots. But now the appurtenances were grown shabby and mean, the aim being—it's a disgrace, really—to stick a person in his coffin (no one will see, they say) in just his socks and some moth-eaten garment. 'If this keeps up,' Shpyn reflects as he picks his way home at night through the puddles from some suburban cemetery, 'before a person's even cold they'll be (they'll figure it out, they will) yanking the gold out of his lifeless mouth themselves, and they'll do it slapdash, in a hurry, without technique. What do they care? But I'll be without a living.' One day Shpyn sets off to work: come to a crossroad, he cups his palm to his ear—are bells tolling anywhere? He can't tell; he hears only dulled rustlings and rumblings. He lingers by a sign that says: COFFINS. Sometimes you can pick up a scent here. No one. He trudges to the nearest church porch: standing on the steps is a woman in black—so he peeps inside: there it is, surrounded by burning candles, and the mourners are neatly and expensively dressed. 'A good sign,' thinks Shpyn, 'only how can you tell what he's got under his lips? Gold or cement? Or maybe nothing at all. He's not a horse—can't look in his mouth.' A priest and deacon come out of the altar gates, one candle lights another, muffled voices float down from the choir loft—Shpyn more divines than hears them—they promise eternal rest among the saints in a land without grief and lamentations. Reflecting that soon he too will be tucked up under a blanket of sod, old Fedos sighs and crosses himself. But with the last prayer, the professional in him awakes: he joins the line, hands pressed decorously to his breast. The file of mourners brings Shpyn up to the coffin. He leans over and—peering into the crack between the blue, petrified lips (jolts have forced them slightly apart)—spies two golden glimmers. Upon kissing the corpse, Shpyn steps aside. His face wears the quiet satisfaction and seriousness of a man ready to perform his sad duty to the end. Someone in the crowd looks respectfully at Shpyn then whispers to his neighbor, 'What beautiful sorrow!' The procession is moving. Shpyn's rheumatic legs barely obey, but he mustn't give up now. He shuffles after the casket amid relatives and friends. A young man takes him deferentially by the elbow. Having mentally counted off all the bends in the paths (he'll have to work by night, after all) and memorized the place, the old man quits the cemetery. The rest of the day he dozes, warming his frozen feet by the stove. That night, he packs up his tools and again makes the final journey. And then... but the ending can be taken alive from the watchman's story. Life is stranger than fiction. Well, shall we go? It's getting late. They'll lock the gates."

We strolled out onto the main path, past the church and office. By the office window, my companion paused and peered inside.

"What are you doing?"

"Go on ahead. I'll catch you up."

And, indeed, by the time I had reached the gates he was at my side and smiling in response to my inquiring look.

"I wanted to see if it was still there. It is."

"What?"

"The wreath for hire. They have one here. The watchman told me so. A wreath for poor people. You pay twenty or thirty kopecks, you see, and a proper metal wreath with porcelain forget-me-nots and long black ribbons is brought out to meet the procession, to attend the last rites, and then repose on the grave, full of dignity and grief, lavish and inconsolable. But as soon as the mourners have gone, the watchman fetches it back to the office: to wait for the next casket. What I am about to say may strike you as funny or perhaps absurd, but I feel a brotherly affection for that wreath. For aren't we, the poets, like elegant wreaths erring from grave to grave? Don't we, too, with all our meanings and with all our being, nestle beside the dead and buried? No, no. I shall never agree with the briefcases' current philosophy: one can write only about the crossed-out and only for the crossed-out."

We walked on, elbow to elbow, along the broad outlying streets. Soon we saw the smooth parallels of tram tracks coming toward us. And hard by my shoulder I heard the quiet remark: "If parallels converge in infinity, then all trains that disappear into infinity must, at the convergence, meet with disaster."

We walked two or three blocks without exchanging another word. I was plunged in my thoughts when my companion's sudden voice made me start. "If I haven't worn you out completely I'd like to tell you my last theme. I've often wanted to write it down, but I'm afraid I'll spoil it. It's not long. It won't take ten minutes; or perhaps I shouldn't?"

With a shy smile, he looked at me almost pleadingly.

"No, by all means."

And the story began.

"I want to call it 'The Funeral Repast.' Only this is not about cemeteries. No, no. It's subtler than that. A fellow with a wife, a three-room apartment, a servant, a good salary, and a good name is entertaining friends. The table is littered with empty dishes and bottles, a small glass of toothpicks. The guests repair to the study, to sit by the fire and discuss a recent film, a recent decree, where best to go for the summer. The fellow's wife produces a box of old photographs and family mementos. The fellow rummages in the cardboard piles and suddenly, from the bottom of the box, comes the soft tap of glass. What could it be? He pulls out a vial: the transparent vial is stopped with a cork and inside is a tiny white crystal. Puzzled, the fellow removes the cork and, wetting a finger with saliva, presses it first to the crystal, then to his lips: he gives his guests a sly and mysterious smile. Understanding neither smile nor crystal, they question their host with a dozen eyes. But he demurs. His brow twitches, his eyes narrow. No longer smiling, he looks as though he were trying to remember a dream. His impatient guests crowd around him: 'What is it?' His wife tugs at his shoulder: 'Stop torturing us.' Then the man says, 'Saccharine.' His friends roar, but he is not laughing. When they have quieted, he says, 'I have an idea, let's organize a funeral banquet. In memory of the days when we were hungry and cold. What do you say?'—'You always were a joker.'—'What an eccentric...'

"Then again, why not? Books have become boring, the new

plays have all been seen, and winter evenings are long and un-eventful. They settle on a day and separate amid hoots of 'No other group of friends would . . .'—'Are the trams still running?'—'What an eccentric . . .'

"On the appointed day, the master of ceremonies wakes his wife at dawn: 'Get up—we have to get ready.' She has forgotten all about it, and besides: 'Why rush about at this ungodly hour? The guests aren't coming till this evening.' But her eccentric joker insists. He wakes the servant and sets to work. 'Glasha, open the casement windows and let the cold air in; raise the dampers and don't fire the stoves. Take the wood out of that box—that's right—and stuff the rug in there. Why? In case there's a requisition. Won't fit? Then roll it up—that's right—there you go . . . Move all the things from the bedroom and dining room into my study. Won't fit? Of course they will—and so will we. We'll all be living in the study because we can't heat three rooms. You? You won't be here—I can't afford a servant.' Stunned and frightened, Glasha thinks she must still be asleep and dreaming some absurd dream. But the joker reassures her: 'Just for today. Tomorrow everything will be as it was, understand?' Glasha goes on gawping. But when the master says she may have the day off once she's finished with the furniture, her face brightens, and bureaus, divans, and tables bang, clatter, and scrape their way into the study. Now fully awake, the master's wife tries to put her foot down: 'What can you be thinking of?'—'Not I, we. Now help me to take this shelf down from the wall.' The whole day the house is bustling: must go to the apothecary for saccharine, can't buy rotten flour any-where, forgot to add bran to the bread and mix in bits of straw—nearly in tears, the eccentric's wife kneads the stiff and dirty dough a second time. The study is crammed and clogged with a fantastic conglomeration of things, and still the stubborn man goes up into the attic to hunt for the small iron stove: that rusty absurdity, jabbing its iron trunk into whatever it can, occupies the last free lozenge of floor space.

"When the man, grimy with smut and covered in rust, gets up

off his knees, he sees his wife wrapped in a wool shawl, huddled in a corner of the divan with her knees tucked under her chin. She is watching him with angry and frightened eyes. 'Marra, do you know,' he touches her shoulder (the shoulder jerks away), 'Marra, that's how you looked seven years ago, like a frozen sparrow, in a shawl and fur coat, miserable and forsaken, and I—do you remember?—I drew your icy fingers out from under your shawl, like this, and breathed on them like this, like this until you said, "That's better." ' His wife says nothing. 'Or do you remember how I brought you that comical ration in six tiny paper cones (a mouse couldn't have eaten its fill), and we did all our cooking on this old pile of rust—more smoke and soot than food.'—'But the kerosene stove was worse,' his wife replies, still facing away, 'this one at least warmed us, but that one... and the flame was dim, "sickly," as you said.'—'And here you won't even look at it.'—'And when only a few matches were left in the box,' his wife goes on, oblivious, 'I'd cut them up lengthwise—so that one match made four.'—'Yes, and I couldn't do that, my hands were so clumsy.'—'No, you've forgotten, your fingers were simply frostbitten, that's all.'—'No, no, Marra, my darling, my hands are clumsier.' The man feels a soft shoulder touch his, hears the tender voice that makes his temples sing: 'Oh, how wonderful they were, those long evenings together, just the two of us: if we stirred at all, so did the flame in the oil lamp and the shadows from things would flicker, up-down, up-down, over the table, the walls, the floor. So silly and merry. Did you get the oil lamp?'—'No.'—'Why not? We can't do without that.'—'It went right out of my head.' The man jumps up. 'Never mind, I'll make one. Meanwhile, you unscrew the lightbulbs, like this—see how easy it is, you don't even need a ladder, just climb up onto the tables.'

"The guests begin arriving. Each one first rings the bell and listens for footsteps, then knocks, and finally bangs on the door. 'Who is it?'—asks their host through the chain on the lock. Some don't understand, others get angry, but still others respond in kind. 'Have to knock louder,' their host explains, 'can't hear you through two rooms.' He leads them—one by one—through the dark and empty room cubes to the last, inhabited one. 'Better keep your coats on, we're working on the stove, but it's still around freezing.' The guests shift uneasily from foot to foot, not knowing where to put themselves or what to do. One thinks with dismay of the opera ticket he gave away so as to hang about—who knows why—beside an idiotic oil lamp, in this bleakness and cold; another regrets not having dressed more warmly. Their host seats them on odd trunks, stands, and stools, and suggests they warm themselves with tea. 'Carrot tea,' he says proudly, pouring the boiling swill into mugs of various sizes. 'Very hard to come by. And here's the saccharine. Help yourselves. But be careful—or the tea will be sickeningly sweet.' Slices of bread cut into identical squarelets are divided up even stephen. The guests bring the smoking mugs reluctantly to their lips. Someone notices that steam is coming out of his mouth. Silence.

"The host tries to start the conversation going. 'What do you think,' he turns to his neighbor, 'when will the warm weather arrive?'—'In two or three months,' says his neighbor, burying his nose in the carrot steam. 'My dear sir,' the man who traded the opera for a funeral bursts out, 'how can you be so cavalier? Throwing months around like that. It seems funny now, but in those years—it's true—we calculated to the day. You'd form a sort of working hypothesis that the spring would arrive the first of March—all at once and for good. Then every morning you'd count the days: fifty-three days till spring, fifty-two till fine weather, fifty-one till that long-awaited day. And here you say: two or three months. At the winter solstice, we would gather in a small group and clink cups of this same carrot mash, drunk at the mere thought that the sun had turned in its orbit and was now coming toward us. And you say: two or three months.'

"The conversation, as if it has been stirred in a glass with a spoon, whirls along, faster and faster, gathering everyone up in its course. Empty mugs reach for the kettle. In the heat of an argument, someone swallows his bread-square whole and tries to cough up the bit of straw stuck in his throat.

"'No, listen. Do you remember,' cries the man who forgot to dress warmly, 'do you remember how during that hard December frost we'd pull on our hats (our coats were always on, after all, even inside), and scramble over the snowdrifts—the only source of light besides the stars—to go and hear that lecturer...what was his name, I've forgotten, he later died of typhoid. He would pace, poor soul, from wall to wall, like a caged wolf—and talk about the cosmos, the Revolution, the new problems, crises in life, in art. And when he paused, his mouth would dive under his muffler for a sip of warmth. The air was bitter cold and flecked with flickering shadows (as it is here). We sat there for hours, shoulder to shoulder, and a thousand eyes followed him—from wall to wall, from wall to wall. Our feet grew numb, our soles stuck to the icy floor, but not a rustle, not a murmur. Hush.'—'I went to those readings too,' the host recalls musingly. 'One day he told us that before the Revolution, we did not see the world because of things, we were lost in our possessions; we would only gain, he said, by giving everything away—from the intelligible to the indoor (let them load them onto carts, down to the bare walls, give the walls away too, and the roof over your head)—all things in exchange for the supreme thing: the world.'

"The guests begin to leave. They all shake their host's hand with warm gratitude. On his way out through the empty echoing rooms, the man who gave his ticket away admits to his companion: 'I gave lectures then, too—to political instructors.'—'On what?'—'On ancient Greek vases.'

"The hosts are alone again. The iron stove has gone out and is growing cold. The draft from a door has doused the flame in the oil lamp. The two sit shoulder to shoulder, in the darkness. The city flashes and rattles on the windowpanes. But they don't hear. 'Breathe on my fingers...the way you did then.'—'Will you say, "That's better"?'—'Yes.' He caresses her small palms—first with his breath, then with his lips. Words are so easy to hide inside those meek and tender palms. And the man says, 'Beyond that door is an empty room, and beyond it another empty and dark room; and farther still are more dark and empty rooms; and beyond them; and you'll walk and walk, and not...' Marra suddenly feels prickly warm drops on her fingers, mixing with his breath and words.

"And here, at the end, I want to show that even these harmless lovebirds, these anonymous people on the sidelines, whom the Revolution only grazed—even they, even they cannot help but understand—"

Something suddenly clanked and blazed three steps ahead of us, blocking our path, and came to a stop with a clang: a tram. A second later another bell, shuddering wheels, and—before our eyes in the empty air—through the gloaming, under three red lights: *Flag Stop*. The theme catcher caught my inquiring look and shook his head.

"No, that's not it. And perhaps there is no 'it' to be invented for this theme. I'm crossing it out: the devil take it!"

I even turned around to look: I had the absurd but distinct sense that the theme was there, behind us, on the rails, cut in two by the wheels.

The city was rushing toward us. Automobiles were droning and rumbling, spokes were spinning, horseshoes were clopping, and along the street—up, down, and all around—people were walking. My companion gave me an anxious look: his eyes and even his bristly beard had an apologetic and ingratiating expression (as though asking forgiveness for the sadness he had inadvertently caused). Almost begging me to smile, he remarked, "I have a friend, a former philosopher, and whenever we meet he says: 'What a life! Don't even have time to contemplate the world.'"

I somehow couldn't smile. We turned into the boulevard where it was quieter and less crowded. The theme catcher trailed behind me wearing a rather caught expression himself. He clearly would have liked to rest on a bench. But I strode resolutely on and did

We passed the bench that had introduced us. Suddenly, at the end of the boulevard: a tight motionless ring of people shoulder to shoulder, necks craning toward the center of the circle. We too walked up: music. The sharp squeak of a bow, up-down, and thin whistling sounds struggling to make a melody. I glanced round the circle, then at my companion; he was leaning wearily against a tree, and also listening; his face was intent and proud, his mouth, like that of a daydreaming child, slightly open.

"Let's go."

We tossed our kopecks into the case, crossed the square, and tramped down Nikitsky Boulevard. At the crooked prospect of the Arbat, we stopped; I was searching for my final parting words.

"I hesitate to call it 'gratitude,' but believe me—" I began, but he—as usual—interrupted.

"And even the Arbat. I always associate it with the Arabat Spit. That sandbar is as curved and as narrow, only it continues for a good sixty miles. You know—you could make a story out of it: summer; southbound trains chockfull ('Where are you headed?'— 'What about you?'); and one passenger who does not answer and does not ask; no baskets, no suitcases—just a light knapsack and a staff; he changes to a branch line—Alekseyevka—Genichesk; very few people at first—an almost empty caterpillar of cars, then a tiny Godforsaken town. But the passenger dons his sack and, having thrown a coin to the boatman who has ferried him across the sound to the end of the spit, begins his sixty-mile walk. People would call this walk strange, but there are no people here: the blade of the Arabat is utterly deserted, legs and staff encounter only sand and shingle, rotten seas are either side, a sun-scorched sky above, and ahead an endless strip, narrow and dead, leading on and on. In effect, in the whole world there is only that . . . but you're in a hurry, and I'm gabbling. I've already stolen . . . a day not mine."

I took his hand, and for a long time we held each other's gaze. He understood.

"So there's no hope?"

"None."

I hadn't gone more than a dozen paces when—through the noise and hubbub of the square—his voice overtook me.

"And even so!"

I turned around.

He was standing on the curb, smiling brightly and serenely, and repeating, no longer to me, but to the starburst of streets before him: "And even so."

Those were our final parting words.

4

As soon as I got home I stretched out on the daybed. But my thoughts went on pacing inside my head. It wasn't until almost midnight that the black bookmark of sleep slipped between that day and the next.

Only in the morning, as I let in the sun waiting behind the curtains, did I remember my non-metaphorical bookmark tucked away in the desk drawer. I must, without further delay, attend to its fate.

I first fetched a notebook, then half opened the drawer: the bookmark was still lying on the yellow bottom, having primly smoothed out its faded silk train, an ironic expectant expression stitched into its design. I smiled at my bookmark and again closed the drawer: this time in earnest.

Three workdays went into recording all of this: with mirror-like exactitude I described our two meetings, banishing all words not his, and ruthlessly crossing out all those fellow travelers who would insinuate themselves into the story and be woven into the truth.

When the notebook was ready, I again opened the door of my solitary blue silk bookmark's prison: and we again began our wanderings from line to line inside the notebook. The bookmark often had to wait for me, as it had in those long-ago years, now at one theme, now at another; we mused and dreamed, we pitted *no against no*, making our dilatory and fitful way—from step to step, from paragraph to paragraph, following the theme catcher's images, meanings, expositions, and endings; I remember we spent nearly half of one night over that short, nine-letter phrase: *"And even so..."*

Of course, my old bookmark's quarters are—for the moment—cramped and squalid. But that can't be helped. We all live flattened, we all live in pinched quadratures, cooped up and resentful. But any corner is better than the long, bare literary pavement of today. Well then, I think that's all. Oh yes, I nearly forgot: over the notebook I must—as is customary—put a visiting card with the tenant's name: BOOKMARK.

1927

SOMEONE ELSE'S THEME

OUR MEETING took place here, at this table at which you and I are sitting. Everything was as it is now: backs bent over soup plates, the nickel tinkle of spoons on the counter, even those same scrolls of hoarfrost on the window and from time to time the whirr of the door spring, admitting clouds of icy steam and customers.

I didn't see him come in. His long back with the dirty scarf hanging down over one shoulder entered my field of vision at the point when he, leaning pleadingly, had lingered too long by one of the tables. It was over there—to the right of that column. We, the canteen regulars, were used to the encroachments of all kinds of lumpen playing their sly game with the salivary glands' reflex. Appearing before a masticating mouth with a box of matches or a packet of toothpicks in a grubby hand held out across the appetite, so to speak, they were promptly waved away with a kopeck. But this time both the stimulus and the response were different: instead of producing a copper, the professorial old man to whom the newcomer had appealed suddenly sank with his beard into his borscht then sat bolt upright, his back pressed to the wall, his forehead lined with surprise. The suppliant sighed and, stepping aside, looked about him: Who else? Two officers in greatcoats by the window and a group of students, jabbing happily with forks around a jumble of shoved-together tables, did not appear to satisfy him. After a second's hesitation he made straight for me.

First a polite slight bow, and then: "I wonder, citizen, if you wouldn't like to acquire a philosophical system? With a double embrace of the world: a precept for both the micro- and the macro-cosm. Formulated according to strict and exact methods. An answer to all the great questions. Well, and . . . the cost is not out of the question."

"?"

"You hesitate, citizen. Yet this philosophy of life—which I could let you have even in installments—is entirely original and not part of anyone else's thinking. You would be the first to contemplate it. I'm just a constructor, you see, an assembler of such systems. That's all."

Meeting silence, the man fell silent for a minute himself. But the stubborn crease compressing his long eyebrows would not relax. Bending down almost to my ear, he finished his pitch.

"Please understand that if I give you this system, I myself shall have to do without. If not for my extreme need . . ."

I confess I backed my chair away in some uneasiness: Was the man mad or drunk? Yet his breath was clean, while his eyes were tucked away under glumly lowered lids.

"I won't hide it: my system is idealistic. But then I'm not asking much."

"Listen," I finally spoke up, having decided to put a stop to this nonsense, "no matter who you are and . . ."

Just then he raised his eyes: their squinting pupils were calmly and brightly smiling. Without even a hint of derision, it seemed. I could only smile back. By now the fingers of this maker of a metaphysical conception were resting on the edge of the table.

"If a philosophy of life is more than you can afford then perhaps you'll be satisfied with two or three aphorisms—of your choice. What is your pleasure: depth or brilliance, wit or brevity, philosophical weight or punning wordplay? We should also agree, incidentally, as to their emotional coloring: Do you prefer sad sentiments, you know, resignation, or—"

"Let's say, sad," I muttered, not knowing how to untangle the conversation.

"Hold on."

His fingers drummed nervously on the edge of the table for perhaps five seconds. And then: "There now—all ready. Your attention, please: 'I know a world where people walk on the sunny side, but only . . . at night.'"

After a pause, he looked at me, his buyer, and added, "You don't like it? Not sad enough? Fine, I'll try again. Just a minute. I've got it. Listen: 'You must live in such a way that not one laurel tree suffers because of you.' And finally . . . But this isn't an aphorism: I haven't eaten in four days. Feed me."

In response to my gesture of invitation, the man suddenly crumpled at the knees and dropped into a chair. I rapped on the table and gave the order.

A deep plate. Followed by a shallow one. The seller of aphorisms pushed away the plates, then his chair, got up and nodded graciously.

"We're even."

Ten seconds later the door swung open, spewing an icy blue cloud. The man walked into it, and the door sprang shut. Thus I found myself the puzzled owner of two aphorisms. When, a little later, I had paid the bill and left the canteen, it occurred to me that this incident was not unworthy of fiction and—in the way of all writers—I began to consider how best to incorporate it into my unfinished story. But I was soon distracted by other things. I had a reading to give that evening. Shall we ask for another glass of tea?

So then, you must know—I'm sure you do—that long table with the dark blue circle of a lampshade at one end where once a week, just after nine, someone's manuscript reposes. Two rows of glasses ranged down the table slowly cool while the manuscript, tumbling page upon page, recounts itself to them. My novella was called *The Thirteenth Fever*. It's a strange title, but about something very simple. A thematic introduction: the ancient apocryphal story of the elder Sisinnii and his thirteen daughters, the fevers, who are unmarried and hunting for husbands. The decrepit Sisinnii takes them far and wide in search of worthy candidates. Those who don't know the charm to ward off fever risk betrothal to the sisters. Fiercely competitive, they tear the intended out of one another's arms: the fair Regardense stares so fixedly into the man's eyes that he cannot sleep; the ardent Shiverlee covers his body with kisses and so gives him chills; Ululalia, murmuring passionate and incoherent speeches, compels him to parrot her gibberish; Bluella . . . but the fairest of them all is the thirteenth—Glacialys: her caresses leave the man gasping for air and stretched taut, white pupils to the sun. Meanwhile, the widowed brides trail after their fastidious old father in search of new suitors. You, as a writer, will understand that I couldn't be content with such a skimpy plot. The myth had to be adapted to everyday life and the charm against the fair fevers reworded so that the pharmacist, scanning it at his window, would say, "In an hour." I had, so to speak, to convince the widow virgins and their intractable father to quit that apocryphal story for a work of fiction. I'm sorry you weren't at the reading—that would spare me having to . . .

"Don't be sorry: I was there and I heard you."

Then you should have stopped me right away. Strange I didn't notice you. Better put that sugar cube in your glass now or it won't dissolve. You see, we're both absentminded. In that case, you must also have heard the exchange of opinions afterward. I think people are willing to exchange opinions because they have none. That's right: what a person *has*, he doesn't give up so easily.

"I suppose you could use that as an authorial rejoinder. But as I recall, you refused."

Yes, but my mental brakes aren't very strong. I did speak up, though by then there were no ears about, not counting, that is, one pair caulked with cotton and tucked inside the upturned collar of a fur coat. I couldn't manage to avoid them: that complicated combination of narrow body, bulky coat, and bundle of books slipping out from under one elbow had gotten stuck in the entrance between the double front doors. I helped him.

"Much obliged," said the old man. "Which way are you going?"

Remembering that this decrepit ex-critic was garrulous and always went to the right, I bowed: "To the left."

"So am I."

It turned out he had moved. There was no help for it. Trying not to show my annoyance, I slowed my step, and we plodded on side by side, slowly and seriously, as though following a hearse. You, of course, know that tiresome eccentric: the drooping gray mustache around his mouth out of which he, twitching rhythmically, shakes endless fistfuls of words. Once upon a time he had written "Critical Surveys," "A Few More Remarks on...," "Another Look at...," but the writers he reviewed were long dead and no graveyard needs "A Few More Remarks."

"Given what people said today about that little piece you were good enough to read...hmm, yes, piece," the ex-critic mused, dragging his feet over the snow, "I should describe you as a literary descendant of Leskov, with his apocryphisms, and of Poe, with his love of the fantastic, and of this one and of that one... but all that's beside the point. To try and explain you, one must close the bookcase door and name just one name."

"Namely?"

"Saul Straight."

"What?"

"I'm speaking of Saul Straight. Is that a smile I see? In that case, you're much more cheerful than your piece. I don't know why, but it reminded me of Straight's remark about a world where people walk on the sunny side..."

I grabbed the old man by the hand, and the bundle of books hiding under his elbow flopped down on the snow, cutting short the quote. Overcome by surprise, I stood inert while my companion, groaning and coughing, gathered up the scattered bundle.

"Then you know him too, the man selling a philosophical system?"

"That's right. First it's 'how' and 'who,' and then it's 'you too.'

Everyone knows Saul Straight, but it doesn't pay to admit it. You say he's selling a system. Well, that means he has one."

Somewhat confused, I hastened to tell the ex-critic of how for a plate of soup I had acquired an aphorism. It wasn't hard to jog the old man's memory. We kept walking and stopping, walking and stopping, the straggling bundle of books shifting from under one elbow to the other and back again. The gist of what the critic told me amounts to the following.

They had met some nine years before in a public library, at the desk where they give out the books. This was in the days when we read a book without removing our gloves and breathed on its text with icy steam. The long tables were punctuated by military broadcloth and worn wool, and the occasional stamping of frozen feet. The librarian, sliding noiselessly about in felt boots, had vanished into the stacks. The people in line would have to wait. Glancing over the shoulder of the man in front of him, the critic noticed the request slip patiently protruding from his fingers: NAME: Saul Straight. TITLE REQUESTED: *A Description for the Edification of Seafarers of the Greatest Shipwrecks from . . .*; but then the librarian's felt boots emerged from the stacks, the request slip jumped from hand to hand, and the critic got no farther. The critic reminded me that at the time he was working on his "A Few More Remarks on the Fates of the Russian Intelligentsia." The armchair in which he established himself was next to that of the student of shipwrecks. "A Few More Remarks" was essentially finished: it only needed some polishing and an epigraph. Having rummaged through various tomes, the critic was just inserting something between title and text when suddenly he heard: "Cross it out. It's no good. That line has been everyone's epigraph for the last fifty years. Let the poor thing rest. I'll lend you a line no one has ever used before. Write this down."

You can imagine how our venerable ex-critic goggled at this un-solicited advice: he was grateful for the comrade's concern, but the comrade who looks over someone's shoulder must know that one cannot suggest an epigraph without knowing the work to which—

Straight interrupted. "Yes, I managed to read only the end of the title: '... sian Intelligentsia.' But are you sure that your readers will want to read more than that? Besides, I have an advantage over your readers: I've met the author and can state that he's a member of the intelligentsia writing about the intelligentsia. Clearly, there's only one possible epigraph, you can't miss it. But suit yourself. As for looking over your shoulder, forgive me. Now we're quits. Wouldn't you say?"

Clapping his shipwrecks shut, Straight got up and made his way out.

The ex-critic didn't deem it necessary to recall the emotions and motives that led, after a moment's inaction, to his decision: to overtake the departing epigraph. Of course, he would have to observe the proprieties and not betray too great a curiosity. Smiling indulgently, he would say, "Now what is it you were, you know..."

I imagine the critic managed to do this with a certain degree of naturalness.

He found Straight in the vestibule wrestling with a foot wrapping that had come undone. Taking the safety pin out of his mouth, but without unbending his back, Straight replied, "If my epigraph should strike you as crude, that's because it's not from a bookshelf. It's a *chastushka* I jotted down in the train. What is your whole title? 'On the Fates of the Russian Intelligentsia'? Well then, how about this:

I'll sit down upon a stone and cry so awf'lly:
No man'll take me to wife, they only paw me."

Having pinned his foot wrapping, Straight stood up.

"Then again, your well-mannered theme will scarcely allow its epigraph to treat it so boorishly. Isn't that true?"

The ex-critic must have made a wry face. But rather than turn away, civility compelled him to show a certain generosity by asking questions: "What are you working on? What is your focus?"

To which Straight replied tersely: "You."

"What do you mean?"

"Just that: you critics. And I warn you: the question of how criticism occurs to a critic is to me less important than the subtler question of how a critic slips into existence. By means of what trick does this passenger without a ticket—"

"But allow—"

"I can't allow any buts, unfortunately, as this concerns literary critics."

The old man could only shrug; Saul Straight meanwhile went on.

"Didn't one of your confreres, the most outspoken of them, I'm thinking of Hennequin, wasn't he so incautious as to admit that 'a work of fiction affects only those whom it portrays'? Open *La Critique scientifique*: that's literally what it says. But a work of fiction recounts the life of its *characters*. If one were to allow a character into life without a ticket, so to speak, if one were to give him the bookcase key and the right to knock on existence's door, then that character would be forced during his sojourn among us—about this there can be no doubt—to devote himself to criticism, and criticism alone. Why? Simply because he of us all is the one most concerned with his own fate, because he must hide his nonexistence, a nonexistence that, you must agree, is more inconvenient even than being of noble birth. And so a creature less real than the ink with which he writes takes up self-criticism in a desperate attempt to prove his alibi with respect to the book: I was never there, he says, I was an artistic failure, the author couldn't make readers believe in me as a type *in there*, in the book, because I'm not a type and not in the book, rather I, like all of you, dear readers, am *out here* among you, this side of the bookcase door, and I write books myself, real books, like a real person. True, when the critic is making a fair copy of this tirade, he always changes 'I' to 'we' ('As we wrote in our article'—'We are glad to report'): all this is perfectly natural and explainable— a creature with a poor sense of identity had best avoid the first-person singular. At any rate, the characters populating books, like us, the people populating our planet, are either believers or atheists. Clearly. What I'm trying to say," Straight went on excitedly (the critic couldn't get a word in), "is that not all characters turn into critics (if that were to happen, we'd all be done for!). No, the ones who become critics are the ones who deny their author's existence—they're the book's atheists. They don't wish to be invented by some inventor and so take revenge the only way they know how: by trying to prove that it's not the author who invents the characters, it's the characters who invent the author. You'll say I stole that from Feuerbach: I don't deny the critic's erudition, I only deny his existence."

Here the ex-critic tried nevertheless to show some existence by standing up for himself and those like him. He repeated to me every word of his wrathful rebuke to Straight. But since you're interested only in the latter, I'll mention just one of his arguments: that Straight's theory makes sense only at the expense... of common sense.

It turned out that Saul Straight, despite the strange glint in his eyes, had nothing against common sense. He explained—somewhat appeasing the ex-critic's wrath—that while characters did not, of course, exist outside books, a character-like psychology, a sense of the made-upness of one's existence, was a genuine, scientifically established fact. Had the notorious student Danilov known, as he prepared to murder, that the libretto of his crime had been completed two years before by Dostoevsky, then perhaps he would have preferred to start with the writer. But Danilov, in all likelihood, had never read *Crime and Punishment*, whereas the critic, as a professional reader, reads and reads until he encounters *himself*. That's when his career takes off. The point is that characters do not, of course, turn into people, but people often turn into characters, that is they serve as material for people who invent people. Turgenev's Rudin, Lezhnev, Bazarov, and Pigasov impress us precisely because life bears them out with its own approximations, if not doubles. And an invented person makes the greatest impression, naturally, on the seemingly not-invented, real person who, upon finding his reflection in a book, feels replaced and redoubled. This person cannot forgive his feeling of double insult: here I, a real, not-invented person, shall go to my grave and nothingness in ten or twenty years, whereas this fabricated, not-real "almost I" shall go on living and living as though it were the most natural thing in the world; more unforgivable still is the awareness that someone, some author, made you up like an arithmetic problem, what's more he figured you out, arrived at an answer over which you struggled your entire life in vain, he divined your existence without ever having met you, he penned his way into your innermost thoughts, which you tried so hard to hide from yourself. One must refute the author and vindicate oneself. At once! The so-called antiheroes are always in a particular rush: Isn't that why Turgenev was criticized mainly by the Pigasovs, Dostoevsky by the Ferdyshchenkos, and Griboyedov by the Molchalins?

The theory was coming to its final conclusions, which the old critic preferred to dodge by throwing a question at them.

"Won't annulling the existence of critics lead to an excessive glorification of writers, to a demiurgification of perfectly ordinary persons? In short, what mystical *something* distinguishes a creator of culture from its consumers?"

Straight's reply was sad and brief: "Honesty. Only honesty."

On seeing the ex-critic's eyebrows shoot up, he must have explained with the same sadness: "Well yes. Has it never occurred to you that the sun shines on credit? Every day it lends its rays to every one of us; it allows itself to be seized by millions of pupils in the hope that it is dealing with honest debtors. But in fact the earth is teeming with free gazers. They know only how to take, speculate, spectate, and squint through their fists. They plunder placers of glints, sounds, and rays with no thought of paying: with daubs, words, tones, numbers. No one dares look straight at the sun: Isn't that because the consciences of the sun's debtors aren't entirely clear? Of course, to give everything back, down to the last glint, is beyond anyone's power, but to try to do what one can, to give at least copper for gold, at least something for everything—that is the indisputable duty of anyone who doesn't wish to be a thief of his own existence. Talent is just that, a basic *honesty* on the part of 'I' toward 'not I,' a partial payment of the bill presented by the sun: the painter pays for the colors of things with the paints on his palette, the musician pays for the chaos of sounds produced by the organ of Corti with harmonies, the philosopher pays for the world with his worldview. Indeed, the word τό τάλαντον means 'balance.' A correctly constructed talent is a constantly maintained balance between what one is given and what one gives back, an eternal fluctuation of the scales that weigh: what comes from without and what comes from within, 'to me' and 'I.' That's why talent," Straight continued to torment the ex-critic, "is not a privilege and not a gift from on high, but the direct responsibility of anyone warmed and lighted by the sun, and only metaphysically dishonorable people—of which the earth is full—shirk their duty to be talented."

"And what did you say to that?"

"'Goodbye.' Allow me to say the same to you. This is where I live."

Walking up to a dark entrance, the ex-critic fumbled about for the bell. No one rushed to answer it, however, so I managed to insert a few more questions.

"Did you meet again?"

"Yes. Two or three times."

"Did you continue your discussion about critics?"

"No. You can't continue anything with Straight. He's always got some new idea."

"Namely?"

"I don't really recall. One time he tried to persuade me that instead of all those patent medicines for toothache and the common cold, science ought to come up with something for remorse.

Bang him on the head with a bell clapper: he still won't open the door, the beast! Another time..."

But just then a light shone inside the entrance.

"'Another time,' you were saying?"

"About 'another time' another time. Ha! Oh no, now he'll be searching for the keys until the Second Coming! The second time that man Straight acquainted me with his treatise on the idea of progress. A very strange book. Beginning with the title, the reader runs into... There we go, finally!"

The door creaked open but I, not wanting to let the title go, grabbed the old man by the sleeve. He tried to pull away, then: "*Advantages of the Empty over the Vacant: A Book of Definitions.* Let go of my arm."

When I got home—the hour was late—I undressed and switched off the light. But I couldn't switch off my thoughts or extinguish my consciousness for quite some time: wandering about my somnolent brain, picking his careful way from cell to cell, was that mysterious "character" who had stolen the bookcase key so as to lock compromising nonexistence away and wander as a likeness among those like him; the subjects and predicates of sad aphorisms kept drawing together and moving apart, trading places to the accompaniment of a crude two-line *chastushka*. And when sleep did finally come, I can't say that it helped me blot out the impression of that day.

The next day, after lunching here at the usual time, I lingered for an extra half hour, waiting for the seller of the philosophical system. I now felt inclined, if not to acquire, at least to examine this philosophy of life, peddled on the sly like an obscene postcard. In any case, this fantastic purchase and sale might serve as an excuse to help the hungry rich man. But Saul Straight did not appear. Not that day, not in the days following. Perhaps he had managed to sell his ware elsewhere: I don't know—I don't read our philosophical periodicals, indeed I'm not sure that we have any.

More than four months passed. First snow, then puddles, then dust on your teeth. And then one day at dusk, walking up Pre-chistensky Boulevard, my eyes on Gogol's bronze back, I bumped into someone's feet. The feet—the toes of their yellow patent-leather shoes stretched out across the boulevard's yellow sand—had no intention of moving. I looked the obstacle in the face and couldn't help but scream, "Straight?"

A dashing black felt hat nodded discreetly in reply. The hands of the lover of aphorisms remained where they were: in his pockets. I sat down beside him.

"I'd like to know how you distinguish the empty from the vacant. If it's not too much trouble..."

Straight was silent.

"Perhaps your manuscript would be more forthcoming."

Suddenly Straight, smiling with affection, gave a long, soft whistle. I looked him in the face: his eyes scanned the grass and path then went back to staring at the toes of his shoes.

"Gone, the wretch!"

"Your manuscript, you mean?"

"Of course not."

"But where is your *Book of Definitions*?"

"In a dust hole."

I felt the need to get even.

"As far as I know, editors pay for manuscripts only sometimes, dust holes never. But then where did you get those shoes, etcetera? Forgive the direct question. Or did you manage to swap your philosophy of life for a hat? Feel free to extend your series of rude answers. I'm listening."

"Oh, no." Straight raised his eyes to me, and a slight smile touched the corners of his lips. "A philosophy of life is more terrible than syphilis and people—you have to give them credit—take every precaution not to become infected. Especially by a philosophy of life."

"But then how, my dear Straight, do you feed yourself? I'm

certainly very happy to see those pink cheeks in place of yellow hollows."

"The secret of my satiation is exceedingly simple: read the paper not front to back, but back to front. And your stomach will never grumble.

"That's right. You must look for guiding ideas not in the lead articles but in some notice about a lost lapdog. You laugh. But it's true. Even this," Straight unrumpled a page of newsprint and pointed to an item circled in pencil: "'LOST... a pug, on the corner of...' that's not important, 'answers to Charles, I beg you, for a substantial...' and so on. The point here, of course, is not the pug or it's being lost, but that deeply lyrical 'I beg you.' I don't much believe words for which authors have been paid, and so once when I found a newspaper on a boulevard bench—this was in my hungry days—I read it carefully, never getting further than the Classifieds, for which, as you know, the authors are not paid, but rather pay themselves; and in among the long columns of words, small and gray as the ink that had printed them, what did I see but a sincere and self-paid 'I beg you.' In among the items, symbols, boxes, and rules, suddenly a cry for help, a raw human emotion, the sort of feeling that usually hides inside sealed envelopes—here it was in an open column for anyone who wanted it. I recall thinking at the time: 'I wish they'd force all those gentlemen who constantly mutter "I must ask you" and "Be so kind" to occasionally remember "I beg you!" Even emotion needs exercise.'

"Immediately a plan formed in my head. I would most likely have rejected it but for the encounter of Opus 81 and Article 162. I'm speaking of the Criminal Code and Beethoven's Sonata in E-flat Major. Perhaps you're in a hurry? Because this is something that must be told either from beginning to end or not at all."

I had a rendezvous in a quarter of an hour. But then I thought: an article and an opus meet more rarely than a man and a woman; if I'm five or ten minutes late, she'll forgive me.

I signaled to Straight: continue.

"This idea happened to me perhaps two months ago."

I listened to Straight without interrupting—people for whom ideas replace facts have the right to use such phraseology.

"Come spring, the music kept in apartments behind double panes of glass manages now and then to run out to passersby. During those May evenings, my ears too were hungry. And when—this was in a lane across the river—an open window let fall into the darkness the first adagio bars, I stopped short, as if over a precipice, and listened. The breathless two-four time eased into four-four: I recognized the restrained sorrow of the first movement, *Les Adieux*. Just then there jingled past, as though through the sonata, a cab and the voice of the cabby coaxing his jade. By the time the noise had faded and abated, the open window was reciting the sonata's second movement: *L'Absence*."

For a minute Straight was quiet, dividing the silence into beats with his hand. And then: "I'm even a little afraid of that *andante espressivo*: it so artfully *absents*, so imperiously parts a person from people and things; a few more bars, it seems, and any return will be impossible. It's that feeling—we've all had it—when wheels are carrying us away, while our thoughts keep coming back, when the space between 'I' and 'you' is inexorably widening, and the closer the one and only, the farther away, and thus, the farther the closer. I understand why Beethoven, striving to drive the E-flat melancholy of this sonata of leave-takings into fingers not his own, could not find—for the first time in his life—readymade terms. Yes, it's here, above the theme of absences, that we see the direction—seemingly lost among the Italian words—in his native language: *In gehender Bewegung, doch mit Ausdruck.** I remember that then too, through the accelerating race of piano keys, in the howling wind of octaves and thirds, there flickered a tiny 'I beg you,' but pounding right after it came the final six bars at *tempo primo*, and before I could catch the signal word, the sonata had veered into its third movement: the abrupt *vivacissimamente*

---

*In unhurried motion, but with expression (*Ger.*).

flooded my ears like a joyful torrent. This was the famous *Le Retour*: the return, the reuniting of the disunited. You recall those oscillating triplets in the left hand, hand joining hand, the fever of notes and lips, the pedal pumping on the upbeats so the piano nearly chokes... but then Stuart Mill was right: to understand is to transgress. The devil only knows how it's all done, but it's done in such a way that when I had finished listening, I stood for a long time under the now-shut window, unable to take my leave of the sonata of leave-takings. At the time I had a fair amount of leisure—so I invited the sonata, as it alighted from the keys, to walk with me along the muddy cobbles in the lanes across the river. In exchange for the emotion the music had given me, I offered to help it finish what it had begun. Happiness, I argued, doesn't like to oblige people because people don't give it (happiness) any holidays. If people knew how to live like the sonata, in three movements, interspersing meetings with partings, allowing happiness to go off for short spells, for a few bars at least, they mightn't be so unhappy. Strictly speaking, music isn't in time, time is in music. Yet we treat our time extremely unmusically. A city knows nothing of separations—that never-dispersing crowd, music without pauses—the people in it are too close together to be close to one another. The narrow streets along which you and I are now wandering, Sonata, are forever knocking into each other for want of space, physical or otherwise; but the roofless sky thrown open overhead reminds us of its boundless and insuperable emptinesses. If orbits intersected like streets, and stars crossed paths like people, they would all have crashed into one another and the sky would be benighted and black. No, up there, everything turns on an eternal separateness. And if we won't unwedge our cramped everyday life with separations, if we won't convert our collectives from a close order to an extended one—we may perish. An old saying compares separations to the wind that douses the candle but fans the flames. So let us sow the wind. Let all the guttering tapers go out, and the sooner the better, all those tiny particles of feeling that produce more soot than warmth or light. The person who doesn't want his soup rattles his spoon and pushes the plate away; but people with no appetite for each other tend to rattle on and on, unable to push away what is unnecessary. The idiotic 'light in the window' should also be put out by the wind of separations: we don't need sitting rooms, or shaded lamps, or round tables. We need strictly enforced rules: on odd days of the month, say, forbid acquaintances to recognize each other in the street; replace two-seater droshkies with one-seaters; impose fines on those who go about in pairs. Equate meetings of husbands and wives with those of convicts; allow children to speak to their parents only on the telephone; give those who abandon their families reduced fares..."

Saul Straight might well have liked to go on with his list, but I protested. He listened closely to my words, shaking his head in time to them.

"Well yes. Well yes. But elements are necessarily elementary. My reforms may be as mechanistic and dead as the ticking of a metronome, but only with a metronome can one nail a rhythm into arrhythmia, can one teach music to the spiritually tone-deaf. Take even that dreary barrel organ of seductions, marriage, that agreement never to part... In the folktale about the Fool who, on meeting a wedding party, says 'Good Lord,' it's not clear to me who the real fool is. In binding lives, one needn't bind hands; the bell at the train station can easily replace the one in the church tower. Double beds are double graves. The Florentine seigniory that banished Dante, wresting him from his *prediletta donna*,* did love a great service. Only by going through the inferno of parting, the purgatory of separation to the edge of a return, could the great master fashion from three canticles his divine sonata, or Comedy—if you wish. I could easily outline my elaborate yet elegant system of separationism, but what interests me now is the art of separationism—not the theory but the practice. I'll tell you about my first experiments in..."

*Beloved (*Ital.*).

"In dognapping," I prompted, preparing to parry curtness with curtness.

"Right you are," replied Straight with complete equanimity. "But what is one to do if one can give people only what has been taken from them? Give a person what isn't his, what isn't included in his life, like an item in a sum, and it will turn out to be not for him. Addition is checked by means of subtraction, and I took it upon myself to play the minus sign. The healthy man, you see, doesn't feel his health, but how keenly does the convalescent. Of course, subtraction—and on a global scale—has long been the occupation of death; the disconsolate black rule around the name subtracted from existence can't move death to pity, what's more, you'll say, death doesn't read the papers. Leaving aside the question of scale, I have the advantage of being beggable and not opposed to paying five kopecks for a paper. I can inspire whole columns of sorrowful, almost funereal notices and then, having allowed people time to grieve, I can hear their prayers, I can soften and return to them their barking, mewing, and yapping delights. At the same time, one mustn't deprive them of the chance to behave decently...at least in terms of a reward. Yes, some days I feel like a small kind god, who, like the evangelical 'thief in the night,' absconds with their limp and skimpy shoots of happiness only to preserve them from earthly drought and hail in his heavenly gardens and then return them flowering with lush blossoms..." Straight suddenly burst out laughing.

Two or three minutes later I no longer knew what he was laughing at: his rhetorical phrase or his first experiment in separationism, which had indeed put him in a rather comical situation.

The first dog to respond to Straight's whistle happened to be of indeterminate breed and equally indeterminate color, but anxious to tag along. The organizer of separations especially liked the dog's intelligent eyes: they seemed to understand the whole purpose of the project, metaphysical premises included. Having gobbled half of Straight's breakfast, the dog began following his kind

god around. God and dog spent the night on a cold boulevard
bench. Come morning, the back page was complaining to scores:
LOST—GONE—DISAPPEARED.

Straight inspected the dog for distinctive markings: he was a
bad judge of canine heraldry, and the stray's indeterminate color
made it fit almost any description. Straight tried out different
nicknames, but again his friend, so eager to please, answered to
them all, ears cocked and tail wagging "yes." This greedy but not
fussy creature pounced on any name and all food, garbage scraps
included. After long deliberation, Straight marked one of the
boxes in the paper, whistled to the dog, and set off for the address
listed. They weren't a hundred paces from their goal when the
organizer of separations was stopped by the thought: Ought he to
rush the tempo so? To replace the languor of the *slentando* with a
harried *vivace*? Longing must be allowed to ripen, no wonder the
E-flat Major sonata has a second movement, no wonder that movement contains tropes of suspension—*quieto* and *ritardando*. An
overly quick return won't have the desired effect. Straight turned
on his heels. He let another day go by. The distress of the person
signaling in the paper was hard to gauge, but Straight's was only
mounting: the voracious animal had cadged a good two-thirds of
his abductor's stores and was continuing to brazenly beg for more.
Next morning Straight exchanged his last copper for a paper: the
notice had disappeared. The moment had come when the hooked
emotion must be yanked fast—out of the darkness into the light.
The person sinking into despair must be caught in time: "Ps-s,
Daisy, let's go." Ten minutes later Saul Straight was ringing the
bell of the apartment listed in yesterday's paper. In response he
heard barking. Then a muffled, "Down, Daisy," then—unhurried
footsteps and a head above the chain. Before Straight could open
his mouth, the head yelled, "This is not a knackery!" Snorting with
disdain, the man slammed the door. Straight said the False Daisy
had a discouraged look. I suspect he did too. Only now did he see
the utter miserableness of the dog's points: a homeless mongrel
with more filth on her than fur. The organizer of separations tried

to leave her in the entrance, but separating from her wasn't that simple. Around the first corner she caught him up, barking frantically. Straight stamped his feet and tried to drive her away. Nothing worked.

"Then it occurred to me that there are worse problems in life," said Straight. "Besides, we were both of us beggars, the dog and I. We've been inseparable ever since. Here, False!"

A shaggy ball came barreling out of the grass and threw its paws up on its master's knees. Shining with a religious ecstasy, the ball's eyes tried to catch the gentleman's gaze.

"Now, now, False, lie down. And you know, the kind deed turned out to be the most practical. (It almost always does.) False earns her keep: since the sheltered canine aristocracy tends to be intrigued by common bitches, she...well, in a word, she makes my job much easier.

"Yes, success belongs to the man who perseveres in the face of failure. Little by little I acquired the necessary skills. The heart, like any mechanism, has a mainspring: make a person wait too long, and he'll stop waiting; the mechanism of emotion, having uncoiled its spring, will stop. 'Nothing in excess,' as the ancient poet said. I studied the habits of dogs, cats, and especially their masters. And I can assure you, few people are welcomed as warmly as I am, often with tears of joy. Some may have their suspicions and may guess, but the emotion of a reunion of bipeds and quadrupeds usually washes everything away—it's for that emotion, for that quickening of the pulse, that people offer money and handshakes. Yes, as a professional purveyor of small homely pleasures, I'm optimistic: I believe that business will soon be booming. When I've set aside the necessary sum, I mean to start a small trade in special aids. I'll put up a sign in black letters: SUICIDE WARES; and in the window: INFORMATION ABOUT NONEXISTENCE FROM 11 TO 4. What does this have to do with what I was just saying? Everything: if you're organizing separations, you must first help all those who want to separate from life. That's right. This is that theme of guttering candle-ends that should be blown out by the wind. The person who, having come to life, waffles between 'not to be' and 'to be' only holds up the general flow; existence doesn't allow visits 'without serious intentions.' Of course, one shouldn't throw the baby out with the bathwater, but if the baby wants to throw itself out, my office will make all the arrangements. Oh, you'll see—sooner or later my experiments will go from the back page to the front page; separationism will be taught in every university; men and women will live on different continents; the classes too will be completely separate. For not until history's metronome has rapped out the last bar of the *Abwesenheit* shall the exultant *vivacissimamente* of the return of all—of all—of all to all—to all—to all, the pan-global *Wiederleben*,* come to pass, and the coda of the sonata of separations ring out!"

A minute later Straight's tall figure, the dog dancing around it, was receding into the distance, dark-yellow shoe polish flashing over the boulevard's light-yellow sand.

Needless to say, I was late to my rendezvous: a small tribute, if you like, to the theory of separations. I spent the entire evening alone. Perhaps it was that evening, I can't remember exactly, that revealed to me the logical vista that led to my decision: to separate from literature. But this, of course, didn't happen right away. And then . . . a lot of this is personal. My story had best go on without stopping at the small stations. At any rate, I felt that I had landed in a boggy place where one thinks from thought to thought, as from tussock to tussock. Many years before, reading notes published by a famous French sculptor, I had come across this observation of the Master's: Beauty is not an attribute, a permanent quality, it is only a moment in an object's development, it cannot be contemplated, but must be caught, struck with one's chisel in flight, like a bird with an arrow. The blossoming of a girl's body, for example, is almost as brief as that of an apple tree or yarrow. Eye and chisel must watch and wait until the model, whose profession it is to bare her body day after day, one day suddenly bares

*Rebirth (*Ger.*).

her soul as well. Then chisel and eye mustn't lose a single session so as to finish their work before that vision—the one thing for which it's worth refining and perfecting one's apperceptive apparatus—disappears. We ask of a thing endlessly, over and over, but a thing responds only once. To miss it, that one time, is to miss everything. Upsurge, peak, chute. Now youth is past, and the nude body is merely naked—bared, if you will, of its nudity. Both Rodin and Altenburg understood this. But if one takes this thought further, it turns out that the artist is a master of *one thing*; to find his one thing, lost in the multitudes, is not easy; to find it at the moment of its blossoming, when it is full-blown, consummate—that is difficult indeed. And to find it when he is at the height of his powers, so that the maximum in subject and object coincide—that is simply impossible. Anything less than that maximum, I cannot accept. That is a step down from art, and therefore not art.

In squeezing my thoughts into these few phrases I have, of course, simplified them. As the number of lines in this crude sketch increased, as it covered itself with more and more strokes, it became fairly complicated—for me, at least—tangling me up most unfortunately in its angles and lines. Having begun to think of how to cast myself ashore out of this inky sea striated with thousands of pens, I, naturally, cast myself into another, broader theme. This happened because literature for me is more than literature. Saul Straight, in his discourse on separations from life, neglected to mention a greater separation: from one's own self. For it does occasionally happen that that je ne sais quoi by the one-letter name of "I" gets away from a person, like a dog from its master, and wanders about the devil knows where. And when your "I" is missing, when you're just the binding from which the book has been ripped out...it's impossible to explain because there isn't enough..."because." I knew that only one person could return my former status to me, but our papers aren't in the habit of printing notices like:

LOST

MY SOUL

I BEG YOU, FOR A SUBSTANTIAL REWARD...

That would be just too un-Marxist. Yes, I had to find a way of finding Straight—it wasn't that simple. People in his profession don't usually leave any traces of their existence in address offices. The chance of meeting him in a city of two million with eight thousand crossroads was, according to the theory of probability, one eight-millionth multiplied by... In short, even probability theory was against me. I began asking writers of my acquaintance: the two syllables—Saul Straight—acted on some like a bright light: they lowered their eyes; others began looking warily about them and were in a hurry to be off, as though this were the name of a creditor; given my desire to be fair and objective, I should tell you that one writer turned red. He was the youngest and not inked through, so to speak. The ex-critic was undoubtedly right about certain things.

Fourteen months went by, bringing us, too, nearer the end. I did finally run into Straight. Three weeks ago. And do you know I had so ceased to believe in the help of chance that I didn't immediately recognize the seller of metaphysical systems. Yes, and it was hard to discern the old Straight in that scraggy figure covered in rags. Only the familiar scarf, the ends of which flapped like the wings of a bird in the sharp October air, arrested my attention and progress. But Straight, who had not noticed me, continued quickly on his way. I rushed after him. At first I could see only his narrow back. Then he must have heard the tramp of footsteps, for he looked around, looked away, and abruptly increased his pace. As did I. Straight turned down a side street. I followed. It was easier for him to walk in his holey clothes and scarf than for me in my heavy fur coat, but I am a person who takes his dinner every day—and that gave me the advantage. Having caught up to within a few yards, I could see that he was giving out: once or twice he tottered, he might push himself another ten or twenty steps, but then he would stop, like a clock that had run down, and I kept on, elbowing people aside. Some of them stared: this must have looked like the pursuit of a pickpocket by the owner of the pocket picked. A policeman on duty raised a tentative whistle to his lips. Two or three bystanders rushed to intercept Straight. But by then he could go no farther: he was slumped against a brick wall, his face wet with sweat and grinning strangely at me. The thick steam of our breaths crossed in the beam of a streetlamp.

"What do you want? I don't owe you even a dog. Leave me alone!"

His voice, broken by heart-leaps, was barking and hoarse; he himself, unshaven and in tatters battered by the wind, put me in mind for a moment of False. But this was no time for associations. The circle of onlookers was ready to close in. I called out to a cabby. Straight evidently preferred the wall pressed to his back. I barely managed to wrest him from the icy bricks and bundle him under the cover drawn around by the cabby—then a pair of sled runners helped us slip away from that absurd street scene. Ten minutes later I was thawing Straight out with tea boiled on the primus and an electric foot-warmer pulled up to the cracked toes of his faded-yellow shoes. The door of my study was tight shut. Straight gulped the scalding water and broke off pieces of bread with red, unfreezing fingers. Only his words would not unfreeze, pause followed pause, like bricks growing up into a wall. Finally I decided to try.

"My dear Straight," I said, looking anxiously into eyes so sunken they seemed imbedded in his brain, "silence, in the end, is not a bad answer to a question about a certain man in service to the word —that is, literature. But I'm convinced that you, and only you, can offer me something more than silence or even a philosophical system. Please, you're the only person I'm not ashamed to ask: help me with a difficult conviction of mine, and . . ."

Straight's eyes looked away. "Did anyone help me with my

conviction? Or do you think that it was easy? That the four laws of thought plus four solid walls and iron bars isn't much?"

This time the long pause was my fault. Finally, and not without effort, I gathered up a fistful of words so as to shy them across the silence. "I only wanted to help you help me. You already did this once. But since you're speaking through your eight walls and since you find me, for one reason or another, unsympathetic—"

Straight, who had watched with patient irony as my request retreated, phrase by phrase, suddenly came in pursuit.

"'Unsympathetic'? Oh, that would suit us both. But that's just the point, I find you sympathetic, you must understand, extremely sym-pa-the-tic, which also repels me."

"You used to joke in a different way, Straight."

"Yes. But now I don't have anything to do with jokes. Gentle humor and a kind smile affixed to one's face—that's the style of sympathetic people. I've made up my mind to end—once and for all—this scandalous affair with sympatheticness, kindheartedness, humanity, and the mealymouthed. To meet with a so-called kind person compromises me. Is that clear?"

"To be honest, not entirely. What has made you so—"

"Conceit. You, a sympathetic person, must understand that neither you nor people like you will ever be able to *do* anything for anyone anywhere. Your very designation, composed of σύν and πάθος, contains not the slightest hint of doing. We, not you, we, the unsympathetic, have only recently learned how to translate this name correctly from the Greek: *compassionate*. We don't mean to deprive you, citizen symps, of your abilities, not at all: thousands of years after science has eradicated the last traces of the concept of the 'soul,' you, the sympathetic, will still be 'unburdening your souls' to each other and 'talking heart-to-heart,' dropping by when you see 'a light in the window' and calling each other 'friend'—that's all you'll be capable of. For centuries to come you'll be offering tea and sympathy, seeking to be the 'evening sacrifice,' and always—at the dawn of ages—poking your

com into things comproletarian, comclassless, comclass, com...
Oh, damn! You'll hang about conflagrations offering to douse
them with your tears; while others are beating drums, you shall
be beating your breasts and standing up for the disappearing culture, for...well, generally for *for*, but not for *against*. I hate that!"

"But there's another verb, my good Saul. And its first-person
singular sounds like this: I love."

"Nonsense: evol—that's if you say it backward, a word worthy
of mollusks, and just as meaningful. In prison I had time to consider all of this from end to end. Christianity collapsed, I say, only
because the world did not. That's right, think in terms of the Four
Gospels. They turn on the belief that soon—within months, days
even—the world will end. The ax laid unto the root is a sorrow to
haymakers...including the man working in the fields when the
trumpet sounds and heaven rolls up like a scroll, well, and on it
goes...or rather it doesn't, it ends, the world, cast out of its orbit
to its death. Given this assumption of imminent doom, loving
one's neighbor as oneself was perfectly sensible and, more important, the only thing to do. There was no alternative. If *you* today
for me are 'I,' then tomorrow...but beginning tomorrow Christianity will lift, like the fog at dawn, because, you must admit, to
love another as oneself for a day or even two, that is doable, but to
love him your entire life and from one generation to the next for
two thousand years straight, that is psychological nonsense. Only
doomsday can set Christianity's affairs to rights. Although I fear
that now even that won't help.

"To the parable about the wise virgins, one might add a vari-
ant about the overly wise virgins who saved the oil in their vessels
till morning when the sun made their lamps meaningless. Loving
day after day with a Christ-like love is like peeling potatoes with
a razor. It's pointless to use such refinements on rough and dirty
skins. If you want to knock together something sturdy—a box, a
society, doesn't matter—you must hit the boards, or the people,
with a hammer until...but we're getting off the subject. Because
the so-called sympathetic person is not even a Christian, not a

creature trying to drag the Sermon on the Mount down into the catacombs, no, he is a thirtieth-generation epigone, a pitiful husk, who has absolutely no idea what to do with himself: he will politely give up his seat in paradise, but will not give up his seat on the tram; he will not give his property to the poor, but will say to them: 'God will help you'; smite him on the left cheek, and he will offer you his ... rights, the letter of the law ... You'll say that this is a caricature, that sympathetic billionaires give millions to charity, that you yourself give coins to the poor, and have just given me tea, but so much the worse for you. Because the more sympathetic you all are, the kinder your kindness, the sooner they'll do away with you!"

"Straight, are you threatening me?"

"Worse than that. I want to propose to the authorities that they take actual measures. All symps must be destroyed. From the first to the last. The good-natured, warmhearted, starry-eyed, sweet, compassionate—they must all be shot and struck from the register. Bartholomew's Day, you say? So be it. The name doesn't matter. I've laid it all out right here."

Pages produced from under an unfastened breast button showed white in his hands. Straight began to read them.

I shan't relay to you the entire complicated contents of that remarkable document. Certain words stood out: "mental viscosity," "other-eyedness," "pathosizers," "piteosity," "heartivism." The plan began by outlining the biological nature of symps, viewed as the cells of a social vestige: like an appendix or an extra-class appendage, they must all be excised before they began to fester; hands were not for handshakes but for work: handshakers must be outlawed. The plan went on to point out that symps, because of their sense of comhumanicity, were not inclined to kill—given the possibility of new wars, this created difficulties; symps were softhearted, their tear ducts responded only on behalf of the so-called insulted and injured, their compassion could be elicited only by the defeated, therefore the working class, so as to elicit the compassion of symps, must be defeated. From this it was clear ...

But I wasn't following the changing pages. My attention had gradually shifted from the progress of the lines to the face of their composer. Straight's sunken cheeks burned with a feverish flush, while in his eyes, which now and then leaped out at me, fear burned like black flames. Rushing from point to point, his phrases evoked in me—or perhaps infected me with—a strange association: the shaft of a chariot straddling a boundary with one wheel still here, in logic, and the other spinning there, over the line.

And although the indictment leveled against me was punishable by death, I, as befitted a contemptible symp, felt a profound and impenitent pity for my prosecutor. After all, the dock in which I sat was, one sensed, very very large—whereas he, a person who walked on the sunny side, but at night, was extremely lonely.

Finally the pages finished. Saul Straight gathered them up with hands swollen from the unaccustomed warmth.

"Well?"

I couldn't help but smile.

"The opinion of a symp oughtn't to interest you. Have you proposed your plan to the people for whom it's intended?"

Straight was silent.

"Well, you see: for sympathy for your plan to destroy sympathetic people you must appeal to those who can sympathize. A circle. Isn't it?"

"Not at all. I don't need this."

"Suppose you don't. Still, I am a man not just of sentiments but of presentiments. And it's not hard for me to predict that this plan and its author will never separate."

"Why?"

"Very simple: because it was written by a *sympathetic person*. That's right. Now don't be frightened. I know this will come as a blow, but you must take it like a man, Straight: you are hopelessly sympathetic; what's more, you're so sweet, you're touching."

"Don't you dare..."

I saw a spasm flick across his face; he wanted to get up, but I held him back as I had then—by the wall—by the hand. This situation was giving me a kind of cruel satisfaction.

"Now calm down. Believe me, if I didn't find you so symp—"

"What slander! You're a shameless liar! That's impossible."

"Then other people are liars too. Anyone who's ever met you". —I rattled off a number of names—"they all say, what a sympathetic fellow that funny Saul Straight is!"

Drawn by reflex into this strange game, I began to lie in earnest. The destroyer of symps sat utterly downcast, with a pale and somehow suddenly pinched-looking face. He muttered something else—once or twice—in defense of his unsympatheticness and fell silent.

Having observed him closely, I already had doubts as to whether I'd calculated the dose correctly.

Now he sprang abruptly to his feet. He had taken command of his voice; only his fingers, nervously jamming a button into the buttonhole over the pages hidden under his coat, betrayed his agitation.

"So then, are you still insisting?"

Without waiting for my reply, he advanced to the door. I tried to stop him, but he pushed me away with unexpected force. A minute later nothing remained in the room of Saul Straight save two large damp stains on the floor before the armchair in which he had sat.

Several days went by, and the impression of our meeting began to fade from my consciousness. We're very demanding of other people's thinking: if their logic comes down with even a slight case of paralogism, we jerk back our brain for fear of infection. Straight had gone down in my estimation: the man from whom I expected help needed help himself... the ordinary help of a doctor. The memory of how I had parried his last idea was to me almost pleasant: after that last, his earlier ones too began to recede, began to seem suspect. Psychologically this suited me.

Then suddenly the other morning something happened, something... I scarcely know how to put it. A large envelope arrived in the mail. It contained—this was completely unexpected—those same pages that had, along with their author, so recently paid me a visit.

Looking through them in bewilderment, I reread that entire phantasmagoria about symps from start to finish. How strange. What more did these pages want from me? I was about to shove them back in the envelope when, on the last page at the very bottom, I noticed a line in pencil that I hadn't read: *You're right: I'm a symp...therefore...*

The next word was illegible. Would you like to see it? I have the pages with me. Here. Strange handwriting, don't you think? What? You're closing? Eleven o'clock? Fine, we're leaving. I'll pay, and...You take the manuscript: easier to give it to you now than outside in the cold. Why? I promise to explain. There now, thank you in advance. We're going.

What a creaky spring! And this blue cloud wafting in—just like then. I love the snow when it crunches underfoot and counts your steps. I love the cold in general. Logic and cold are undoubtedly related.

So then, I've told you almost everything. I've only to finish with *almost*. That line in pencil which you now have in your coat pocket will play a certain part in my...then again, to play a part in what's done—that's bad style, even for an ex-writer. I remember that when I read that line, I rushed to the telephone to try and elicit any facts about Saul Straight. But the telephonic ear had heard nothing of him; no one—in the last ten days—had seen him anywhere. Then, thinking harder about the meaning of the postscript, I understood what I had refused to understand at first: Straight had been forever excluded from all meetings, and it was even too late to look for him in the cemetery since the graves of vagrants are usually unmarked.

Instantly, the realization of my guilt came crashing down—with all its force—on my brain. For what, in essence, had I done? I had pushed a sick and helpless man to his death. Why? Because he had given me thoughts without asking anything in return, thoughts that were, in any case, better than my own. I wasn't the only one, you say. That's right, perhaps I wasn't. All against one. And now—this will strike you as strange—now that it's no longer possible to meet that generous giver of philosophical systems, aphorisms, formulas, and phantasms, that dispenser of ideas wrapped in a raggedy scarf, our entire literature is finished—that's how I feel—finished. Then again, all that mousing about with pens no longer concerns *me*. And the only thing I ask of you, the writer of my choice, is that along with the manuscript you accept the theme. You say it's someone else's? Well all right then! This much I did learn from Straight: to give without asking anything in return. In memory of him, you must do this. Your language is succinct and seamless enough to support the weight and not fall silent under it. Well then, I need only wish the *theme* a good journey.

From this point on, reading this manuscript presents a certain danger. The person writing it must warn you: given the least carelessness in dealing with this text, you may confuse several "I"s. This is because of an oversight by the author, who allowed his character to narrate the story in the first person, who lent him his own personal pronoun—"I," so to speak—and now doesn't know how to get it back so as to finish in his own name.

According to the law, possession of a thing—honest possession, of course, bona fide—turns that thing after a certain period of time into the property of the possessor. In literature, however, it has yet to be established on what page the "I" that has passed from author to character becomes the personal property of the latter. The one person who could have answered that question, Saul Straight, can no longer answer.

So then, since the right of the person in possession of the manuscript and theme to the first-person pronoun is debatable, we shall have to content ourselves in these last paragraphs, despite the stylistic disadvantage, with the word "he."

Once installed among "his" themes, someone else's theme had to fight for space on the page. The busy man in whose briefcase

Straight's plan had landed had first to finish *his* story and to satisfy two or three contracts. The theme had to take its place in line, at the very end. And when its turn finally came, it somehow felt utterly alienated from literature and loath to yield to a strange man. This man, something of an expert in dealing with plots, knew that to use force in such cases was futile and that without the necessary impetus any attempt would only lead to a definitive estrangement from the strange theme. He put his pen aside and began to wait for the impetus.

A number of weeks went by. Then one day, as he was moving with the crowd down one of Moscow's busiest sidewalks, he noticed ahead of him a familiar shape. It was the man who had entrusted him with those useless pages. Here was a chance not to be missed: to return the theme to the proper party. The man calling himself *he* had already made a move—to catch up and call out—but then something in the very outline, in the pitch and pace of the shape walking ahead of him, made the writer pause. The stooped shape was moving in a strange way reminiscent of a corpse being carried along by a river current; rhythmically rebounding from the buffets of the people all about, the shape bobbed along the sidewalk, tilting stiff shoulders now to the right, now to the left; it did not look ahead and did not glance back when wheeled around by the vortex of a crossroad; its swollen face, exposed for a second to the observer's gaze, wore an expression of excludedness and wordlessness.

"Could a Bartholomew's Day of symps have really begun?" flashed through the observer's mind. And hard upon that thought, another: "I've found the impetus; I'll try again."

The theme did not return: to "its" brain.

Still, the man calling himself *he* had overestimated the power of the impulse. The widowed theme refused to come out of mourning. No one knows how long this might have gone on if not for the help of Beethoven's Sonata in E-flat Major. The meeting with the sonata came about, like so much in this story, by chance. The man known here as *he* attended the concert of a touring pianist whose name always drew large crowds and was startled to find the words *Les Adieux* staring up at him from the program. As a non-musician, he had of course forgotten the key and number of the sonata that had brought Straight to his theory of separations.

And when the pianist, after a series of preliminary numbers, pulled his bench up to the first chords of the sonata of separations, among the thousands in the audience there was one person who, covering his eyes with his palm, tried to restrain the nervous lump rising in his throat. That very evening, he became not "he" to the theme, but "I."

1929–1930

THE BRANCH LINE

THE RAIL joints clacketed, rapping out the staccato of the route. A service cap hanging by its visor from a hook swung from side to side as though trying to shake a migraine from its cloth temples. Quantin unbuckled his briefcase and pulled out a newspaper. But in the quavery incandescence of the carbon filaments overhead, there was just enough light to prevent sleep. The dingy breviers refused to become comprehensible as words. Quantin put the paper away and turned to face the window: the hunched frames of pines, huddled against the light under branches like black stretchers, were sinking into night. He felt a chill: must be a draft from the window, or perhaps he was feverish. He tried lying down with his head on his briefcase and his legs under his coat. But the short slithery material, weighted by the sleeves, kept slipping off, while under his shoulder a hard board shuddered. Best sit up and stay awake the rest of the way. He was nearly there. The locomotive let out a hoarse, weak-chested wail and choked. "Like someone lost," thought Quantin, raising himself up on one elbow. The cap on the hook continued, if a bit more slowly and musingly, to swing back and forth, looking as though it were hiding a pair of eyes. "Imagine a country or a world where outermost thoughts closest to the skull would occasionally, by dint of proximity, stray up under the crowns of hats, under their leather linings, trivial thoughtlets whose flight from head to hat would go unnoticed by people's thinking, then..."—a gentle jolt, as though not of buffers against buffers but of pillow down against down, brought the train to a halt—"then (must be a semaphore)...no, best take not that line, but the branch line. Suppose our brain sits on top of another brain, the way a hat sits on one's head, and suppose that other, subcortical, genuinely reflective brain tips the thinking hat in greeting whenever it meets..." Falling across Quantin's thought like the shadow of a lowered semaphore, a downy sound grazed his ear.

"All dreams, please."

Quantin looked up. Under the conductor's canting a red beard bubbled, and through the beard a smile.

"Be so kind as to have your dreams ready."

In bafflement, Quantin—following the rhythm, not the meaning—took his ticket out of his pocket.

"This?"

A puncher perforates the cardboard and regains the conductor's palm; from below gleams the blue circle of his lantern and through the perforations, as through tiny windows, tangled threads of light stream—parti-colored points, lines, and silhouettes; Quantin squints, trying to get a better look, but now the tiny windows too have leapt into the palm, the blue lantern has turned away and through the beard, alternating with a smile: "Hurry up now. Don't over-stay-awake. Must change trains."

Quantin wants to ask why and what dreams have to do with it. But the conductor's back has already slipped out the door, and from down the line of carriages through a dozen partitions comes his merry: "All dreams, please."

There's no help for it. Quantin gets up and makes his way out. His legs feel oddly cottony and hollow, the briefcase under his elbow soft and springy, like a pillow plumped for sleep. Carriage steps tumble his feet to the ground. His soles sink into warm earth. To one side of the stopped wheels stands a new train. Quantin walks through the darkness toward the column of sparks above the panting locomotive. Like an iridescent bonfire, the sparks fountain and fall away in dying showers. In their brilliance, he traces the lines of the smokestack. It's an old, distended funnel, a round moon crater propped up by a crooked leg harking back to Stephenson's time when trains were just learning to run and parting with their pistons the sleepy space sprawled across the rails. And the carriages: under low-sagging roofs, their fold-out accordion steps were of a kind no longer made. "The branch line," thought Quantin, "is a rusty, narrow-gage affair, sarcophagi on wheels, bound, no doubt, for disaster." But down the dark, low-roofed rank, the lantern's blue eye was already gliding. A whistle pierced the gloom on a high crickety note. Stumbling on a step, Quantin grabbed the railing and leapt aboard. The buffers clanked with a percussive panache, and the train started up. At first the carriage windows grated slowly against the air. The old locomotive, trailing steam, moved through the night as though shuffling soft slippers that would keep falling off. But by degrees the wheels gathered speed and the rails unwound from them like threads from fast-spinning spools. The carriages' crooked springs groaned at the rail joints; from every crack came the hiss of air cloven by the locomotive's chest. Leaving the night behind, the windows slid through the first blue glimmers of dawn, which chased after the racing wheels, waving to the colliding corners and curved shapes flickering past so fast they blurred. Catching hold of the jiggling partition, Quantin tugged the window by its leather lug; with a thin tinkle, it slid down. A soft, damp, tropical wind pummeled his face. Past the train in the azure-tinted air flashed the outlines of unfamiliar trees clustered here and there on hills and bending their bare scaly bodies upward so as to explode at the top in gigantic green laminas. "Palms"—the word slipped over his brow with the wind. Quantin wanted to understand: How in the midst of marshy willow thickets, shivering birches, and needle-covered conifers could there suddenly be...? But the train's speed—by a half-thought, by a half-turn—was somehow outstripping logic. And then that warm wind, like a wing against one's soul. Along with the sparks from the incandescent smokestack, flocks of gaily colored birds rushed past his eyes, their clangs and cries battered his ears; crashing in at the open window came now the din of a distant landslide, now the burst of strings ripped from an invisible soundboard by the wind; a smell of mysterious herbs, bitter and spicy, assailed his nostrils; buffeted by the blue wind, a butterfly fluttered into the carriage and began beating its crumpled wings against the ceiling light's wire mesh. Quantin recognized the patterns on its scales: *Urania ripheus*, a subtropical species not found above the twentieth parallel. A page from an entomological atlas flew into his head—with its many-colored likenesses—then fell back under its hard cover. Quantin noticed that the train was losing speed. The carriage's overheated flanks still swayed from inertia, but the creak of the springs was lower and rarer, the shapes in the window more leisurely and distinct; beneath the wheels, rapping the rail joints one by one, a yawning bridge span droned past. Then the clicking of a switch, a long whistle like a breaking thread, the locomotive's asthmatic wheeze and shriek, and the carriage steps were hanging down above the ground. Quantin found his tumbled briefcase on the floor and, gazing about him, issued out. Beneath glass walls, the platform was empty and silent. "Can I have been the only one on the train?" The puzzled passenger looked about him once more. No one. Not a soul. Not half a soul. Only a flat hand suspended in air pointing the way. As Quantin walked past, he sensed an enormous, blue-lacquered fingernail aimed at his back. The light was too limpid for dusk and too hazy for day. The solitary passenger sought out a clockface: but the numbers and hands, hidden beneath an overhang, seemed swathed in the black crepe of night, and he couldn't make out the hour. Now the walls funneled into a corridor. Glancing around yet again at the emptiness, Quantin went where the walls led. First there was nothing but paving stones and the sound of his pounding footsteps and then, in the tunnel's distant aperture, an approaching shape. "I've got to get out of here"—Quantin quickened his pace and saw looming toward him from under the stone vault a large paper placard. He had only to look up at the letters:

!ALL HANDS TO THE HEAVY INDUSTRY
OF HEAVY DREAMS!

Two black, mace-like exclamation points posted either side of the slogan stood guard over the words. "I'd better turn back"—but the silence closing in from behind urged him on. His heart beat faster and louder, his footsteps became quieter and slower.

Suddenly the tunnel ended. Quantin was standing on steps leading down to a wide square. In place of the stone vault overhead blue sky yawned, and before his eyes—above swarms of agitated people, amid ropes and gossamer nets hurled high in the air—bizarre, smoke-colored masses kept changing their ballooning shapes. The people were working in silence and with great concentration. Uncoiling lasso-like, the gauzy threads gradually ensnared the billowing sides of the masses drifting over the square. Some of these tried to rise up, but hundreds of hands pulled them down like harpooned whales, dead hulks heaving in the foaming waves. Quantin didn't understand at first. Only when one of those netted shapes happened to slip free, sail up over the roofs and, caught by a gust of wind, quickly disappear, did he realize: these people were hunting the clouds scudding through the mountains in dense shoals.

Quantin descended the steps and, hugging the square's perimeter, tried to find a way out of the confluence of clouds. The hunting was in full swing, all eyes and hands on work; no one noticed the wary visitor, a briefcase under one arm, stealing into the web of city streets.

At first Quantin kept knocking into the ledges and corners of buildings, but then gradually the air became less brumous, colors and outlines clearer and more distinct. Before him stretched a broad avenue under a canopy of branches. Clad in the shadow and light of a slightly dimmed sun, the avenue beckoned him on and on. It was daytime, evidently, yet all the windows were hidden behind blinds and folds of draperies. Here and there people sat on benches, a soft litter of shadows at their feet. Now and again Quantin came across unhurried passersby. One of them, his face eclipsed by the broad brim of a hat, passed very close, almost shoulder to shoulder. He was breathing—long exhalations between short breaths—the way one does in deep sleep. Quantin wanted to turn around and follow him, but just then something else caught his attention: a man standing at the foot of a telegraph pole was tying heavy metal crampons to his shoes. For an ordinary fixer of wires, his attire was somewhat unusual. An elegant tailcoat, white vest, and patent-leather pumps wedged into the cumbrous semicircles of his climbing irons; and beside him—in place of a box of tools—a sheaf of music. Quantin stopped and went on watching. Having tightened the last strap, the man in the tailcoat gripped the pole with one crampon then the other and began his slow ascent, ankle over ankle, up to the wires. Several people who had been sitting motionless on benches now raised their heads. Two or three passersby paused. A cuff fluttered up over the parallels of the telegraph strings, and a metallic arpeggio rang out over the street. Blinds cracked open their green eyelids and waited. Then the musician, flapping tails buoyed by the wind, burst into song:

> Ladies and gentlemen, dreamers and dreams,
> The sun is but a coin from a beggar's torn seam,
> It falls away at sunset, as through a crack,
> And again the fir dreams of palms, alack,
> Life is a litter of shadows, years leap o'er the Lethe.
> To sleep—to die: "For the power of the poets."

A muffled chord hummed down the wires, from pole to pole. The performer made a bow to the newly lowered blinds and began his descent.

The street was silent and still once more. So as to break the soundlessness, if only with the sound of footsteps, Quantin walked on.

Suddenly he saw a brisk black figure come mincing out of a black door and across the pavement, whisking into the shadows then out into the light. Gathering up the long skirt of his soutane, turning a sharp-nosed profile now right, now left, the figure, as if it had squeezed between two buildings, disappeared. But in the engraving-like outline of that vanished face, in the forehead squared by a rectangular headdress with shoulder-length folds, there was something strangely familiar, exuding the musty smell of old, worm-eaten books. Quickening his pace, Quantin went in pursuit. This was in an alley. A blind alley beneath a double canopy of shadows: it glided straight along then veered off. Diving after the figure between walls, Quantin glimpsed a black back turning a corner and a sharp elbow hitching up a black hem. Pursued by a memory and a man, the figure walked faster still. But the stride of his pursuer was longer and stronger. Pitching forward on the defeating folds, the soutane dashed from wall to blank wall and then, like a mouse overtaken by claws, turned around to reveal a sharp-nosed grin: on his neck, which craned spitefully but frightenedly out of a collar, a razor-thin slit from Adam's apple to nape showed red with blood. "More!" cried Quantin and stopped short, as though he had tripped over the name. Thomas More, not wasting a second, dodged down a flight of steps leading to a cellar. Hearing nothing behind him, he turned around again and eyed the foreigner. A wizened finger straightened up like an exclamation mark, and the threads of his lips moved.

"A useful bit of hygienic advice: don't wear your head out on your shoulders. First it gets an idea then it gets the ax. And they're even. The head with the Head, I mean."

Before Quantin could open his mouth, the cellar doors had clapped shut. Coming closer, he could see only an old, ragged-edged sign hanging above the deserted steps. Half eaten away by rust, its letters said:

WHOLESALE SUPPLIERS OF UTOPIA SINCE...

The year had been obliterated by time.

"Now if that man's in charge of exporting utopian socialism, then..." Quantin was about to descend the sinking stairs when an odd noise startled him: coming right for him—down the alley's winding course—was a choir of glassy, bubble-blowing, and loudly popping sounds, a discordant but merrily gurgling and cackling orchestra. In another minute, through the singing glass, he heard the steady tread and tramp of feet; then swinging around the bend he saw a flagstaff, and finally the actual procession. Quantin's eye was caught first by the slogan swaying between poles, GLORY TO THE UNWAKEABLE, then by the people staggering after it. The disorderly orchestra straggled on like a pile of leaves in the wind; sticking out of the musicians' mouths were large, upraised bottles without bottoms; their cheeks, swollen with blowing and bloating, belched through the inrushing liquor to produce a resounding march of bursting bubbles. Grazing the unemptying glass funnels were purple noses tumid with erections of desire. Grabbing at the walls with hundreds of palms, the procession, losing bodies, lunged on like a long and slithery centipede fond of damp and narrow cracks.

Quantin followed the procession for a few minutes out of morbid curiosity. The choice of narrower side streets, where it was easier to enlist the walls' support, was probably deliberate, he thought, but then a long notice stuck to the stone exactly at eye level arrested his attention and, with it, his progress. The notice—in the manner of a proper, not overly pushy advertisement—listed the advantages of so-called *heavy dreams*. Having come across this subject once before, Quantin read the fine print carefully, line by line: "The main advantage of the heavy industry of nightmares over the light industry of golden threads plunged into brain fibrils, over the production of so-called sweet dreams, is that in marketing our nightmares we can guarantee that they will *come true*, we can hand our customers 'turnkey dreams.' Sweet dreams cannot withstand reality, sleepy reveries wear out faster than socks; whereas a heavy dream, a simple but well-made nightmare, is easily assimilated by life. Where dreams unburdened by any-thing disappear like drops of water in the sand, dreams contain-ing a certain harshness will, as they evaporate in the sun, leave a hard kernel on the roof of Plato's famous cave: these deposits will collect and accrue, eventually forming a swordlike stalactite.

"Speaking in more modern terms," the fine print went on, "our nightmares, weighing as they do on the brain, gradually form a sort of moral ceiling that is always about to come crashing down on one's head: some of our customers call this 'world his-tory.' But that's not the point. The point is the durability, un-wakeability, high depressiveness, and wide availability of our nightmares: mass-market products good for all eras and classes, nighttime and daytime, moonlight and sunlight, closed eyes and open." Quantin wanted to read on but the bottom of the notice had been torn away—probably by a passing drunk. He looked up from the text and listened: the hymn of the unwakeable was barely audible in the distance. Afraid of losing his way, he fol-lowed the echo. But then he came to a fork. Right or left? Quan-tin chose at random and soon saw that he had erred. Arching its stone ribs, the street led away from the noise and clamor. Rather than the fissured gills of blinds: the blank stifle of shutters. One sensed that if a sound wave were to stray in here, even it would slither, suppressing its curves and shying away from all ears in fright. Quantin trudged on resignedly. Not a crossroad, not a per-son. His muscles ached with exhaustion; leaden blood throbbed in his temples.

Suddenly from around the bend he heard a soft but audible noise. He flicked the weariness from his brain, like the dust from a hat, and rushed greedily to meet it. A door in a wall stood wide to the street. By the steps was a cart on stopped wheels. Several men, running up and down the stairs in silence, were stacking the cradle-shaped cart with softly bulging bundles. It wasn't hard to guess what these were: plump, quadricorne pillows clinging to each other with downy bellies. Quantin went nearer. A man in a green apron, straining the smoke from his pipe, occasionally unclenched his teeth to give an order, and the mountain of pillows quickly grew. Seeing the stranger, the man turned his pipe to meet the other's gaze.

"Yes, sirree, in the dream business there's no time for sleep. We're always working. Day and night. A completely dreamed-out pillow is an old dream-producing tool that has served millions of headboards. You have only to touch the down hidden inside and ... Here—wouldn't you like to see?"

The man wiped his hand on his apron then pressed it to one of the pillows. Through the cracks between his fingers, parti-colored smoke curled slowly up into the air in hazy, tenuous shapes. His free hand dove under the apron—and out came the bulging, transparent eye of a magnifying glass.

"You'll see better with this."

Squinting through the glass, Quantin now clearly saw seeping out of the pillow images of people, trees, coiling spirals, bodies, and fluttering clothes; the parti-colored air swaying above the man's fingers formed an open lattice through which a host of worlds flowed and intertwined.

The man put away the glass.

"There. Now the feathers filling these pouters, what are they? A wing torn into a host of tiny wingednesses, a flight exploded in eiderdown. Once they've been sewn into pillows, these tiny wingednesses fight to free themselves and take flight. Without success. They go on struggling until someone's brain lies down on their atomized flight, and then ... As for the human brain's affinity for pillows, it's entirely natural: they're related, after all, the pillow and the brain. For what do you have under the crown of your head? A grayish white, porous-plumose pulp wrapped in three pillowcases. (Your scientists call them membranes.) Yes, and I maintain that in the head of any sleeper, there is always one pillow more than he thinks. No point pretending to have less. No, sirree. Off you go!"

This last was, apparently, addressed to the cart. Lazily turning its spokes, it trundled off, rocking the piles of dreamed-out pillows to sleep on its springs. Tipping his hat, Quantin made to follow the wheels, but the man in the green apron detained him:

"Come inside a minute. Mind the step. There. I want to show you our latest model—*Somnifera Ultima**—a sort of pillow in disguise."

He pulled a cord and one of the warehouse's partitions came down to reveal a black cascade of bulging, quadrangular briefcases tumbling end over end.

The man's hand caught the taut corner of a somersaulting briefcase.

"Here. Won't you try one? Our new and improved Undermind. But I see you already have one. I recognize our label. So then. A black leather pillowcase stuffed with numbers, plans, drawings, totals, and forecasts—this, believe me, is a big step forward compared to the ordinary, old-fashioned bed pillow. No mattresses and no lights-out necessary. No need even to trouble your head or close your eyes. Just tuck this thing under your elbow, and you—while standing up with your eyes wide open in broad daylight—will sink into the deepest sleep: you'll dream that you're a manager, a mover and shaker, a public servant, an inventor of new systems, and this briefcase-shaped pillow straining under your elbow will propel you from dream to dream. Everything will swell up: your liver with ambition, and eventually your brain too will balloon: its convolutions and creases will become smooth and free of thought, like a well-plumped pillow. Yes, sirree. True, this under-elbow pillow is only in its first clinical trials. But the results thus far have been so encouraging that we can already say this: in the technology of lulling people to sleep, the future belongs to the briefcase!"

Coming out of the warehouse, Quantin noticed that the street's blue air had turned slightly darker and duskier. He looked about him and walked on. Soon the narrow street flowed, like a stream into a lake, into a public square banked around by steep

*Exceedingly soporific (*Lat.*).

buildings. Quantin's gaze was immediately drawn to a grassy knoll in the middle of the square, where, beneath the limpid branches of a fountain, poppies grew in thick profusion; their wide-open, moistly bloody lips exhaled a spicy, narcotic fragrance. Benches were crowded around the grass; on the benches, shoulder to shoulder, figures sat slumped: faces hidden in hands, heads lolling on shoulders, arms dangling, mouths gaping at the purple poppy mouths.

Quantin crept closer to the knoll. A pungent smell passed through his nostrils up into his brain. Attracted by the poppies' scarlet smears, he was about to take another step when he felt a hand on his elbow. A man in a poppy-red jacket, his pupils dilated, smiled warningly.

"No strangers allowed. Go away."

"I don't understand..."

"Understanding is strictly forbidden. Even dreams have the right to dream. Isn't that so? Now go away."

Just then a light wind fretted the poppies, their exhalations grazing Quantin's brain, and before he could step back a diaphanous cloud of poppy pollen was skimming along the ground. Caught up by the air, the cloud quickly became denser and began to take shape; now the lower edge was touching the ground—and Quantin was astonished to discern a slim bare foot; swirling above the foot he saw a knee and the suggestion of a hip; amorphous flakes fluttered about the female outline, but then a last gust of air dispelled them, and the wind-driven figure slid helplessly forward. Quantin, afraid of losing sight of even a single glint, followed, scarcely daring to breathe. Without looking around, the woman slipped—like the mist along a crag—slowly past the closed doors. Trying not to make a sound, Quantin quickened his stride. He was already close, his breath brushing her shoulder, when suddenly a door slammed open. A strong draft struck the vision's body, confusing and crumpling her contours; Quantin caught a glimpse of her face, thrown back in the throes of vanishing, her outstretched arms and melting breasts. Before he could rush to her aid, nothing remained but empty air.

The door that had killed the phantom continued to stand open, as though inviting Quantin in. He looked up: over the door a neat inscription showed black:

EVENING CLASSES FOR NIGHT VISIONS

He stepped inside. A flight of stairs, spiraling upward, was deserted; from somewhere through the walls he could hear a monotone voice punctuated by occasional pauses. Classes, evidently, had begun. The stairs led up to a dim and empty choir loft. Quantin went to the railing and looked down: a high and decorous pulpit. Above the pulpit, a circle of subdued light recalled the slow discharge of Crookes tubes. Under its cascading rays, a bald skull, glistening with sweat and crowned with a blister-like bump, was giving forth. Leaning over the pulpit toward several dozen attentively cocked heads, the skull swayed methodically in time to the words.

"So then, we know it and they know it: the time has come for the kingdom of dreams to go on the offensive. Until now we have been forced to live cooped up between two dawns, between neurons, in dark cracks, in a mere 'third of life.' And that third, ceded to us by their sun, is rather oppressive. High time pillows and heads changed places. If for thousands of years we've allowed their mouths to snore on pillows, now we'll make them wheeze beneath the press of pillows. This, of course, is only an image. The point being that it's time to stop. It's time. Our millions of nights have amassed a stockpile of dreams sufficient to oppose their armies of facts, to attack their facts and put them to flight. Our battle plan is as follows: to drive reality into the 'I' and cut off all the loose ends, to shear the sun of its rays, so to speak, having first put it to sleep, as Delilah did Samson. Oh, people in their wildest dreams have never guessed the danger of dreams!

"Until now we've engaged only in deep reconnaissance, in skirmishes between heads and headboards. Armed with darkness, we've managed to overthrow and flatten the enemy, but only for a few hours at a time. With every new dawn we landed inside millions of open pupils and were forced to fall back, into the night. Our enemy is strong—there's no sense hiding it—he knows the technique of creative insomnias, he is sharp-eyed, enterprising, and a quick study. Isn't it from us he learned how to attack a man when he's down?

"But the situation has now changed dramatically in our favor. Pascal was the first to separate the world of reality from the world of dreams. 'Reality,' he asserted, 'is constant, whereas dreams are flimsy and variable; if a man always dreamed the same dream, and if he woke up every day among new people and new surroundings, then reality would seem to him a dream, while his dream would have all the qualities of reality.' You can't be clearer than that... But it is no less clear, to us and to them, that reality since Pascal's time has lost much of its constancy and invariability, events of recent years are rocking it, the way the waves do a boat; nearly every day the morning papers give waking up a new reality, whereas dreams... Haven't we managed to unify dreams? Haven't we hoodwinked humanity with that sweet million-brain dream of brotherhood, a united dream about unity? Flags the color of poppy petals flutter above the crowds. Reality is fighting back. But its blazing suns don't frighten the newly ascendant underground. Sleepers' eyes are shielded by eyelids. Yesterday's utopia has become today's science. We'll break the backs of facts. We'll rout their status quos: you'll see those status quos turn tail and run. If an 'I' should rise up against our 'we', we'll hurl him down a well of nightmares headfirst. We'll hide the sun behind black blots, we'll plunge the whole world into a deep, static slumber. We'll put even the idea of waking to sleep, and if it resists, we'll gouge out its eyes."

The speaker's bald crown leaned closer to the craning heads.

"At this hour when night is silently advancing, when our enemies' ears are smothered in pillows, I may reveal to you this secret. Listen: when reality is finally vanquished, when we see it blind and powerless in the shackles of never-ending dreams, we shall carry out our long-concealed plan and..."

The lecturer's voice, while no less clear, now sounded as though it were coming through the cone of a mute. Quantin leaned forward, resting his elbows on the loft railing. Drawn by the words, he forgot about his briefcase: the leather satchel stuffed with papers suddenly slipped out from under his arm, described an arc, grazed a glass shade, banged into the pulpit, and tumbled away, landing on the floor with a loud plop. A light dashed about the walls. The speaker's outstretched hand froze in air. The heads all looked up in alarm.

"A scout! A spy! Stop him!"

Quantin understood: every fraction of a second counted. His muscles made his body jerk. Pounding down the spiraling stairs, he heard voices racing to cut him off: "Seal all the exits!"—"Search the loft!"—"Hurry!" Quantin threw a leg over the banister and, nearly pitching into the stairwell, slid down the spirals past the onrushing stampede and leapt out into the street. Less than a hundred paces off was a crossroad. Breaking his trajectory, Quantin ducked through a low gate: a courtyard; another gate; again the polygon of a courtyard; a street. Happily, not a dead end. Quantin slowed his step, and only his breathing continued to race. Glancing warily about him, he noticed that the city was quickly changing out of its blue air into the black work clothes of night. Under the arcs of lamps bent over the street, glassily transparent spools were spinning and unwinding diaphanous black threads of gloom. The black-thread rays gradually suffused the entire space, while the streetlamps' whirling, barely discernible bodies began to look like frightened cuttlefish secreting sepia. This suited the escaped "scout." That word, suddenly said out loud, now sounded to Quantin like the click of a key, like a password to reality, still more like a slogan to explain all the fears, wanderings and dangers in this mazy city exporting dreams.

"Scout," he mouthed the word and felt it blend with a smile, the first to have crossed his lips inside the oppressive walls of this factory of nightmares; the word pulsed, beating in time to his heart. Yes, as a scout he would trace all the twists of their designs, he would burst the million black bonds even if it cost him his life, he would stop those accursed spools unwinding night. "Who was it who said—I think it was a German pedant: 'Oh, if only the day knew how deep is the night.' Well, the day will know, we'll measure it to the very bottom. No need to turn over in your grave, Herr. If I'm not a spy for the day!"

And suddenly he saw—here, in the lightless city of night—his diurnal, sun-drenched world: the swaying fields reaching up their gilt-edged rays to meet the sun's golden spikes; the dove-colored dust dancing around the spokes of wheels; bright cascades of roofs and colors of clothes mixing on public squares, as on gigantic palettes; ruddy cheeks, red banners of slogans above the swaying crowds and then the eyes, human eyes, ringed with iridescence, squinting brightly out of crow's feet at the sun, while here... Quantin felt his throat contract and clenched his fists.

The darkness, rousing owls and bats, was disturbing the torpor in this city of dreams. The streets—so recently dead, like the paths in graveyards—were now full of an increasing animation. Blinds crept up to reveal black holes of windows. Only here and there in the open casements did a dim, decaying light begin to smolder and fade away. Doors flung wide, like the wings of nocturnal birds taking flight, cast people's hurrying silhouettes out into the streets.

The hour of the night harvest was evidently approaching, and manufacturers of visions, nightmare makers, and dispatchers of phantoms were rushing to work. Their stooped silent shapes disappeared through the cracks in gates or dove down cellar stairs into the ground. One gate had been left ajar. No one was going in or out. Quantin looked around to see if he were being followed then ducked his head inside: stretching the length of the courtyard was a rank of round wellholes, their openings weighted down by massive, cone-shaped covers that looked from a distance like the giganticized lids of outsize inkwells. Around one well-hole, he could see several figures now crouching down, now straightening up. The cone, slowly rotating under pressure from their shoulders, was gradually unstopping the stopped throat of a well of nightmares. One more turn—and...behind him Quantin heard footsteps. He quickly crossed the street and continued on his way, trying to keep to the most shadowy places. One window, half hidden in a cellar, shone brighter than the others. From behind the lattice came strains of music seemingly stifled by the ground. Quantin leaned over: through the lattice he could see the clinging spirals of a plant creeping from windowsill to pavement, and the flashing of a violin bow sewing a melody into the air with long stitches. He recognized it from the first strokes—this was that song lost and found in the city's nervures, the song of the aerial wires:

TO DIE—TO SLEEP: "FOR THE POWER OF THE POETS"

Quantin leaned against the wall and listened. He couldn't understand what it was: sorrow or simply weariness. Suddenly he felt something brush his hand. He jerked his hand back. And again he felt it—just barely. Quantin bent down: a coil of ivy that had reached his palm with its shaggy tendrils was humbly and shyly reminding him: without words—without words—without words.

Quantin peered down the street. In the distance loomed a gigantic arch. He made straight for it.

Chains of lights blinking from behind the arch and muffled but long whistles heralded: a train station. Quantin's attention was suddenly elastic and focused. Finally! Now he would see the freight ramps for shipping dreams. The loading of nightmares, the transit of images wrapped in night—the whole technique of exporting phantoms would unfold before him.

A minute later the arch's light framework was floating over-head, while underfoot a floor pitching glassily forward shone with mirrorlike glints: reflected in them were the arch's interlacements, the bustle of elbows and backs all about, and blue pinpricks of stars. Afraid of slipping, Quantin treaded gingerly, trying to brake the force of the incline. Suddenly his outstretched hand was grappling ... air. Yes, it was air, a vaguely delineated emptiness which, however, resisted his jabs and would not let him proceed.

"Watch out, will you!" the hand of a gray-smocked man fell on his. "What the devil! You'll smash all our goals in life. A consignment of top-quality goals. Etiquette: ethics. And you go kicking it as if it were a sack of sand."

"That's right," a voice behind Quantin concurred, "goods for connoisseurs. Not everyone can afford a goal."

Yielding to the strict and strong hand, Quantin went around the bale of compressed emptiness. His eyes, searching for a clue, chanced on a handful of letters stuck above a low, dismal doorway:

BUREAU OF INVISIBILIFICATION

He knew from experience that dreams, like the thieves in the parable, come unseen, they slip under foreheads, trying to avoid the eyes, and only there—under the cranial roof, safe and sound, sprawled on the brain—do they throw off their invisibility.

And indeed, under the station's gigantic arches one could see nothing but bent backs, cocked elbows, and straining shoulders which, pressed against air, were pushing that air through the air. Rather a strange sight: it diverted one's thoughts from station ramps to theater ramps. But when Quantin looked down, it was all he could do not to scream: the floor's mirrorlike surface was pelting his pupils with myriads of the most fantastic shapes and flashes, a barrage of sparks. The Bureau of Invisibilification, while invisibilizing goods, evidently left them (in the form of an optical tare) the ability to be reflected. Quantin wanted to avert his eyes from the florid flood, but had to overcome his fear and look down more and more often. The glassy incline, barely noticeable at first, like a slanting silver deck, was becoming steeper and steeper. The soles of his feet, like skis down a snowy slope, began to slip and slide and suddenly he was gliding. With nothing to hold on to: below was a flood of reflections; all around him, air and dreams. Workers' smocks flashed past less and less often. The multicolored flux gathered speed. Before he knew it, Quantin was outside the station. Scanning the empty space, he finally saw struggling toward him a figure. The figure was clambering up the slope, occasionally collapsing on his hands and dragging his left leg after him. Swooping down from above, Quantin grabbed the lame man by the shoulder, nearly knocking him off his good foot.

"Sun and damnation!" the man cursed, lifting up a frightened face gray as his smock. "My right suction cup has gone all to hell. And now you—may the sun shine in your eyes. Let go!"

Felled by the blow of an elbow, Quantin managed to grasp the lame leg. Now he saw, bulging under the man's right foot, a hollow, stake-shaped sole recalling the rubber tip of an arrow shot from a toy pistol; stuck to the slope, the foot was barely able to keep the two fright-linked bodies from falling.

"Let go!" the worker tried to free himself, but Quantin's fingers had worked their way up the lame leg; he had already caught hold of the smock's gray hem when from above—right between the eyes—the blow struck; Quantin's fingers unclenched, dropping his body.

Now there was no hope. He was slipping down and down, faster and faster. Beneath him, down the glassy descent, rushed flocks of gaily colored reflections. His speed was such that he could no longer make out their shapes: the eddy of blinding blurs was tumbling with him into the void. He wanted to cry out, but the onrushing air had stopped up his mouth. Only for instants could he glimpse his flight-fractured reflection in the slope's incandescent silver. An invisible bale banged him on the head. Down and down. Then suddenly he saw looming up—like a dam across a silver cataract—a wall, a monolithic stone mass racing toward his body batting about like a wood chip in the whorls of a waterfall. For a second he imagined his head slamming into the stone and the splatter of his brain. The wall, expanding in width and height, was hurtling noiselessly toward an impact. Better not look. He shut his eyes tight and ... But then something sharp and bright, like the blade of a knife forcing a tight lid, was prizing his eyelids apart; yielding, he opened them—and brilliant daylight flooded his pupils.

Right in front of his eyes—not three feet away—was the yellow wall of a carriage. Above were metal-edged bunks. Quantin raised his head from where he lay and, screwing up his eyes, looked about him. The train had stopped. In the passage, he saw a porter's back bent under a bale, and out the dusty window, the familiar glass canopy of the Moscow Station. Propping himself up on one hand, he still hesitated to enter into the day.

But it was time. He swung his feet down onto the floor and reached for his briefcase. What? His palm banged into wood— his briefcase wasn't at the head of the bunk, or by the wall. And instantly, through layers of memory, he saw: the dusky choir loft—the blue light—the bald man's outstretched hand—and the bulging black briefcase tumbling down. And then, with another turn of the carousel—one by one—the night's played-out images.

"Off with it?"

Quantin shuddered and looked up. Above the apron and badge shone a merry face flecked with freckles and beads of sweat.

"Your briefcase ran away from you. Look where it wound up," the porter bent down, dragged the briefcase out from under the bunk, and dusted it off with his apron. "Don't have anything heavier? Off with it, then."

"Thank you," muttered Quantin. "I'll take it." He remained seated with the briefcase on his knees. The porter's back vanished behind the overlap of bunks. The carriage was emptying. Outside, the tap-tap of a gentle hammer wandered down the stationary train, leaping from wheel rim to wheel rim. Quantin placed a hand on his briefcase and gave it a cautious squeeze: between his fingers there was only air. He stood up abruptly and made his way to the door. A battered and belated bale, belted around with ropes and lumbering lazily, bumped down the carriage steps. "And even so," thought Quantin, "the only possible technique for replacing a light card with a dark one, day with night, is celerity, a twinkling faster than the 'twinkling of an eye.'"

1927–1928

RED SNOW

RESIGNATION to one's fate takes practice. Like any art. Or so citizen Shushashin maintains. He begins every day—after putting on his shoes and washing his face, before throwing on his jacket—with an exercise. Again, the expression is his. This exercise works like this: he walks over to the wall, puts his back up against it and stands there in an attitude of utter resignation. For a minute or two. And that's all. The exercise is over. He can begin to live.

So it was this murky winter morning, more reminiscent of a night gone gray overnight. Having finished his exercise requiring no special equipment save a person, a wall, and a readiness to make oneself an open target, Shushashin threw the noose of his suspenders over his shoulders, took a deep breath, then yawned and squinted out the window: opposite his window was another window, and in that window was the yellow haze of a lightbulb that seemed to have lost its way between day and night. Shushashin crossed off yesterday's date and slipped his arms into the sleeves of his coat.

Seven turns of the stairs, the rusty whine of the door spring, the courtyard, the long vaulted passage from courtyard to courtyard, the gate, the street.

Shushashin has a very hard job: being out of a job. Every day he must call on ten-odd promises, ask into the telephone of a dozen five-digit numbers—"Any news? You too? Not possible? Tomorrow?"—and beat down doors while trying not to wear down the soles of his shoes, which day by day are becoming, along with his hope, thinner and thinner.

The asphalt and stones lay beneath a glaze of glare ice. The fog walked forty paces ahead of the eye, swathing all things in itself. Snaking around the house on the corner, like a long listless tapeworm, stretched a line: for something. Dodging between automobile horns, Shushashin crossed the crossroad. Another line: baskets hanging from arms, shawls and caps. Shushashin turned down a side street, his eyes seizing on occasional squares of paper showing white on the wall: just in case. "Will dye your things black"—"Will dye anything black. Cheap"—"black"...what the devil... Shushashin jerked his pupils back and walked on, picking out the yellow patches of sand on top of the ice. Then suddenly he nearly knocked into these words emanating from the fog: "Oh, dear sir, from your apartment, you say... But I've been evicted from my own head, and I'm all right. But you..."

Speaker and spoken-to passed quickly by. Shushashin looked around. Two backs: one in a heavy winter coat, head half hidden by bristling fur, the other in a thin and tattered topcoat whose lining gaped below the hem.

Then the side street turned, skirting a silent stunted belfry and wrought-iron fence on the left. Another minute—and rising to meet Shushashin was a gloomily familiar outline with grand granite steps leading up to it. Shoving noisily out the door was a tangled group of tourists, while on the bottom step, apart from the others, two men stood stamping their felt-shod feet. One was young and comely, with earflaps turned down under a fur hat, the other, his hoary blue-gray beard the color of the fog, was short and bent, and seemed with every word to trample himself still farther into the ground.

"So there. Seeing Moscow at an off-hour. You must be joking! This line is for museum coat checks from 11:00 to 4:00. But Moscow prefers visits at an unwritten hour."

"What do you mean 'unwritten'?" the earflaps flapped.

"You know: black—when it's night both in windows and in

people, and not a living soul anywhere, not in the lanes, not in the squares."

"Why?"

"That's easy: because there isn't a soul in Moscow."

Batted by the wind, the earflaps balked: "But..."

"*Pravda, Pravda, Pravda!*" cried a little boy, bursting through the fog with a thick bundle of newspapers; a second later his voice had become faint and indistinct.

Shushashin went around the end of the conversation. At a distance too great to hear, he again looked back at the outline of the museum: the two men were climbing its steps, the bent man's beard was becoming enfogged in the fog, and with every step he trampled himself lower and deeper into the stone. "Will he last until the entrance or won't he," crossed Shushashin's mind, but a wary reflex tugged at his neck muscles and, without waiting to see, he turned the corner. Not far off, as it happened, behind the cut glass of a street door, lived a five-digit number that had promised to put in a word to the right people. And off he went. Shushashin scrambled up to the fourth floor, back down, back up to the fifth floor, sliding down the banister, to the third, fourth, fifth, third, grabbing hold of the banister, to the sixth—and stopped on the checkered landing's gray-and-white stones, panting and glancing back at the banister's seismogramically crooked yellow line wound around the stairwell. This time he imagined the elusive something that kept changing its five-digit number to be a nimble mouse hiding inside a receiver with a long—miles long—telephone-cord tail slithering from side street to side street. He went slowly back down the stairs. Briefcases shoved past him. Two floors below, a door flew open and a shriek rang out: "I'll break your legs in so many places you'll never put them together again!" Shushashin, his feet falling wearily away from the steps, wondered: if a man needed x amount of time to put his two legs together, then how much time would an octopus need to put its eight legs together or, say, a millipede... and suddenly, ripping this irrelevance from his brain, he looked around: Where was he and what was this? Tall yellow double doors; and on the doors a nameplate:

DOCTOR SINGER——THREE RINGS
U. U. ANGELIKOV——TWO RINGS
NOSELESSKY——ONE RING
M.E.——NO RINGS

Shushashin's hesitant hand described a circle by the bell: it would be interesting to glimpse this M.E., only how was one to get hold of him?

Shushashin's hand dropped; his feet finished counting the stairs. His reflection, slippery on the slippery glass, stood aside at the push of his palm; he stepped out into the street and swung around down the sidewalk. The fog had thinned, but the crowds were denser. The sun made to force its way through a throng of gray clouds in military broadcloth, but they sailed on shoulder to shoulder. Now Shushashin had no reason to hurry. Let the plumes of smoke rise and fall over the smokestacks, he had nowhere to run up or down, he had scaled all the verticals, there remained only the hopeless horizontal, long as an inexhaustible ball of thread.

Without warning, the streets banged into a square. Automobiles. Tram bodies. In the center, where the rails intersected, a woman wrapped in shawls was jabbing at joints with what looked like a poker, uncoupling cars as they rolled up. Beside her bustling figure was a campstool, but the clanging numbers gave her no rest.

Shushashin didn't care where he went, and the spinning of wheels drove his steps to the curved white rim of a boulevard. Here it was quieter, but more mournful. Leafless trees and empty, ice-covered benches. Walking past a row of trunks, Shushashin suddenly noticed: on one of them hung a backdrop like a straight sail; nearby a street photographer, his straight whiskers twitching, was adjusting camera to shutter. Gathered around the sail were several gloomy people with bared heads. What could this be?

Shushashin went closer: facing the camera's bulging glass eye, in front of a yellow palace entwined with roses and swans swimming above blue lakes, was an abbreviated coffin with a yellow infant inside. A woman's hand slid for the last time along the coffin's wooden edge, adjusted a cold little heel in its yellow stocking, and withdrew. The diaphragm clicked. "Yes, it's cheaper that way," Shushashin mumbled as he went on bending and unbending his knees past the trunks and benches. But weariness was hanging on his feet like weights and fogging his mind. He had to rest. The nearest bench offered a cold back and allowed him to stretch out his legs. A man and woman seated at the other end stopped talking. But Shushashin didn't even look. Only a minute later, compelled by their newfound words, did he give the pair a sidelong glance.

The man, in fact, not counting the odd rejoinder, was doing all the talking. His shoulder—turned toward the worn and withered plush under which his companion's ear was hiding—shook with anger.

"They sent me a questionnaire: Your attitude toward religion? God, you see, is a disfranchised person who must be evicted from the world he created. Isn't that so? But seriously now. I've drafted an answer. Here's what I've written: 'God, of course, does not exist because if he did, he, in all his wisdom, could have created more intelligent adversaries for himself than the fatheaded hacks at *The Atheist*.' Well, what do you say?"

The worn plush touched the man's hand.

"Don't mail it. You mustn't."

"But I have to tell them the—"

"You mustn't."

Hunching forward, the man squeezed his hands between his knees and stared at the tamped-down snow on the path.

"I suppose you're right. As always. Why be stupider than the stupid. As an adolescent I used to think: if that gigantic tri-hypostatical shadow should have doubts about people, then people will have no choice but to respond to that unbelief with unbelief.

Well, that too is nonsense, an archaic three-letter word that I put out of my head long ago. But now I'm beginning to believe again, yes, I'm beginning to, but...in something else. I think, no—I know, only don't be frightened, I *see* that there is an afterlife. That's right, it's a fact."

"Vadik—"

"A fact, I repeat. Haven't you noticed how in the last few years our life has been permeated by nonexistence? Little by little, on the sly. We're still immured in our old space, like the stumps in a felled forest. But our lives have long since been stacked in piles, and not for us but for others. This wristwatch with its pulsating minute hand is still mine, but time is not, it belongs to someone else who will not let you or me into a single one of its seconds. What is death, after all? A special case of *hopelessness*. Nothing more. And aren't we, members of the intelligentsia, whose name still recalls the ancient word *intellegentia*,* aren't we all inscribed in hopelessness? More and more people, less and less land. It's becoming so crowded that one cannot be and be conscious at the same time. Well, they can have being; I prefer not to be, but to be conscious. Only your fingers are trembling. That's not good. There's nothing to be afraid of: in hopelessness, too, you see, there's a razor-sharp delight. Look at those trees with their fingery branches drooping down to the ground: they're grieving for us, the ones who knew how to see them. Or the early-winter twilight—have you noticed how it's like a cindery powder sifted through the air's pores? And in that window in the distance, there's the first light—like an icon lamp for the dead. Never mind, never mind, never mind. We'll learn not to live, we'll..."

Trying not to get caught by the leg of the bench, Shushashin rose and crept soundlessly away from the conversation. For a minute or two he walked along, strangely avoiding objects and people, with the look of an inexperienced ghost who had strayed by mistake into the daylight.

*Understanding (*Lat.*).

Now the air was indeed touched with cinder, while the sunset coming toward him burned like gigantic yellow bonfires. On crooks of branches, a flock of black crow blots burred. Shushashin's stiff legs, gradually limbered by walking, undeadened and stepped more quickly. At the end of the boulevard, he came level with three men walking side by side. The man in the middle, turning now to his right, now to his left, was finishing a story.

"So then, he was nearing his building. His entrance—this is important—is in a courtyard that connects to another courtyard through an archway. Anyway, he was nearly there...it was late at night and all the windows were dark, but in his a light was burning. You know why. And whether he went up or he didn't: either way he was done for. He put his hand in his pocket, and in his pocket he had this thing you need a license to carry—and..."

Shushashin wanted to come level with the end of the phrase, but his feet were suddenly stuck to the ground, he grabbed hold of a post and remembered that he hadn't eaten since morning. The three backs disappeared into the crowd. To his left Shushashin saw a door flanked by tin-backed menus. He made to push the door handle, but found his way barred by a piece of cardboard suspended from a string:

CANTEEN CLOSED FOR LUNCH

He would have to go elsewhere. Another quarter of an hour's walk, and Shushashin was sitting in front of a soup plate set out in a row with a dozen others along the edge of a narrow, oilcloth-covered table. In the little canteen the lights were already on. Above the soup plates hung steam and a burble of voices. Shushashin bent over his soup and tried to listen only to the clatter of his spoon against the earthenware, but the voices of his neighbors kept intruding. From across the narrow board came an explosion of merry laughter. Shushashin peered through the soupy steam: several bright faces with the visors of their caps cocked back. Must be college students, or from the Literature Department. A youth with prominent cheekbones sopped up the remains of a rust-colored sauce with a crust of bread, swallowed the crust and said with a sly look: "Or take this. From a story he's writing. Can't remember the title. 'We were walking down a Moscow side street late at night. The black windows were fast asleep. Every sound seemed to have been pressed into the ground by the darkness. If not for the crunch of snow underfoot and the poignant protracted song of twice-crowing cocks...' Ha-ha, he certainly muffed it with those cocks, hmm?"

The others ho-hoed in assent.

"But why do you..." Shushashin started to say before hoarseness cut him short.

Under his cocked visor, the youth narrowed humorous eyes.

"Because, citizen, all of the capital's chanticleers, if you'll pardon me..."

Fumbling unhurriedly about the tabletop, the youth picked up a knife, described an arc about his throat, then carefully replaced the knife. A fresh flight of laughter accompanied this stunt. Shushashin looked back down at his soup plate.

The chairs opposite him, legs scraping the floor, drew back. But then from somewhere off to the side, from behind a pot containing a paper palm, a muzzy voice muttered: "According to city statistics, every twelve thousandth person is run over. Therefore, if we allocate this equally and in all fairness, so to speak, one twelve thousandth of any one of us has been crushed by an automobile. And so..."

In an effort to wrest his ears from the hubbub, Shushashin slid the mustard jar over to his plate and poked the little spoon through the sticky brown scab sealing its neck; but the spoon bumped into something hard and elastic; Shushashin dug deeper and up came—gummy with mustard and stuck fast in the hole—an old cracked condom. Shushashin pushed his plate away and got to his feet. A nauseating lump rose in his throat. The suffocating steam with its oily stench fogged his eyes. He lunged for the door.

The street air had already changed into its evening crepe. The singsong voices of paper boys sang out. From around the corner, yellow lamp eyes flashing, an automobile wailed: as if it too had been run over.

Shushashin walked past lights and faces and longed to be back in his room, lying facedown in the dark. But the familiar blocks kept strangely lengthening, stretching out like caoutchouc. He thought he had already passed the toy store—yet here it was again invading his pupils with its vulgar variegation.

Finally he saw the familiar gates in the distance. A building—another building—the apothecary's signboard—then the bright window of a shop whose bare counters displayed wooden cheeses, round and red like heads with the skin peeled away—then steep brick steps tumbling down to the "Quick Repair"—and through the drafty archway—the courtyard—the tunnel of the second archway. But under the second arcade, he was suddenly accosted by the thought: What if my window...?

Shushashin stopped short in a cold sweat. But then—along the tunnel wall—a figure slid past and didn't look back. Then another: this one did look back and slowed its step. Shushashin willed his muscles to move. From the depths of the second courtyard, the stone frigate of his building, studded with sidelong rows of windows, sailed into view: *his* window was dark. "My infernal nerves," he mumbled and sighed with relief, "the nonsense that flies into your head, and..."

In his room with the door locked it was warm and almost restful. True, the neighbors' voices grated, in the kitchen dishes clattered and the roar of a primus grew louder, but even so he could bury at least one ear in his deaf pillow and pull the darkness up over him. Only the window opposite slightly irritated Shushashin: now the square was red-lit, now the light went out, then again. "Like a broken lighter," thought Shushashin, shielding his eyes with his palm. Lying face to the wall, he tried with flagging thoughts to untie and throw off his day, as he had untied and kicked off his boots. But the ties became tangled and knotted, and the crowded day continued to bear down on his brain: flights of stairs rippled their steps, boulevard trees held out their wretched branches, begging passersby to know how to see them, while the bent little bearded man from the fog doggedly trampled himself into the ground, muttering all the while that not from eleven, and not from twelve, and not from one, and not from . . . the numbers, like the blue-and-white number plates on gates, glided by in an endless succession as the little man shrank from three feet to one foot, from one foot to a few inches, from a few inches to one, from one inch . . .

Peering tensely about with eyes tight shut, Shushashin wanted to catch the tiny trampling man as he flattened himself from a millimeter into naught, but just then he felt a warm wind whistling through his temples, and the millimicrons, followed by the hum of the primus and everything down to the last resonance from the spots in his eyes, sank into . . . into what? He tried to wrest his ear from the pillow, to overtake the tiny man with his pupils, but his head either slumped back down into the darkness or raced along, knocking into yellow lights, so as to vanish into the void once more. Suddenly the wind shifted, tossing his temples up into the air, and Shushashin saw himself sitting on his bed, palms dug into the flimsy mattress.

The room was dark. Through the walls: not a sound. In the windowpanes: not the slightest echo of the streets. The silence was so complete that you could hear the timbres of your thoughts: yes, of course, this was that black hour when, while everything sleeps, the meaning keeps watch. Shushashin smiled into the darkness: the millimicrons would not return, not now. He pulled on his boots. His body felt strangely light and pliant. The door opened soundlessly. In the corridor and in the kitchen all the corners and things seemed to move out of his way. The stairs. The courtyards. And again the street: but now different and new. Black eye sockets of windows above deserted swathes of ground. Not a cart, not a footstep. Only a warm but insistent wind whistling along the pavement and through his temples without a moment's respite. Shushashin threw open the flaps of his coat and the wind, filling them like sails, propelled him along, guiding his sliding steps from this street to that. The ice, now past melting point, was breaking up into puddles, but under the blows of Shushashin's soles the puddles were plashless and still. Everything was stereoscopically cold and inert. So that the rhythmically swinging shadows atop an approaching wall made Shushashin raise his gaze to what was casting them: in a stunted belfry, in complete silence, rope-pulled bells were swinging to and fro. Now the wind turned the right flap—and again coming to meet his sliding steps, but from another belfry, this time tall and ornate, was the furious swinging of tongueless bells calling to church with a ringless ringing.

Shushashin hadn't yet apperceived this when, in defiance of the wind, a step from his eyes, someone's cap waved its visor and a voice from under the cap, rushing into his ear along with the wind, introduced itself.

"ME. No periods. That's right, me. I always come when I hear no rings."

Shushashin surveyed him: an indistinct figure with an unremarkable face.

"I still have many places to go. So I'll be brief: thoughts are as mute as fish, they sink to the bottom, but if you stun them, they float to the surface."

Swinging Shushashin around to the left by the flap of his coat, ME made a sign to the air. The air complied—and Shushashin slid quickly on ahead.

Just as suddenly the gust of wind subsided. His coat sank back down, like a sail becalmed. Standing at an unfamiliar, evidently, outlying crossroad among fences and low roofs, he looked in bewilderment at the shapes surrounding him. Stretching the length of a fence to a low porch and the square sign over it was a line like a long tapeworm. The people, their single-file shoulders pressed into the fence boards, might have been mistaken—at a distance of twenty or thirty paces—for water stains or the smudges of shadows, but tonight Shushashin's eyes were especially sharp and he instantly knew: people.

Wishing mainly to free himself from possible unexpected-nesses, he buttoned his coat, hitched up the flaps, and only then approached the line. "I wonder what it's for."

Simplest of all was to inquire of the sign. Shushashin did just that. In each of the square's four corners was a symbol—A, E, I, O—and at the intersection of the diagonals the Latin word *con-tradictio*.

Shushashin's puzzled gaze passed from the square to the file of people. More puzzling still: they were standing nose to nape in good fur coats, above astrakhan and beaver their collars shown white, and glinting here and there was a pince-nez; tucked under elbows Shushashin saw not baskets and sacks but gleaming leather briefcases and bundles of papers and books. He would likely have felt shy of asking straightaway, if not for a heavy fur coat under a Cossack hat that he recalled having seen that morning. Why yes, this was the man who'd been evicted from his own head.

"Excuse me, what is this line for?"

"For what-for," the fur coat muttered, turning away.

But the thick English woolen two places ahead shifted a bulky bundle of books from under one elbow under the other and kindly explained.

"You see, it's for . . . hmm . . . logic. If you still have your M coupon, you can exchange it for middle terms. Be quick, though, the terms may not last. Only, please, go to the end of the line."

"Say," a low forehead on a giraffish neck popped up from behind, "is it true that the middle term is meant—for purposes of rational explanation—to unify?"

"I have no idea."

"Of course, you don't, since they didn't give you one. I think one ought to welcome uniMness with open arms: M, after all, never ends up in 'S are P' no matter what, therefore, what does it matter what it is. Why the Kant do we—"

"But even so," someone grumbled through a wiry grayness of bristling whiskers, "philosophy, if I may call it that—"

"Philosophy?" the neck flinched. "What a silly name: in Russian it would be 'love of wisdom.'"

"Well what should I call it."

"Nothing at all—that would be simplest. But if you must call it something, call it 'sympathy for wisdom' or something of that sort. Or else you risk ... truisms and tomthoughtery."

"That's right," a rather hoarse basso profundo chimed in from the line's last vertebrae. "I agree. But even so, the allocation of syllogisms isn't well organized. They mix them up. Judge for yourselves: last time they slipped me a 'Barbara' instead of a 'Baroco' and a 'Bramantip' instead of a 'Bocardo.' Why the dickens give me a universal affirmative when my article calls for a particular negative!"

"Ah, so that's it," the neck drawled, "a particular negative. And did you know that all manner of particularization is being abolished, hmm?"

For a minute there was silence. Then suddenly someone's timid falsetto: "You seem to know everything. I, you see, am a writer. And I've heard that our thoughts are going to be put to a recount and that those writers whose 'collected works' contain a total of three, not two or four, but three—"

"Naturally," the other enunciated. "Next you'll be saying 'five or six,' like that landowner Chatsky home from Europe. In our thinking, too, we must aim for the poorest minds. As for all those ... as a matter of fact, writers' craniums ought to be searched. We need to know what you've got in there."

"Good gracious, absolutely nothing!" the falsetto pleaded.

"Hmm, you may have nothing. But the number of scribblers needs to be whittled down. Keeping literature in a thousand heads—that's more than we can afford. Judge for yourselves: we tend to have one topic at a time, and never more than one ideology. Now if one worker with one shovel can dig out one cubic meter in one workday, then a thousand workers *with one shovel* will dig out that same cubic meter in the same period. Therefore, once we've reduced our literary staff, our one topic can be handled by the one writer on duty. Instead of a hundred advances, we'll pay one, instead of a hundred editions of ten thousand, we'll print one mass mega-edition of a million copies. In what order will writing duty be assigned? Alphabetical, I suppose, or— "

"But my last name begins with a 'U,'" the falsetto bleated.

Just then the door under the intersecting diagonals swung soundlessly open, releasing a blast of icy logic. Shivering and stooping slightly, the line began to creep slowly inside.

Shushashin went around the end of the line and continued on his way along the narrow sidewalks of outlying lanes between cellars half trampled into the ground. Overhead, through the black night, snowflakes floated down like soft moist osculations. Skirting a porch whose three steps leapt out onto the sidewalk, Shushashin noticed a motionless, sunken-shouldered figure. Slumped on the top step, his breath hidden inside the collar of his cold coat, the man appeared to be sleeping. His bedroom, if one took into account the abbreviated overhang, was missing three walls and one bed, not counting the bedding. Bending down, Shushashin touched the man's chest, and under his fingers something rustled: either the man's breathing or a manuscript hidden under the cloth. But the man didn't stir. Shushashin bent down even lower: the man's face was...the face of a *man*, except that across his bony brow ran a tight cord from which hung a small lead fastening. Shushashin straightened up. Of course: the thinking under this broad frontal bone had been sealed. He could only go on.

Shushashin took his way, hoping to come across a familiar street. But everywhere black cavities of windows stretched in endless rows, like the recesses in a gigantic crematorium, and he began to notice something strange: the damp warm snow trailing after him in slow relentless flakes down the suffocating soullessnesses of these lanes tasted, when it settled on his lips, slightly sweet and ferrous. Shushashin pulled out a handkerchief and wiped his mouth. The handkerchief bore a dark stain. Looming up from around the corner was a streetlamp with a murkily green nimbus. Shushashin entered the circle of light and saw...red snow, slowly fluttering to the ground in innumerable flakes. The cobbles blinked with red puddles. Downspouts bubbled with a fusty, crimson swill. And from his fingers, purple drops dripped. Shushashin shut his eyes tight and groped his way blindly forward. His hand knocked into the lamppost, then empty air, then a wall. Shushashin stood there, trying to catch hold of his heart jumping up into his throat.

Suddenly a hand grazed his elbow. Shushashin walked on, palms patting the wall. But the hand—also patting the wall—followed. Shushashin spun around—and pressed his back against the wall: his exercise had some use after all.

Two or three seconds of silence. Then three steps away, he heard a harsh metallic voice: "For the last time." Shushashin opened his eyes. Facing him was a man of an exceedingly peaceable, if slightly hunched appearance: having set his briefcase down beside his left overshoe, he took hold of his head and began—using the even, circular motion one does with an electric lightbulb—to unscrew it from his collar. Shushashin tried to glimpse the hunched man's face, but his head flipped so fast—nose-nape-nose-nape—it couldn't be apperceived. Twist, one more twist, and the hunched man's hand was holding out his head to the shocked Shushashin, exactly as a beggar does his wooden bowl for a well-meaning coin. Shushashin made to back away from the bald ball with the discomfited pince-nez askew on its nose, but just then the ball's lips moved.

"Give a philosopher something for a philosopheme. God the former will reward you. I used to write about Kant. But now I can't: Kant is cant."

Shushashin ignored the request and tried to pass by, but the begging head barred his way. So he pushed it. The head slipped out of the hunched man's hands, plopped into a red puddle, and rolled between Shushashin's feet. He tripped over the red ball and nearly lost his balance before giving it a good kick. The crimson head of cheese bounced away with a wooden clatter over the cobbles.

Shushashin all but ran—on and on—without looking back. A premonition of dawn was striating—with dark blue veins—the heavy black marble of night. By chance he saw a familiar crossroad. Breaking into an all-out run, Shushashin raced down one block, then another; flashing past his eyes in the damp daybreak he saw the window with a dozen such bloody wooden heads, the "Quick Repair" steps running down into the ground, the archway, courtyard, archway, courtyard—and suddenly he stopped, transfixed, heart pounding fit to burst its venous bounds. All the windows opposite were dark, all but one—his own—in which a bright light burned.

Shushashin screamed in terror and...awoke. His room and the air outside were black. But across the way, like a red gash in the night, someone else's light was burning. Shushashin lay on his back, his head sunk into his hot pillow. Before he could raise himself up on an elbow, the light had snapped out. Sitting up on his bed, chin between his knees, Shushashin thought: "Yes, if you stun them, they will float to the surface, only dead."

1930

THE THIRTEENTH
CATEGORY OF REASON

THAT'S HOW it always is: first you call on your friends, and then—when the hearses have delivered them—on their graves. Now my turn too has come to exchange people for graves. The cemetery where I go more and more often lies behind high crenellated walls and looks from the outside like a fortress: only when the fighters have all fallen will the gates open. You walk in—first past a chaos of crosses, then past the inner wall—to the new crossless cemetery: gone are the monumental statics of the old human sepulchers, the massive family vaults and stone angels with their penguin-like wings grazing the earth: red metal stars on thin wire stems fidget nervously in the wind.

It's early spring and the earth clings to my boots, gently retaining me: stay longer, if not forever. This is my fourth time meeting him: the slow squelch of his spade as he digs out the dense and difficult earth—the old gravedigger. First he's visible from the waist up, then from the shoulders, a little more, and his head will vanish into the upturned clay. But I come closer, dodging the lobs off his rhythmically ringing spade, and say, "Good day!"

"Well, all right, good day." He surveys me from his pit.

One circumstance draws me to this old man: he is clearly out of his head and lives inside an apperceptive tangle whose knots Kant himself could not untie. For you see, all those who are off (I won't look for another definition) or, rather, out of their heads, evicted, so to speak, from all twelve Kantian categories of reason, must naturally seek refuge in a thirteenth category, a sort of logical lean-to slouched against objective obligatory thinking. Given that this thirteenth category of reason is where we entertain, in essence, all our figments and alogisms, the old gravedigger may be useful to my projected cycle of "fantastic" stories.

So then, I propose a smoke, and he reaches up a sweaty hand for a cigarette; I squat down, light to light—and the thirteenth category of reason throws wide for me its secret door.

"What's that alley over there, under the poplars?"

The old man squints at the column of trees and says, "Actors' Row. When it warms up, the young ladies'll come with their keepsakes, and heaps of flowers, and read aloud to one another from little books: not grand-like, but with respect."

"And over there?" I cast an eye farther down the wall.

"That's for penmen: 'Writers' Impasse,' they call it."

The old gravedigger wants to go into greater detail, but I interrupt and shift my gaze to the joint of two walls: the graves there are shielded by a long crenellated shadow, the rust-yellow mounds interspersed with odd patches of unmelted snow.

"Speakers' Corner," the voice from the pit explains. "Best keep away from there at night."

"Why?"

"Mighty restless. Speakers, you know: soon as it begins to get dark, they all start talking at once. Sometimes you walk past that corner of theirs and the ground's just whispering away. Best keep your distance."

"I guess it's true what they say about you, old man: you're out of your head. Who's ever seen a buried man start to whisper?"

"I'm not talking about seeing," the old man balks, "I'm talking about hearing, and it's so. Something happened just the other day. They were burying the deputy chairman of some...right here, in Speakers' Corner, down the end on the left. Got another cigarette? A red coffin, more wreaths than you could count, and slews of people. A great speaker, so they said. Well now, they lowered the coffin into the pit, pulled up the ropes, and launched into the usual speeches. They went on and on, and then we, that's me and Mitka (my helper), we fetched our spades. I spat on my palms—and suddenly, what do you know: from under the lid: 'May I have the floor. Having heard out the previous...' But then—oh my Lord!—them previous ones, and all the rest, they took to their heels. Even Mitka, the fool, threw down his shovel and turned tail. I looked about me: nothing but two or three galoshes sticking up out of the snow and some forgetful body's briefcase swinging from a crosspiece. But that deputy chairman— he couldn't see anything, of course, being in a pit and under a lid—he was talking a mile a minute: 'Citizens and comrades, don't bury me in the next world—whatever happens, when the trumpets of judgment sound I'll pull the lid to and refuse to be recalled; as a recallist, I'll...'—is that a real word, or did I dream it? I'm not educated—"

"It's a real word. Now go on."

"Go on? Not likely! He wanted to go on, but I was so nettled I grabbed my spade and without waiting for Mitka I buried that driveler and his speech in one swoop. Only imagine how restless people have become. Have you ever heard of such a thing happening before?"

"Oh, grandfather, neither before nor not before. You're raving. You should see a doctor. Have you been to the local clinic?"

"The earth will cure me, son. I don't have much longer to live. But if you don't believe me, come on and I'll show you the grave."

Setting aside his shovel, the old man starts to hoist himself out of the pit by his elbows, but I restrain him.

"Oh, all right, I believe you, I do."

"There now"—reassured, he goes on with his tangled tales. "Now that one who swallowed the good earth from my shovel, he shut up. But with another of them undecedents, I had an awful wrangle. I live out that way, just beyond the gates—the hut with two windows by the wasteland. The hearses, they all go past me, one after another. One day about dusk I had lit my night lamp and set down to the table to have my supper when suddenly I heard a sound at the door: knock. 'Who could it be?' I wondered. I went to the door and hallooed, and again I heard it: knock. I undid the latch and peered out. Well now, I've seen a lot of them, so I knew right away who it was: he was standing there, arms all rigid and pressed to his chest, tall and yellow. 'You keep away!' I says. 'Where'd you come from?' 'From a hearse,' he says. 'I saw your light. Let me in.'

"'Well,' I thinks, 'Not likely!' I barred the way with my arm: 'It's not right: dropping dead then dropping in—besides, they'll catch on to the fact they're burying nothing. How'd you manage it?' 'Well,' he says, 'as soon as we began to bump over the potholes, the lid slid sideways—and through the crack a light winked at me: my last light, I thought, my last. I looked back: some were lagging behind and straggling (it's a long way to your cemetery, grandfather), others were still trudging along, but with their eyes on the ground because of all the puddles. I gave the lid a shove then closed it again and quietly... Let me in, grandfather.' 'But what if you're not in time,' I says, 'what if you don't make it to your funeral?' 'I'll make it, the hearse can barely turn its wheels, don't refuse me this last light before the eternal darkness.' He pleaded with me so, I begun to feel sorry for him. 'Come in,' I says, 'only make it quick—then into the pit.'

"I went over to the night lamp. He followed me with his arms still crossed and bent his waxy face to the light. Then he says: 'Feel behind my lashes, grandfather: my eyes have turned glassy. I may get lost and not be able to find my coffin. Oh, it's time, my hour has come. It's time.' And he left the way he came: through the open door. I watched him out of sight: everything was hazy in the dusk and the bells had tolled. 'Will he make it,' I wondered, 'or won't he?'

"It grew dark. I re-latched the door. Then I said my prayers, got into bed, and was about to blow out the night lamp when again I heard a sound at the door: a rustling. 'Oh no, not at this hour of the night.' But there was no help for it—I opened the door. 'Didn't make it?' 'Didn't make it,' he says. 'By the time I got there they were smoothing my grave over with their shovels.' 'It's not right,' I thought, 'but the office is closed, have to wait till morning.'

"'Now don't stand there like that letting all the cold air in,' I says, 'be my uninvited guest, never mind, you can sleep in the passage by the wall: it's a bit tight, but don't judge it too harshly, a coffin's tighter still.' I threw him some matting. And we went to bed. I woke up around midnight—maybe I'd dreamed it all?—I wanted to turn over, but just then I got a whiff of something rotten. 'Oho,' I thinks, 'dreams won't protect you from that.' I lit the night lamp—couldn't fall back to sleep anyway on account of my uninvited guest—and I went out into the passage. 'You all right?' 'Fine, thanks,' he heaved a sigh, and was silent. 'Did they read the Gospel over you,' I asks. 'No.' 'There now,' I opened the book and begun to read the best I knew how. I could see he was listening, he was, but then he says, 'It's moving, grandfather, but it misses the truth.' Now that got my goat. 'Now look here,' I says, 'the decedent is supposed to lie still—and not bat an eye or move a muscle, but you keep on, like a cuckoo in the nest. You don't know your place.' He fell silent and didn't stir. Next thing I knew it was morning. 'Well, get up,' I says, 'let's go and be buried.' 'I can't move; I'm stiff.' 'Come on now, get up. You got yourself into this mess, you get yourself out: no use complaining.' I pulled him by his arms and shoulders—and finally he moved; rigid and ice-cold, he got up and staggered after me on legs like stilts: click-click.

"We walked into the office. 'Missed the boat,' I says, but the clerks they begun laughing and accusing me, just like you: 'You're out of your head, grandpa.' They told us both to get lost. 'Oh, what a lazybones!' they winked at each other. 'Wants to hire himself out as a dead man. Go back where you came from!'

"'Where did you come from?'—Soon as I got him out the gates, I asked. 'Krivokolenny Lane, apartment 39, my house is number...' I took him by his crossed arms and bundled him onto a tram and the other passengers, they pitched in: 'Citizens, move up!' 'Make way, citizens!' Alive or dead, they didn't care. Then I got on and whispered in someone's ear, 'Won't you give up your seat to this nice decedent?' The ear leapt aside. I bent my uninvited's knees (now stiffer still), pushed his back against the bench, and the tram lurched off. Well, we crawled and we crawled and finally we came to Krivokolenny. Stairs. 'I can't,' he says; 'let them come down and carry me up.' I could see how hard it was for him. So I leaned him against a wall, and went up myself—from number to number: 39. I rang the bell—the door opened. 'You didn't finish burying one of your tenants,' I says, 'take him back.' 'What tenant? From where?' 'You know from where: from the cemetery. I barely got him here; he's waiting downstairs.' Oh, how they screamed at me, all ten of them at once: 'He's drunk! Can't you see he's out of his head?' (Like you just now.) 'Call the Antireligious Commission, they'll put him where he belongs! Here we are, already packed in like sardines, with a dead man at our door! Get out, you flimflammer, before we break both your legs!'

"There was no help for it. The hell with them. I went back down to my vagabond and tapped him on the shoulder. 'Let's go on,' I says. And he—slack-jawed and white-eyed—he whispers, quiet as quiet, 'Maybe this is my soul going through its trials?' 'Don't be silly,' I says, 'your trials are still ahead of you, waiting under a cross. This here is what they call life...'

"Well, it's a long story. Next day I hauled him back onto the number 17 tram, and off we went; a hearse would have done better, but where were we to find one? As we were getting off at Teatralnaya, the people behind us begun to shove and shout: 'Get off, will you!' 'You're holding everyone up!' 'The man moves like a corpse!' I turned around and I said, 'Right you are, because he is a corpse.' Again they begun shouting and elbowing me in the back: 'And now you!' 'Get off this tram, you so-and-so!' Well, I understand, people are busy and rushing about with their absent eyes, what do they care that a person hasn't been properly buried?

"I struggled along with my unlucky-come-lately—hugging

one wall then another—all the way to the employment office. There, in Rakhmanny Lane, it got easier: I stood him in line— when the person ahead gave way, the person behind pushed— and saw things were looking up. I poked his certificate between his fingers and said to myself, 'Think I'll run out for some tobacco and then look up an acquaintance nearby, he may have some advice.' And off I went. Well that acquaintance, he told me: 'Listen,' he says, 'you better get rid of your stiff because this kind of thing hasn't been *decrimiligaturitized*.' (That's what he said.) And that word—*decrim*... can't even pronounce it a second time —I tell you, it gave me the heebie-jeebies. Wasn't scared before, but now...

"As I dragged myself back—along Rakhmanny—I just hoped his certificate would do the trick. I begun looking for him among the backs behind backs behind backs, all so rigid and stock-still you couldn't tell which was dead and which was alive. I climbed the steps, went inside, and there he was jammed up against the wall with his head stuck fast in the window: couldn't budge. So I went up to the window—the clerk, he was fuming: 'What are you, citizen, deaf and dumb? That's the wrong certificate, we can't register you. Stop holding everyone up! Next!' I yanked my laggard out by the elbows, my old arms could barely support him—he'd gotten so heavy with wanting to pitch over—and then people begun to talk: 'They didn't register him? Why? What certificate? Show us!' I showed 'em. 'Good people,' I says, 'what is this? He's got his death certificate, and suddenly they won't register him. Now if it was irregular, that I could... but this one's got a number, and a stamp, and everything. How can that be?' Straightaway we had, you know, acres of elbow room.

"So back I went with my graveless good-for-nothing out into the hurly-burly and the hubbub: motorcars hootering on all sides, people rushing this way and that, briefcases banging into briefcases, eyes absent. In my anger, I gave the thing up as hopeless— that acquaintance's '*regrim*...' Drat! I still can't pronounce it."

"*Recrimiligaturitized*," I prompted.

"That's it . . . that '*turitized*' had shook me up. 'Goodbye, Un-invited,' I says. But by now he couldn't open his mouth. Then a wave of people swept us up and tumbled us apart—him to one side, me to another—and I saw my come-lately go bobbing off like a bubble in the gutter, being carried farther and farther away by the crowding crowds. I took my cap off and I crossed myself: God rest his soul. Amen.

"After that, anytime I chanced to be in town, any man I met, I stared: might he be my graveless wanderer? But I never did see him again, fate willed otherwise. Don't suppose you ever came across him?"

For a minute we are both silent. Then we have a smoke. And the old man takes up his spade.

"But that's nothing out of the ordinary. Whereas once I . . ."

Just then the bells in the tower above the gate gave a shudder and from behind the wall there wafted, like a draft, a length of quavery choir song. The old man's back dove down into the pit— and over the smack of his shovel and clods of clay upon clay, I heard: "You got me talking and now the grave's not ready. Things go awry like that: first you have a pit with no departed, then you have a departed with no pit. Now step back, else the earth'll hit you."

I turned toward the way out. One set of gates, then another. Under the stone archway in between, I stepped aside to let the procession pass. And walking out of the gates, I thought: Leonardo was right in saying that one can sometimes learn more from water stains than from the creations of a master.

1927

MEMORIES OF THE FUTURE

I

FOUR-YEAR-OLD Max's favorite tale was the one of Tick and Tock. Straddling his father's knee, palms buried in the nap of a tobacco-redolent jacket, the little boy would command: "Tock."

The knee would rock in time to the pendulum beating on the wall, and his father would begin.

"The tale goes like this: Once upon a time there lived an olden clock, the father of two sons: Master Tick and Master Tock. So as to teach them how to run, he allowed that he be wound, though it made him moan and groan fit to be bound. Meantime the minute hand—maintaining a measured pace—took the boys for walks around the clockface. But suddenly Tick and Tock had become young men: they griped and they sniped and they left their father's ken: not ever to return, not ever again. Now the old gray clock searches for them by hand, groaning and calling out in his no-man's-land: 'Tick-Tock, Tock-Tick, Tock!' That's how it goes, right?"

Little Max would dive inside his father's jacket, squint through the woolen eyelids of a buttonhole, and invariably reply, "Wrong."

His father's warm vest would twitch with laughter, tickling Max's ears; through the buttonhole he could see a hand knocking out a pipe.

"Then how does it go? I'm listening, Master Max Shterer."

Max Shterer did reply in the end: but only thirty years later.

Max's first attempt to make the leap from word to deed occurred when he was five.

The house in which the Shterer family lived looked out on a large mustard plantation that stretched away in green squares to a distant bend in the Volga. One evening—this was in July—the child did not appear for dinner. The servant circled the house, calling out the lost boy's name. Max's place at table remained empty throughout the meal. Evening turned into night. Max's father and the servant went in search, having left a light burning in the house. Only the next morning was the runaway found: at a river crossing some ten miles off. He had the look of a true traveler: a sack on his back, a stick in his hand, and in his pocket four coins and a crust of bread. To his father's irate demands for a frank confession, the runaway calmly replied, "It wasn't me who ran away. It was Tock and Tick. I went to look for them."

After he and his son had had a good meal and a good sleep, Shterer père resolved to radically revise his educational methods. He summoned little Max to him and announced that fairy tales were stuff and nonsense, that Tock and Tick were just the knock of one metal plate against another and that that knock had nowhere to run. Seeing the bewilderment in the little boy's round blue eyes, he opened the wall clock's glass case, removed the hands, then the face, and running a finger along the mechanism's serrated edges, explained: the weights, because they are heavy, drive the gear train, the gear train drives the gear wheels, the gear wheels drive the gear teeth—the purpose of all this being to measure *time*.

The word "time" appealed to Max. And when, two or three months later, he was made to learn the alphabet, e, i, m, and t were the first letters out of which he tried to make—pushing his pen along the slanted rules—a word.

Now that he knew the way to the small whirring wheels, the boy decided to repeat the experiment performed by his father. One day, having waited until everyone was out, he put a stool against the wall, scrambled up onto it, and opened the clock case. His eyes were level with the pendulum's yellow disk swinging to and fro; the chain, drawn by the weight, kept disappearing up into the darkness and the murmuring cogs. It was after that that something strange began to happen with the clock: as they were sitting down to lunch, Shterer the elder glanced at the clock and noted the time: two minutes past two. "Rather late," he muttered, hurriedly taking up his spoon. In response to another glance between the first and second courses, the clock said: two minutes past four. "What the *zum Teufel!** Can we really have been eating our soup for two hours?" Shterer the younger, keeping his eyes on his plate, said nothing; when they got up from the table, the hands showed five past seven, and by the time the servant had fetched the clockmaker, who lived nearby, the clock claimed it was nearly midnight, though the sun was still shining.

The clockmaker first removed the hands and asked little Max to hold them. He then uncovered the mechanism and set about inspecting the screws and wheels with the father, giving the mischievous little boy ample time in which to pull a tiny prosthesis off the hour hand. Having carefully examined and checked everything, the clockmaker pronounced the clock in perfect working order: they shouldn't have troubled him, a busy man, for nothing.

Incensed, Shterer the elder began to shout; he said he believed his own eyes more than other people's knowledge and demanded that the clockmaker repair the clock gone mad. Now the clockmaker took umbrage; he said that if someone had gone mad, it surely wasn't the clock, and that he did not intend to spend his time and Shterer's money mending what wasn't broken. Having replaced the hands, he slammed first the clock case then the front door. At which point the clock, as if to crown the insult to its owner, took a new tack and began tapping out the minutes with chronometric accuracy.

*What the Devil (*Ger.*).

Father and son spent the remainder of the day without exchanging a word. Now and then, now one, now the other glanced anxiously at the clock. Night was already curtaining the window when Max, overcoming his embarrassment, went up to his father, touched his knee and said, "Tock."

Thus the legend of Tick and Tock, all but banished from Shtererdom, returned home. In conducting his first experiment, Shterer the younger had forced the clock hands to exchange axes: hour hand for minute hand, and vice versa. And he had seen how even such a simple inversion disturbs the running of mental mechanisms.

The experimenter had reached out and touched one of the hands—the shorter one. The other hand was leading its long black tip into the upper recesses. He must study that hand too. Standing on tiptoe, he could just reach it. Above his head something had cracked, and in his fingers the hand's broken-off end showed black. What should he do? From a seam in his jacket a black thread was hanging down. A minute later the broken-off end had been neatly attached to the nearer tip. True, the short hand was now long, and the long hand short—but what did it matter. Just then he heard steps in the passage. The little boy shut the glass case, jumped off the stool, and put it back where it went.

The patient old Swiss clock did not become angry with the inquisitive little boy. Pacing incessantly from corner to corner on its long leg inside its cramped glass cage, it graciously allowed that pair of childish eyes to visit it in its solitary confinement. Rhythmically rapping out the seconds, the mechanical teacher from Zurich, like most teachers, was energetic, precise, and methodical. But a genius doesn't need to be taught imagination; suffering from his own excesses, he looks to people for only one thing—limits. Thus teacher and pupil suited each other perfectly. Every day after lunch, as soon as he heard his father's snores through the wall, Shterer the younger would draw a stool up to the problem of time and begin his questioning. He pulled his teacher's weights, felt his round white face, and stole with curious fingers inside his hard, sharp-edged brain. Then one day his mechanical teacher—evidently baffled by some difficult question—let his leg drag and stopped rapping out the lesson. Max assumed the clock was considering its answer and waited patiently, standing on the stool. The silence stretched on. The hands remained still. And from behind the cogs: not a sound, not a peep. The frightened little boy leapt to the floor and rushed to his sleeping father; tugging him by the sleeve, he stammered through sobs: "Papa! The clock is dead. But it's not my fault."

Shaking himself awake, his father yawned and said, "Don't be silly. It's not that easy to die. Calm down, pet: it's only broken. That's all, and we'll mend it. Now stop crying."

The future master of durations dried his eyes with small fists and asked, "And if time breaks, will we mend it too?"

His father, following the old clock's lead, fell silent. He sat up and eyed his child with not a little uneasiness.

2

These incidents from Max Shterer's childhood—and there were many—attest to one thing: to an early established mental dominant, to a focus that appears to have fused with its object, to a passion for one idea or, rather, its first inklings—the basis, some researchers say, of a natural gift. The child, and later the youth, strove to see down the road that stretched ahead without taking a single step along it. The father viewed his son's bent for contemplation—for listening to his inner voice, his reluctance to run about and play games—as ordinary apathy. He supposed that life, like medicine, must be shaken: else it wouldn't have the desired effect. At the age of nine, Max was shaken: sent off to Moscow, to a preparatory school. Father Shterer, left to his own devices, made up for the lack of conversation with twice the number of pipes; he smoked and he pined. One long winter evening he had even to resort to the bookshelf. The dozen books sprawled there included an odd volume of Dal's proverbs. (A Russified German colonist, Shterer considered it proper to converse with the Russian folk by means of their proverbs, *Sprichwörter*, diligently learned by rote in alphabetical order.) Leafing through the volume, Shterer discovered a note in his son's childish hand. Next to the saying "Time marches on" was the scrawled remark: "But I'll make it dance in a circle."

Shterer père never did learn to what "it" in fact referred, but Max Shterer's biographer, Joseph Stynsky, calls this jotting "the first threat" and notes the image of the circle, which the inventor later used—as opposed to the straight line that typically symbolizes time—in realizing his plan. The first two or three years Shterer was away at school, father and son met and parted at the start and finish of every vacation. With each new visit the son would be taller and thinner; his sleeves and trousers could scarcely keep up with him; even his hair, once fair and shoulder-length, now stood up on end no matter how often it was cut. But the year 1905 soon separated the Shterers in earnest. First the father, fearing peasant unrest, asked the son to delay coming, then the son, pleading a project of his own, postponed his visit. The mysterious "project" consumed the next vacation as well. The father sent a telegram and money for a ticket, only to receive a telegram back: "Time is taking all my time. Don't wait," while the money turned quickly into books and reagents. Maximilian Shterer, to the horror of his landlady and the fascination of his fellow boarders, had long since set up an improvised physicochemical laboratory under his bed. He guarded the contents jealously: the box of retorts, electrostatics equipment, and other scientific paraphernalia. In summer he carried the sealed tubes, vials of reagents and spirit lamp out into a corner of the yard, behind the shed; in winter he worked only on Sundays and holidays when the other boarders were absent. Busy with his thoughts, fourth-former Shterer had little time for lessons. Teachers and classmates considered him a loafer of only average abilities. Still, certain incidents somewhat confused the general impression: once when he was called with two other boys to the board and didn't have enough room on his third for the geometric symbols needed to solve the problem, Shterer, in a fit of pique, erased the long line of equality and arrived at the answer in a few chalk strokes using analytic geometry. The physics master who taught fifth formers capillarity and Rupert's drops as well as Newton's universal laws was a little afraid of a certain pupil found to be annoyingly conversant with the latest scientific discoveries. For his part, Max, who ignored the top marks meant to fend him off, was not opposed to helping teachers broaden their horizons: one day he handed his mathematics teacher a German memoir about elliptic functions. The teacher wouldn't likely have understood anything even if he had understood German. A week later he returned the book with a patronizing pat on the back and, coattails flapping, ducked into the teachers' room. Shterer, who had spent a sleepless night rebutting the memoir's main points, never did find anyone to discuss it with.

Indeed he was very lonely, even in his early youth. In the boardinghouse dormitory, ten beds stood side by side; next to the beds were small tables; and on the tables, green-shaded lamps. The dormitory's older inmates spoke in voices breaking from bass to treble, scraped the down on their chins with penknives, and hoarded kopecks for the eventual acquisition of condoms. The younger natives, known disparagingly as "swarmers," spent reverent evenings eavesdropping on their elders, who, squatting by the open stove, inhaled the smoke while discussing broads and the best system of brass knuckles.

Only two boys took no part in either the discussions or the eavesdropping: Max Shterer, shut away with his books and his thoughts, and Ichil Tapchan, Ichya for short, a spindly-legged, sunken-chested youth with the face of someone not fated to live. Ichya would sit hunched on his bed, pupils turned inward, yellow-knuckled hands wrapped around his knees. His blue eyelids quivered like a bird's ciliary membrane, while through his fine protuberant ears, if one squinted, one could see the green outline of the lamp.

Schoolmates sometimes tried to tease Ichya.

"Should be carting you off to the cemetery any day now, Ichya."

"Better write home and tell your mother to send you your tallith."

Ichya never said anything back; only his birdlike membranes quivered, while his sharp cheekbones bloomed with ruddy blots. Max Shterer, who paid Ichya more attention than did the others, did not mock him, but neither did he feel compassion, he simply observed him and pondered the process of deterioration now gaining on that of regeneration; here was a problem about a difference in speeds, like the arithmetic problem about the freight train overtaken by the express. He must adjust the conditions accordingly, solve the problem, check the answer, and go on to the next. The investigator of time most likely saw the sickly Jewish boy from Gomel as a vessel from which time was fast escaping and running out, or as a mechanism whose faulty regulator had released the starter too quickly. In Ichya's frequent fits of resonant coughing, Shterer learned to discern a succession of distinctive intonations: it was as though Ichya were talking to someone using short aspirated words composed entirely of sibilants and gutturals; having waited for the rejoinder that only he could hear, he would answer with a new paroxysm—all whistles and wheezes— of protests. Listening closely to these conversations, Shterer sometimes—so it seemed to him—guessed to whom Ichya was talking: the name of the other was, after all, always in his thoughts.

Early every Sunday the boarders went off and the dormitory stood empty, save for the two boys: Ichya sat hunched on his bed, while out from under Shterer's bed there crept, all tinkling glass and metal, the box laboratory. One boy, narrowing birdlike membranes, observed in himself the spread of death. The other boy—bent over tangled wires, a system of contacts and switches, glass-necked retorts, and a cipher jumping from atom to atom—dreamed of a trap that would catch time. They never spoke to each other. Only once, sensing that he might, Ichya asked shyly, "You don't go for walks, do you?"

"I have no interest at all in space," said Shterer, and again bent over his box.

"I thought so," Ichya nodded, and waited.

"People move about in space. From any point to any point. They ought also to move through time: from any point to any point. Now that, I tell you, would be a walk!"

Ichya grinned excitedly: that's right, a walk as never before!

He began coughing into his handkerchief. Max, putting the wordless but to him intelligible bursts together, heard: "You go on and get there without me—because I'm done for."

Max made to take a step toward Ichya's protruding shoulder blades and held out his hand. But just then voices sounded in the front hall. The box laboratory slid quickly back under the bed.

A week or two went by. Walking into the dormitory one day at dusk, Shterer noticed the rectangle of a book on his pillow. He turned on the light—the yellow cover said: *The Time Machine*. From Ichya's mischievous smile it was easy to guess who had left this mysterious present. Shterer did not feel gratitude—flipping quickly through the pages, his hands expressed, if anything, rage. Someone, some fabricator of fictions, had dared to invade his own Shtererian idea, an idea that could be taken from his brain only with his brain.

The whole evening book and eyes did not separate. Ichya, following the movement of the pages from his corner, spied first a forehead glowering above them, then brows that had moved calmly apart, then an almost disgusted smile playing about pursed lips.

Sunday came and Ichya, who had been feverish since morning, lay down with his back to the light. Suddenly he felt a hand on his shoulder. Squinting up, he saw Shterer's face bent over him.

"You should pull the covers up. I'll do it. There. And take your book: I don't need it."

"You didn't like it?" Ichya mumbled, dismayed.

Max sat down on the edge of the bed.

"You see, it's not a matter of pleasing people. It's a matter of attacking time, striking and destroying it. Shots at a shooting gallery do not a war make. Besides, in my problem, as in music, being off by five tones creates less dissonance than being off by a half-tone. Take, for instance, the machine's appearance: the wires, even that absurd bicycle seat. Nothing of the kind: even the externals of my time-traveling machine will be entirely different. Oh, how clearly I see it."

Pressing his temples, Max broke off. Ichya leaned forward in anticipation.

"What does it look like?"

"The temporal selector, as I now see it, will have the shape of a pointed glass hat snugly covering the frontal and occipital bones. The focuses of the temporator's exceedingly fine flint glasses will intersect in such a way as to exclude the apparatus from sight even before launch. Optically this is entirely possible. Then, once the machine is in operation, this invisibility should gradually spread from activator to activated, that is, to the brain in its transparent vise, the skull, neck, shoulders, and so on. Thus a bullet's nickel-plated cap is excluded from sight by its flight, despite being present in space. Still, that's not the point: the time hiding under one's skull must be covered with a hat, like a moth with a net. But time has a billion wings and is far more easily frightened—wearing an invisibility hat is the only way to catch it. I can't understand why the significance of the invisibility cap invented by storytellers remains to this day...invisible to scientists. I get my material from all different places. As you can see, even fairy tales may have their use."

"But then how—"

"How will it work? Very simply. Actually, no: very complicatedly. Take even this aspect—the easiest to explain: any textbook on physiological psychology recognizes the principle of the so-called specificity of energy. Were it possible to detach the auditory nerve's internal ending and graft it onto the brain's optic center, we would *see sounds* and given the reverse operation *hear shapes and colors.* Now listen carefully: all of our perceptions, which flow along countless nerve wires to the brain, are either spatial or temporal. Of course, the durations and expanses are so entangled that no surgeon's knife could ever separate them. My idea too, evidently, isn't sharper than a steel blade, it can't uncouple the instants and glints, but at least I'm on the right track. I can already guess, albeit vaguely, the difference in intension between these two types of perception. And once I learn to separate seconds from cubic millimeters in the brain, like molecules of oil from water, it will only remain for me to finish work on my neuromagnet. You see, even an ordinary magnet diverts electrons from their path; my neuromagnet, enveloping the brain in the form of a hat, will do the same thing, not with a stream of electrons but with a stream of durations, of temporal points, rushing toward their center: intercepting the stream midway, my powerful neuromagnet will redirect the flight of temporal perceptions past the customary paths to spatial centers. Thus the geometrician wishing to turn a line into a plane must divert that line away from itself to form a right angle. And in that instant when it jumps into the glint, so to speak, and becomes three-dimensional, present, past, and future may be made to change places like dominoes, a game requiring at least two dimensions. The third dimension is for safety's sake. After all, for the canoe that has lost a paddle, there's only one solution—to float downriver with the current, from past to future. Until the skiff is wrecked on the rocks or swept away by a wave. What I'm giving people is a plain paddle, an oar with which to restrain the racing seconds. It's as simple as that. Use it and you, or anyone, will be able to row against the days, or ahead of them, or even across time . . . to the shore. But your cheeks are burning, Ichya. You don't feel well?"

Damp, hot fingers gripped Shterer's palm.

"I do feel well. Better than I'll ever feel again."

Shterer smiled.

"That's not true: when I've built my machine—even if it's ten or twenty years from now, it doesn't matter—I'll come back, I promise you, to this exact day, to right now: we'll be sitting here like this, your fingers, though you won't exist anymore, will be damp and hot, and you'll say, 'I do feel well. Better than...' But then I'll pull the lever and take you—"

"To the shore?"

"No, Ichya, past it and beyond. Through time's flight."

Shterer's subsequent declarations never came to pass. Ichya's health grew worse by the day. His family came to take him home to Gomel. One morning, as if in confirmation of the snide predictions about the tallith, Ichya, wrapped in a stripy blanket, was sitting in a carriage, his head thrown back on the leathern pillow. Max Shterer hopped up onto the footboard and gave Ichya's frail fingers a cautious squeeze. The lilac birdlike membranes fluttered in gratitude. Shterer hopped down.

They exchanged two letters. A third letter sent from Moscow was returned unopened: Addressee Deceased.

Stynsky, who used, among other sources, Tapchan's diary and a copy of the first Moscow letter, which Ichya had lovingly copied into his notebook the day before he died, maintains that this first attempt at friendship was Shterer's last.

3

Very little is known about Shterer's first two years at university. Classmates recalled a reddish goatee and the same short light coat summer and winter, but what Shterer spoke about and to whom, or whether he ever spoke to anyone at all, none of Stynsky's respondents could say. One suspects the latter: that he never spoke to anyone about anything. We now know that Maximilian Shterer, like many outstanding minds of his generation, was afflicted with the black philosophical pox of Schopenhauerism. At any rate, certain confused jottings in his lecture notebooks refer to a rather strange theory explaining the origin of the past. According to these jottings, the past results from the *displacement* of perception A by perception B. But if one increases A's *capacity to resist*, then B, rather than replace A, must stand *beside* it. Thus a symbol in musical notation may join the preceding symbol both horizontally and vertically: in the first case, we have to do with melodious time; in the second, with its harmonious form. Given a consciousness so vast that the perceptions accumulating in it did not displace each other, there would be enough present for them all. When two objects are equidistant from the eye, one will appear closer than the other depending on the light, the brightness of its color and the distinctness of its shape. What compels one's consciousness to move this or that element of the accumulating present into the past or, to use Shterer's terminology, what compels one's consciousness to build a past into which elements may be *moved*? "Pain," replied "the then Shterer" (as Stynsky reconstructs). In space, any organism naturally moves away from an object that causes pain: since I can throw away the match burning my fingers, reflex does just that; but since I cannot throw away the sun burning my body, I myself hide from it in the shade. And since—pessimism was entering into the argument—all perceptions are pain, differing only in degree of painfulness, then in both time and space one's consciousness has no choice but to remove those perceptions or to remove itself from them by means of what is called perspective and the past. Commenting on this passage in one of Shterer's few manuscripts, Stynsky notes the influence of Spencer's theory, which describes perceptions of pain as signals sent by the nervous periphery to the center to warn of external dangers. Having marched with the English evolutionist right up to the abyss, says Stynsky, Shterer then marches into the abyss: a consciousness that doesn't warn of danger with pain is superfluous; therefore, all its perceptions are signals and all those signals are distress signals sum-SOS; it must avert its death so as to live.

In his own definitions of the concepts of time and pain, the

Shterer of this period strove to superimpose them one on top of the other. "Time," he wrote, "like a ray of light racing away from its source, is a departure from self, a pure placelessness, a minus from a minus; pain is a test imbued with a tendency to avoid being tested."

At this remove it's hard to account for all the considerations and semi-considerations that blocked the way with metaphysics, what's more a metaphysics that had cast its "meta" through the gloom into the brume. Shterer must have felt a certain disappointment in the strength of his sling once he came to terms with his opponent's size and might. His miniature box laboratory couldn't compete, naturally, with the equipment in university laboratories; new, more exact and extensive experiments did not confirm his first, primitive semi-experiments; a number of bold conjectures turned out to be false; many many things had to be crossed out and begun again. In one of his notebooks, Shterer remarks bitterly: "Today I am twenty-two. I delay and demur and, at the same time, time is gaining time in the fight for the theme of time." And a few lines down: "Time always wins because it *goes by*. Either it will take my life before I take its meaning, or..." Here the entry breaks off. But that pessimism, like the shadows of clouds entrained by the wind, soon left Shterer's consciousness. Perhaps it had to be so: one must pull the bowstring back to shoot the arrow ahead, one must slow one's thoughts to determine their meaning. In the first eighteen months after this break, Shterer made great strides in concretizing his plan. Unfortunately, most of the material from this period—destroyed in part by Shterer, in part by the Civil War—has survived only in odd fragments, and even these need decoding.

This period begins with Shterer's article investigating the question of time's so-called diameter. Submitted to his psychology professor as a term paper, it was two or three years ahead of American scientific findings on "the duration of the present" and intended to overturn conventional notions of the present as a point of "zero duration." Time is not linear, it is an "anachronism of *chronos*"—it has its own diameter known to "consumers of time" as the present. Since we project our *nunc** across durations, we can, by changing our projection, range our nunc down durations: thus we can calculate how many presents will fit into the space of, say, a minute. The so-called tempograms appended to Shterer's paper showed "time's diameter" or, rather, its typical range: from tenths of a second to three whole seconds (later the Americans' more exact measurements would allow one to observe the length of a present of up to five seconds). Be that as it may, this second-year student's attempt to measure the interval separating "the end of the past from the beginning of the future" (I quote from the paper) did not meet with his professor's approval. Shterer's department, as one might have expected, turned out to be wooden and hollow inside.

Whether it was this circumstance that caused Shterer to turn his back on official science is unclear. We know only that the money sent the following semester by the father to pay for "the right to study," the son elected to spend on compounds so that, in due course, he was expelled for nonpayment.

To this brief period at university, scholars usually ascribe Shterer's invention of the *hiemsetator* and his *month-of-Sundays* project.

The hiemsetator, according to Stynsky, was a singular sort of scientific toy. Shterer supposed that winter and summer, succeeding each other as they do at several-month intervals, might be administered to the percipient nervous apparatus "in a powderlike form." The calendar year—the metamorphosis of leafy green canopy into snow-white cover and consequent stimulations of the eye's retina—could be ground up in the hiemsetator, like coffee beans in a hand-cranked mill, while retaining all of its properties in every grain. This "toy" worked like this: the subject's eyes, sealed off from all other sources of light, were fitted with a disk that spun at different speeds and was divided into two sections:

*Now (*Lat.*).

green and white. Entering the subject's field of vision by turns, the green and the white succeeded each other, like the leaves and the snow in nature's cycle. A set of disks with all different ratios of white to green, similar to an optometrist's set of lenses, allowed the subject to select the ratio best suited to his or her own eyes. Some one hundred and fifty experiments conducted on inhabitants of different climactic zones in Russia produced—so Stynsky tells us—the following results: for inhabitants of regions where statistically the ratio of snowy months to green ones is 2:1, the most comfortable disk was that on which the ratio of white to green was also 2:1; the eyes of southerners were least fatigued by the spinning disk on which the ratio of green to white was 3:2; and so on. Since Shterer himself attached little importance to this whirligig and its extremely crude imitations of the changing seasons, we needn't discuss it any further.

The project jokingly referred to by Shterer as his "month of Sundays" came down, in essence, to the problem of designing an *artificial day*. "Days," according to this unfinished manuscript, "are inserted into the apperceiving apparatus like the pipe valves in a barrel organ. Days, however, differ from pipe valves in that the pins on them—that is, the stimuli affecting psychophysics—shift continuously. But if one consolidates those stimuli into clusters, if one turns those days into uniform constancies and rotates the perceptions, like the hands on a clock, then the circular course of time or, rather, its content will also be transmitted—after a certain number of revolutions—to the psyche, circularizing even it." The isolator for producing the artificial day was supposed to be a hermetically sealed room cube insulated from all outside sounds and influences by a double layer of cork. The ceiling (fairly high—in case of encroachments by the subject) would act on the subject by means of various light- and sound-signaling devices suspended from it. The clockwork inside the cork-lined room would rotate sounds and rays in strict succession; upon completion of the twenty-four-day cycle, it would repeat in the same order and at the same intervals, and again repeat. It is curious the zeal with which Shterer worked at mechanizing not only the cork lining but also, as far as possible, the movements of his subject, encased in a system of elastic traces designed to control him and his bodily functions.

Stynsky rightly remarks that this looks more like torture than experimentation, and smacks of prisons not the lab. Yet he immediately qualifies this by saying that apart from the obduracy of a young mind, this project shows Shterer's reluctance to give up his childhood dream of "making time dance in a circle." In the end, "this bizarre plan to create a month of Sundays, all of them . . . Bloody" (Stynsky's words) may be the lyrical impulse of a man caught inside himself by one persistent idea spinning around him, of a man who gave all his days to the problem of days.

At any rate, once he had freed himself of the ceiling with the pendant signaling devices, once he had discharged the image in sketches and numbers, Shterer finally arrived at that bloodless, light-filled mode of thought comparable to a quiet dustless day when the horizon, flung wide by the sun, discloses the ordinarily invisible shapes of distant islands and mountains. The first idea to put him on the road to realizing his plan was that of *simulating time*.

Starting with the assumption that a measure always resembles what it measures (a number of analogies bore this out), Shterer hypothesized that a timepiece (or, rather, the design of its mechanism) and the time that it measures should resemble each other in some way, as a yardstick does a board, a bucket does the sea, and so on. All mechanisms marking time—be it with grains of sand or gear teeth—are constructed according to the principle of *returning*, of turning on a real or imaginary axis. What was this, chance or expedience? If the yardstick unfurling a bolt of cloth winds the fabric around its steel ends, then its movements are strictly determined by the *nature of the material being measured* and are in no way random. So why not assume that the circular motion of yardsticks measuring time (in other words, clocks) is determined by the nature of the material that they measure, that is to say, time? Shterer jabbed his pen into the inkwell and quickly revived the ancient Pythagorean notion of time as a giant crystal sphere that encompasses all the things of this world with its ceaseless spinning. Of course, the proto-philosopher's rudimentary image bore no more resemblance to Shterer's notion of the multiaxiality of time than does the embryonic blastula cell to the fullgrown organism, than do a dozen geometric theorems discovered by that early forerunner to the complex system of subtle mathematical stimuli that triggered his follower's idea. The genius who settled relations between the hypotenuse and the catheti would scarcely have been able to immediately understand how Shterer's formulas intersected, and Stynsky's position too, in trying to keep pace with the thinking of his contemporary, was extremely difficult. In his desire to come level with Shterer, he often resorted to a library ladder. Thus, with reference to Shterer's hypothesis about time's multiple axes, Stynsky recalls Leibniz, creator of the *monadology*: in answer to the question of how any changing of places, any motion is possible given that matter is continuous and fills all of space, given that all places have been taken, Leibniz said that the only motion possible within such a continuous world was the rotation of spheres about their axes. If one imagines (Stynsky was now inferring) that the continuousness of this world is not of matter but of movement (time is just that, pure movement), then the world cannot be seen as other than a system of circular motions rushing out of themselves into themselves. As in the mechanism of a clock where wheels turning wheels relay—in a certain spatial *sequence*, from gear tooth to gear tooth—the impulse of the mainspring, so in the mechanism of time a sequence specific to it bandies the "spinning instant" from axis to axis into the everreceding *beyond*; but the axes, for all their spinning, remain where they are—in short, time is given to us *all at once,* whereas we peck at it one grain at a time, in split seconds.

Stynsky's account may be guilty of impressionisticness. Shterer, after all, made his case without going into either impressions or metaphysics, as the following excerpt will illustrate:

On a single-track road one cannot *pass* without swerving to one side. So long as we conceived of time as a straight line, points along it blocked the way of other points. The discovery of *time's diameter* has allowed me to build a *second track*. Now points will have to make way when I want to pass them.

A clockface. Inside the clockface is a minute dial, around which a hand travels in 60 seconds; but a clockface has room as well for a second dial (this wouldn't be hard to construct)—the hand on it would have to cover 60 fractions of a second in one second; but were the clockmaker to construct a 1/60-second dial, whose hand had to make 60 successive movements in 1/60 second, we would apprehend those 60 movements as *one* since the time allotted us for their apprehension would not exceed in duration that of our *present*. If—having adjusted the hand's speed to our apperceiving apparatus so that it went around the circle, divided into fractions, in one instant—we were to focus on one particular fraction marked with, say, red paint, our consciousness would merge the moment of the hand's departure and that of its return into one *present*; the hand would have time, so to speak, to dash off, run around the circle, lingering at dozens of other fractions, and return, without ever having been "missed." Inside every instant there is undoubtedly a complexity, what I would call an untimely time. One can cross time the way one crosses the street—one can dart in among the streaming seconds the way one darts in among the rushing automobiles, without ever being run over.

A few lines down: "I need a wheel that goes from axle to axle. This will be a bit more difficult than Aristotle's famous conundrum about two radiuses. Yes, my wheel goes not around an axle, but from axle to axle. This is the specific nature of transtemporal journeys."

And farther down: "Our brain tempers time. If one untempers *tempus*,* then..." Then comes a formula that begins with the curve of an integral, but its symbols have all been scored out, and above it Shterer has written in pencil: "Crossing time here is dangerous!"

But on the other side of this page we find a fresh attempt at a breakthrough: "Time's energy manifests itself as a difference in potentials, $T-T = t$: one may pass down the minus sign, as down a gangway, from the big T to the little t and back again. If one accepts..." There follows another formula, in among whose symbols it is easier to get lost than in a forest. Even in fiction, one must hug the forest's edges.

These quotes culled from Shterer's few surviving notebooks are impossible to date. Shterer, who sought to overthrow the power of dates, never noted days or years. One can only hazard the guess that all these scraps of ideas, which happened onto paper by chance, relate to 1912–1913 when Shterer, expelled from university, was still living in student digs, in a tiny room hard under the eaves of a huge stone pile whose windows gave onto Kozikha. The monies from home had become rather meager, forcing Shterer to find work in order to support himself. It was at this point that he began giving lessons which, in exchange for twenty rubles monthly, cost him ten thousand paces a day. Elbows sticking out of his pockets, Shterer patiently made the daily journey from Kozikha across the river and back to Kozikha; and when, after six months of lessons, he happened to meet a smiling lady in the street with her school-age son, who gave him a friendly nod, he couldn't think who they were, though they were his pupil and his pupil's mother.

Meanwhile the lady from across the river had made repeated attempts to steal under the lowered eyelids of the glum young man. Every day, an hour before Shterer's arrival, she would sit down at her dressing table and prepare her face with far more care than did her son his lessons. Crimping irons and a red lip pencil

*Time (*Lat.*).

reflected in the looking glass, but nothing reflected in the tutor. The advantage of the small goal over the great, however, is in its attainability. One day Shterer, having walked the first five thousand paces, learned that there would be no lesson since "the child asked to be let off today, do forgive him, so as to go to..." Without waiting to hear where, Shterer turned on his heels only to feel a light pressure on his elbow: he was invited to sit down and drink some tea with lingonberry jam: "What's your hurry?" Shterer agreed or, rather, his weariness agreed. An empty birdcage hung on the wall. Watching the sleepy blue roses on the lady's peignoir rise and fall, Shterer asked, "Why is it empty?" There followed the mournful story of an overfed canary, which segued seamlessly into that of a premature widowhood and the difficulties of managing a mischievous little boy alone, without a man's firm hand. Then came several desultory sighs to which Shterer responded by jabbing with his teaspoon at the lumps of sugar refusing to dissolve in his glass.

"You never know, you may make a hole in the bottom. Besides, why hide your eyes in your glass? That's where the jam goes, not your eyes. You're always thinking, but what about? About different things?"

Shterer replied, "No, not about different things."

"About one thing then? Or perhaps one person?"

Through her smile two silver fillings winked. The blue roses smelled of bluing. Jerking back his pupils, Shterer remarked that in a game of checkers it was possible for both players to win: when one tried to capture the other's pieces, while the other played giveaway. For all that, our theoretician didn't notice that one of the pieces had already been touched.

A quarter of an hour after the first aphorism an outside observer might have acquainted himself with the theory of *time's cuts* as set forth in the batting eyes of the lady from across the river.

As applied to love, the theory went like this: memory, "unrolling its long scroll," may, like a reel of film, be edited. One may cut

bits out of both time and the reel and dispense with the lon-
gueurs. Thus if one were to make cuts between a woman's first
meeting with her first lover and her first meeting with her second,
her third, and so on, that is, if one were to leave what was purest,
most sincere, and deeply embedded in memory, the film reel onto
which we had transposed this series of spliced-together first meetings would show us the woman—with the speed of a roulette ball
skipping from number to number—whirling from embrace to
embrace and aging before our eyes. To a lawyer, of course, this
would recall the article in the Criminal Code dealing with mass
violence. Try editing the superfluous out of anything at all, leaving
only what is essential, and you'll see that it won't be to your...

An hour after that last aphorism Shterer was persuaded of its
cruel accuracy. Whereas an outside observer... actually, in situa-
tions like this such people are superfluous.

The next day Shterer surveyed his pupil for the first time:
bending his eyebrowless forehead over his arithmetic book, the
boy tugged at his bushy hair as though trying to pull the unknown quantity out of his head; the lamplight shone through his
small red ears.

"Just like Ichya's," thought Shterer.

Inside Shterer's "I" it felt like an unheated room.

4

This happened in February 1914. Having walked his usual route,
Shterer failed to notice the porch jutting out onto the sidewalk in
the lane across the river, and the snow continued to crunch underfoot. He looked like a person dogging someone's tracks. Two
or three female heads turned to stare, whitening their furs with
their breath. But Shterer was trying to catch up with his own head
or, rather, one of its thoughts, skimming along like a dusky shadow
over the snow. The lanes were deserted; his steps, extricating themselves from crossroads, crackling through the blue air, were over-

taking a syllogism. The city's ice-covered gates had been left behind. The snow slithered up his ankles and began to confound his found rhythm; the syllogism's major and minor premises, seizing on the pause of a snowdrift, came apart, but just then, blocking their path, along parallels of steel, a spiral of smoke came thundering up followed by round racing wheels. Shterer stopped, gasping for breath; his face burned with a furious joy: he had caught the last symbol in the last formula—finally!—under his frontal bone.

Standing knee-deep in snow, he picked up a stick stuck to the frozen crust and etched his formula in the white field. Next day a thaw set in, and the document revealing the secret of Shterer's machine was scored out by the sun's rays. From then on the inventor worked without confiding in either people or paper.

Then again notes were no longer necessary: the time had come to build the machine that would trap time. For this he needed money. Shterer calculated his expenses: they hovered in the high five figures. Father and son exchanged letters in which the son asked and the father refused. Shterer pared his estimate to the minimum: four figures winked gray from the fold in the telegram. His father ripped the spectacles from his nose and flung them to the floor. The first page of his reply threatened disinheritance, the third advised patience—upon his death his son could have everything, and the postscript promised half the sum forthwith.

When the money arrived, Shterer the younger, without waiting for more, decided to begin building his machine. The hundred-odd doors around his own struck him as a threat to his secret. He must get away from people's curiosity, guesses, and peerings. On the outskirts, in a lane that crossed the Khapilovka, he found quarters that were fairly quiet and isolated: a wooden mezzanine with three tiny windows, two low-ceilinged rooms, and stairs down into the yard. The outer room contained a bed and a pile of books (here Shterer received the very rare visitor). The inner room, where no one was allowed, was home to his machine.

The neighborhood's new resident seldom appeared on the steps leading down from the mezzanine. But when he did, he always had bottle-shaped and cylindrical bundles tucked under one elbow, while the other slid down the steep railing. His windows were invariably curtained, and even when spring had flung wide all the casements in all the walls, the mezzanine's three remained shut.

Hiding under the ice, the sickly Yauza burst its banks not far from Shterer's abode and tried for a week or two to remember what it had been in bygone centuries when riverboats and sails— not parti-colored patches of oil and dung—glided down it, in the centuries' wake. The sun, staring into the puddles, like a drunk into his drink before drinking it, drained them all.

Mouths chewing sunflower seeds by Khapilovka porches discussed the strange settler once or twice. First it was decided that the man in the mezzanine drank alone and all the time, emptying his bottles and cylinders. But then one day a woman was seen climbing the stairs. And every night a light burned in the three windows. The mouths, construing the curtains another way, grinned with satisfaction.

By the end of May Shterer's money had all but run out. He had drawn a radius with his idea—from nowhere, from no single point. Now his eyes chanced on two or three letters lying unopened in the corner. He unsealed them: the red translucent ear, hot blue roses smelling of soap, the empty birdcage, and again the edge of an ear bent over numbers. He must finish building his machine. No matter what. Blinking in disgust, Shterer scrabbled in his desiccated ink-swill for a few lines, as a consequence of which idle neighbors did indeed see a female figure climbing the stairs to the mezzanine. The meeting produced something like a game of checkers in which both players lose: this happened because the takeaway side, on reaching the last move, suddenly decided to give in, while the giveaway side balked, striking back with a stubborn merchant-class stinginess. In short: on learning that a certain machine would require a particular sum, the lady from across the river became very suspicious of Shterer's reasoning: she knew perfectly well what sorts of machines young people spent their own and other people's money on nowadays. When

Shterer opened the door to his inner sanctum, suggesting she see for herself, the lady from across the river, clutching her reticule to her bosom, asked why this contrivance so compelled him. Shterer patiently explained that he needed this construction so that he, Shterer, might transport himself to other centuries and millennia.

"But what about me?" asked the lady from across the river.

Shterer looked abashed.

"There's only one seat. You'll have to wait until I return from—"

"From the millennia?"

"Yes."

The reticule refused to open its small, metal-clasped mouth: this did not suit it. One side was left without kisses, the other, without money. But a week hadn't gone by before yellow showers of acacia began filling the lanes across the river with their fragrance; the evenings were close and complicit. Like the fish that throws itself upon the shore to spawn, the reticule kept gaping in despair and disgorging hundred-ruble notes. Shterer could resume his work. The advancing July heat finally forced the mezzanine's six panes open so that in the dead of night the casual passerby could hear a tremor-like sound that seemed to cleave the air, to riddle the silence with a staccato stipple. Listening more closely, the belated passerby would notice that in the changing shots of sound the... but Khapilovka's belated passerby was invariably drunk and would rather drown out the silence than let it into his ringing ears.

Immersed in his work, Shterer, because of the one thing coming slowly into existence, did not see other things; he lived past the facts accumulating around his three windows. The word "war," lost at first in the fine print, had gradually enlarged its type to fill all the headlines in all the papers. The word caught Shterer's eye for a second or two only because of its resemblance to another word: "warp" (as in "time warp"). The three letters skimmed over his retina then left the way they had come, and for the next few days he continued to substantiate his exquisitely conceived trap for catching time.

Shterer had grown accustomed: toward evening the street noises would abate, allowing him to work with greater concentration. He would postpone the most difficult parts of putting his apparatus together till nighttime. But one day the dusk came, then the darkness, and still the noises under his windows did not subside. He could hear shards of steps, swarms of voices. Shterer first frowned then—despite the heat—pulled the windows shut against the unusually loud night and went on with the painstaking assembly.

Little by little the absurd clamor and racket outdoors died down. But the night had scarcely retired when the windowpanes began to rattle with the clatter of wheels. Shterer glowered and put his work aside, waiting. But the fracas of wheels would not stop. The shuddering ground kept jostling the implements set out on the table and rocking the levels inside the retorts and vials. Unable to go on with the assembly, Shterer went to the window and twitched back the curtain. The street was full of carts loaded with long flat boxes. Ranged under the half-torn-away lid of one, like the teeth in an outsize comb, were bayonets.

By midday the cartwheels had quieted. Shterer could go on with his work. But now a dull and logy feeling was confounding his fingers and thoughts. He lay down on the bed: first came a decelerating whirl of numbers and symbols, and then, like a tight black blindfold, sleep.

His weariness, accumulated during countless vigils, might well have lasted into oblivion and beyond if not for a knock at the door. Awakened by the sound, Shterer raised his head: the room was full of dusk; down the stairs, a creaking was slowly receding. Shterer went to the door, opened it, and peered out. The creaking crept back up, and the hazy shape of a man held out a white slip. It only remained to return to the room, turn on the light, and read it: in the upper left-hand corner, he noted the stamp of the military high command, and in the three-line text requesting an "appearance," the name "Shterer."

This he had not expected. Taken unawares by the lines, he stared at the slip of paper: a card slipped out of a sleeve, a card-sharp's trick, a marked death trying to corner his machine. Then again . . .

Shterer pushed open the door to his inner sanctum: rising up from a glass tripod in the grip of micrometrical screws that were as links in a chain of transparent spirals, looming over time as a sword looms over the shield of an enemy, was a light and powerful construema.

Shterer sat down at his desk, pencil in hand, and counted the days. If he worked nineteen hours a day, then in two to two and a half weeks the time machine would be finished; checks of its operation, spare parts, and double braking system would have to be done without. Better to crash into the future, having ejected oneself into unknown centuries, than to surrender one's device, than to allow oneself to be crushed by a page from a tear-off calendar, than to have one's idea crossed out by the flight of a random bullet, eternity by today's date.

Now began an odd sort of game *a tempo* between man and time during a fitful and sleepless week: time made its moves with events, man with the development of his machine. For the man it was clear: if time outpaced him, the time machine would be lost; if he outran time, time would lose its own self.

At the end of the contest's third day, a second notice arrived. The draftee considered: he ought to move his workshop.

Impossible: the construction was too fragile and unfinished for that. Perhaps he should go into hiding for a while himself? But they might come and break down the door, and the machine would be discovered. No, he must grit his teeth and go on fighting.

Shterer's exhausted consciousness could see the instant when, having attached the last clamp and inserted the last component, he would pull the lever and—shaking off the days that had hunted him, hearing the rumble of war fall away, overtaking lengths of longevities on furiously whirling clock hands—hurtle headlong into the future.

The morning of the seventh day Shterer realized he had run out of a reagent. He would have to buy more. Scraping together his last rubles, he threw on his coat and pushed open the door: standing outside were two armed soldiers in gray broadcloth. The paper barring his way said: Take into custody. Within two days Shterer was pronounced fit and inserted into the war: they numbered his shoulders, marked his forehead with a cap badge, and shaved his head. The few hours left him "to put his personal affairs in order," Shterer spent disassembling his nearly finished machine: in his frantic rush, some of the most delicate parts were destroyed, while others lay low in a deep box studded with sharp nails. Thus it was that Roland, trapped in the pass of Roncesvalles, struck his sword against the rock.

5

Private Shterer, like other privates, marched for the requisite number of weeks to "Hep, two!"; at the command "Attention!" he clicked his heels, while at the command "About-face!" he spun about on his left heel, turning his body 180 degrees; with his rifle at the ready he rushed the straw man, while at midday he tore with his teeth at his "ration" threaded on a stick. One might add that since he usually got to the dispenser's hamper last, Private Shterer received a puny piece of bony gristle previously palpated by all forty of the platoon's palms and rejected by all forty—it tasted not unlike the wooden stick on which it was impaled.

The mechanically numbered greatcoats were then transferred from a reserve battalion to a company in the field. And one bright autumn morning Shterer marched off—shoulder to shoulder—under rows upon rows of bayonet stalks, swaying like a field fretted by the wind. Onlookers waved hats and handkerchiefs as the column made its way to the station, and Private Shterer reflected that a white handkerchief raised on his bayonet was his last chance.

The first days of soldiering found Shterer depressed and somewhat stunned by what had happened. But he soon managed to regain his calm and will to fight: even if time had outstripped him by half a length, even if his machine was in pieces and nailed up, his idea had yet to be thrown with him into a common grave; even if the action brought by a man against time was hidden under military broadcloth—so be it; he would wait for a moratorium and bring it again.

The position met Shterer with a maze of subterranean tunnels and the blue arcs of missiles. In front of the trenches, on the field sentries' line, shots crackled. But if one listened closely, one could hear the chirr of grasshoppers and the friction of the wind against the grass. Acting with caution, but determination, Shterer did not allow the bullets to hiss his idea off the stage; what he had hidden under his cranial bone was weighty enough without adding an ounce of lead. He took advantage of his first combat operation and, as he put it later, "gave himself up to the Germans for safekeeping."

The next two and a half years of Shterer's life were circumscribed by the barbed wire of a concentration camp. Captivity oppressed him less than the other prisoners in his barrack. Even the star-shaped barbs down the parallels of wire, inside which he liked to take himself and his idea for walks, irritated him no more than the real stars overhead, swaddling Earth in concentric orbits. Shterer's approach to space and its contents tended to be that of a *nonspecialist*, indifferent and inconsistent, confusing the capacious with the cramped; he could never remember whether his ceilings were high or low, and invariably miscounted stories. But then the concentration camp had no stories, only long low roofs of blocks containing four rows of bunks. In all those many months, Shterer never did learn to tell apart the men occupying the bunks to his right, to his left, and in front of him; this seemed to him as needless as the ability to tell apart the boards from which the bunks were made: he might have learned with practice, but what was the point? On the other hand, the other prisoners must have long remembered the chevron-shaped furrows on Shterer's brow, bent over some persistent thought, his fingers entwined in his shaggy copper-colored beard, and his eyes squinting through people as through glass.

The long leisure of his captivity afforded him the chance to thoroughly rethink all of his old thoughts; the imagined construction modeled itself, unmodeled itself and again took shape in his head. Only now did Shterer see how imperfect that unfinished, war-stolen machine had been: to have set off across time in it would have been as foolhardy as braving the ocean in a pleasure boat. Turned out in a hurry from cheap materials, his vessel could not have withstood the blows of the onrushing seconds and the terrible battering of an eternity churned up by the machine's spirals. It was all too flimsy: he hadn't calculated the resistance of a material that was made of durations, just as he hadn't accounted for the friction of time against space. Shterer had discovered this last principle only in the camp, during his long meditative walks beside the wire wall. Perhaps it was the war that, having scored the globe with fronts, had forced him to realize the enmity, the conflict between time and space. "In the classic 'Raum und Zeit,'"* Shterer would later report, "I investigated the *und* and saw that time, since it appears as an annex to space, invariably lags behind and doesn't manage, owing to a sort of friction of seconds against inches, to harmoniously correspond, to be correlative to its space." In Shterer's terminology, this means that "events lag behind things," making for a general discordance in the world's design. This discordance manifests itself, incidentally, in the unattainability of so-called happinesses, which are possible only when ideal time and real time coincide. Wars and other cataclysms, says this theory, come of an increase in the friction of time against space.

All of this rather bizarre terminology conceals a mysterious system of improvements aimed at mastering the time machine's center of equilibrium. The new, streamlined version of Shterer's machine promised not a short hop across one or two hundred days, but a long and smooth flight. Shterer's fingers, again itching to carry out his plan, traced zigzags and angles in the air, but the

*Space and time (*Ger.*).

camp's barbed-wire fence barred the way to their realization. Days piled up into weeks, weeks into months; the air, swallowing the angles and zigzags, remained empty. Sometimes, in an effort to lessen his inactivity, Shterer tried to distance himself from the ideogram rubbing against his brain. Thus in a matter of days, with the commandant's permission, he rewired the rheostat in the pocket power station lighting the camp, effecting a 30 percent savings in electricity; next he tackled the automatic alarm system, so as to rule out all possibility of escape. His fellow prisoners now fell silent at his approach, whereas the corners of the commandant's mouth turned up as he saluted smartly. But Shterer, his pupils staring back into his idea, was oblivious to all worldly achievements. Everything that was not his idea he imagined only from the outside as a variegated uniformity (Russia—Germany; theirs—ours); he saw all work unrelated to his idea as a game of solitaire, and debating the advantages of one kind of solitaire over another as senseless.

Shterer spoke German fluently. His several acquaintances outside the camp (the authorities, who favored him, had allowed him the occasional absence) meant that—when the war was over—he might settle down in the neighboring town and go on, in calmer and more cultured surroundings, with his work. Shterer, who did not like unnecessary journeys and peregrinations in space generally, felt inclined to do just that, but two pieces of news from across the front lines in quick succession made him change his mind.

The first, which arrived in March 1917, apprized him of a revolution in Russia; the second, two months later, of his father's death.

Shterer imagined the "revolution," like the "war," as something rumbling, a clattering of cartwheels, munitions, and millions of feet pounding the ground so that floorboards trembled, instruments jiggled, and one's work was thrown off or ripped out of one's hands altogether. A jar in which crystals are precipitating will not bear jolts; while the facets are growing, it must be protected from shocks and blows; naturally, Shterer's mind shunned revolutions, mass disturbances, and war.

But the envelope bringing news of his father's demise complicated matters in the extreme. The executor of the will wrote to inform Shterer of the inheritance awaiting him in a Moscow bank. To complete the formalities, the legatee would have to appear in person. The amount named in the letter would make null and void all material difficulties in realizing his life's ambition. Once in possession, Shterer could begin and finish construction—using the very best and strongest materials, without cutting costs—of the machine long since sifted through every brain cell, his high-speed, seconds-skimming timecutter with power to spare.

Yes, the money was his, as good as in his pocket, he need only hold out his hand. Striding excitedly around his usual route, he reached out—and his fingers cannoned into metal barbs; a bee-like siren droned to life overhead, through the twilight's crepe came blades of beams and pale-blue patches of onrushing soldiers—Shterer didn't immediately realize that he had set off his own alarm system.

This incident, put to rest outwardly after questioning in the commandant's office, gave Shterer a better, clearer sense of the situation. The serried line of wire around him, the broken line of trenches beyond, and beyond that the chaotic course, the twisted and crisscrossing lines created by the revolution: he must break through all these, one by one, or else the hand that had run up against the first obstacle would remain empty, and his invention unrealized.

After a day's reflection Shterer wrote the executor asking that all measures be taken to secure his inheritance in case his captivity should prolong his absence. The executor's next letter informed Shterer that his case had been turned over to a Moscow attorney. Entering into communication with the attorney, Shterer soon received a sheet of paper with a stamp in the left-hand corner: a court had approved the will and suspended the statute of limitations.

The confusion of lines blocking his way seemed to be straightening itself out into parallels, orderly and intelligible and somehow similar to the parallels of the lines on the stamped sheet.

However, rumors about events on that side of the front forced Shterer to abandon his system of passive anticipation; who knew where the facts of the next few weeks might veer, one could fight the unknown only by outrunning it; if before it had made sense to give himself up to the so-called enemy for safekeeping, now it was imperative that he get himself back, and his guarantor could be—or so at least he thought—the letter about the inheritance awaiting him.

In a series of official and unofficial notes, petitions, and letters addressed to his executor, the camp commandant, his attorney in Moscow, the *Amt* in Berlin in charge of prisoner exchanges, the Red Cross, and the medical commission, Shterer asked, demanded, and again asked that he be exchanged, that his return be helped along, that pressure be brought to bear, that the distance separating him from the wealth that was his by rights be removed. Half of his solicitations were waylaid by the military censor; the other half straggled from office to office. Several months went by. Shterer stuck to his pen, firing off one petition after another: now he wanted to remind them, to ask them to append this letter to that, to inform them as well, and so on. At first he got nothing but two or three forms to the effect that "your request dated . . . has been received." Then one morning—by now it was nearly fall—Shterer was called into the camp's main office. A strange man wearing a wispy mustache and a crisp uniform was leafing through a thick file; he asked Shterer several meaningless questions and then said, smiling, "I have yet to meet a fellow, *mein Kerl*,* as in love with his bride as you are with your inheritance."

To which Shterer, staring at the ground, replied, "Yes, but what if it wants to betray me?"

*Here: My young friend (*Ger.*).

The mustache twitched with laughter: not a bad *Witz*.* The man checked something off in the file. A month later "prisoner-of-war Private Maximilian Shterer" was included in a party sent to Russia as part of an exchange.

An elementary arithmetic problem begins, "How many revolutions will a wheel make given a distance of..." The train, its axles creaking musingly, its hundred broad-browed bumpers swaying, seemed to be slowly dividing the distance by the circumference of its wheel rims; having miscounted, it checked its addition by means of subtraction, creeping slowly backward as the bumpers met head-on; there wasn't one siding at which it didn't stop while solving this problem. At first the station roofs loomed steep, but then their dihedral angles began to splay, replacing the acute with the obtuse; instead of the straight courses of causeways traversing the railroad, now the elaborate windings of a cart track that plunged under the barrier: Russia. The contents of the heated freight car containing Shterer was systematically counted or called out. Sixteen times in a row Shterer had answered to his name. The seventeenth time, he was silent. The night before, during a long stop in a long siding, while raising his iron extremities in wooden stocks to the sky, Shterer had felt a fever droning in his ears, a needlelike chill threading its way through his body and a bitter taste in his mouth. After that, dark spots began to cloud his consciousness, and by the evening of the next day a stretcher had shifted the burning body from the freight car to a hospital barrack. The diagnosis was quick and simple: typhus.

6

The illness would have gone farther: from the barrack to the graveyard. But Shterer's stout heart put up a desperate fight, refusing to surrender body to pit. The typhoid poison went up into

---

*Joke, witticism (*Ger.*).

his brain: six weeks of fever were followed by several more of mental disarray. When Shterer's mind had finally cleansed itself and he, thin and waxen, had tied up his sack of belongings so as to continue on his way, he felt as though he hadn't yet begun: German trains kept trundling past the platform and everywhere he saw the same blue-gray broadcloth. The German *Reichswehr** was positioning its battalions, cutting the Ukraine's winter crops—now asleep beneath the snow—off from Moscow.

Many more days had to pass before Shterer, getting off the train, saw overhead the long semicylindrical canopy of Moscow's Bryansk Station, like an outsize barrack. Hoisting his sack onto his back, he trudged after the other sacks and backs into the city. The streets were dim and dirty, with only here and there red patches of flags. Above the backs hunching along the sidewalks, tall letters towered on posters and slogans. Dragging his recent illness after him, Shterer staggered on, scarcely able to bend his stiff knees and wincing from the air's blows to his lungs.

First he must find his attorney. Shterer raised his eyes to the blue numbers: odd on the right, even on the left. He turned down a side street: even on the right; odd on the left. This must be it. A long building. By the entrance, next to the bell's exposed coil, a convex square had been papered over. Shterer scraped at the paper with a fingernail: first "Atto," then "at-law." Leaving the name under the paste, Shterer pushed the handle of the door leading to its bearer. But the door would not give, the entrance was locked. He would have to go around the back. In response to his knock someone first spoke to him through the door, then eyed him over the chain. This man in felt boots, with gold-rimmed spectacles on a ruddy nose, didn't invite him even to take off his coat. Unlocking the desk drawer with two tinkling turns of a key, he took out a notarized copy of the will and handed it to the heir.

"A blank sheet of paper," he said, smiling politely, "is worth more today."

*German army and navy, 1919–35 (*Ger.*).

And in phrases round as zeroes the attorney explained that the events of October and the subsequent nationalization of the banks had deprived Shterer of his right to the sum bequeathed him and that, legally speaking, the sole heir to all inheritances now was, so to speak, the people.

Seeing his client's contorted face, the sympathetic attorney made a helpless gesture: even a month ago, he might still have managed to extract the money—just as the cashier's window was, so to speak, slamming shut, but now...

The attorney bowed his head—either in resignation to fate or in farewell to his visitor.

Out on the landing, Shterer stood for a minute with his back to the black stairwell; he moved aside to let a slop pail pass; then, hand on the banister down the steps' steep turns, he took his way out onto the street.

He understood all the words that had been said to him yet he didn't understand their meaning: how could something lesser block the way of something greater, how could their minor revolution impede his major one, the one he carried between his temples, the one that was above all, that was *above*; what could they do, the people who had put up those flags, other than avenge three or four hundred years and call out to the future—only call out? He, on the other hand, or rather his machine, would catapult humanity centuries and centuries ahead.

An old woman, her back bent beneath a sack of potatoes, toiled past him up the narrow sidewalk. Toward him now strode a stagger of gray caps bestarred with red; rifles and sawn-off guns hung from belts, barrels pointing at the snow.

Shterer shuffled on, hugging the walls. The air was choked with the smoke from hundreds of stovepipes sticking out of the stone and glass. The buildings seemed to be breathing—with much difficulty and soot—through a multitude of tracheas. Now and then, here and there, words clung to the stone. Pausing by one of these texts, Shterer noticed that the lines at the end were shorter and capped with exclamation marks:

LONG LIVE THE POWER OF THE SOVIETS!
LONG LIVE THE DEATH OF CAPITALISM!

From among the poster's parti-colored platitudes flashed a slant-lettered word: avant-garde. Brought to a near halt, Shterer's thoughts latched onto this word and again got under way. Before he knew it, he was in front of the house of a man to whom he had entrusted parts of his machine. But as it turned out the man didn't live there anymore and was no longer alive. Shterer found the yardkeeper and demanded to be given the things he had left in storage. The yardkeeper had a vague memory of two boxes that he thought had been taken up to the attic. But for the key he would have to go to the House Committee. Shterer didn't know what that was. Only that evening did he finally find his boxes—among piles of dusty junk under the eaves. They had obviously been knocked about before being shoved under a heavy, metal-edged trunk: the slats were broken and half torn away, while the fragile parts of his beloved design, woven into a gossamer garland of spirals, had been smashed and killed.

Shterer wiped his dusty palms on his greatcoat and silently descended the crooked stairs from roof to ground. Night had entered the kitchen garden. But neither windows nor streetlamps defended themselves from the darkness with light. Only here and there, through a cloudy pane, could one see the faint, moldering glimmer of an oil lamp. Shterer walked on, encountering occasional patrols. Some let him pass; others studied his "document" with the glowing end of a hand-rolled cigarette. He spent the night on a wooden stoop, his legs tucked under his coat, his head pressed against the felt-padded door. Next morning he and his document were batted from one long line to another and, two or three days later, having attached this document to that, he received seventy-four square feet on the fourth floor of a building at the confluence of two Zachatevsky lanes.

The new occupant of that square room made do without words. The only thing his neighbors heard from him was footsteps. The footsteps inside the square room sounded suddenly, usually in the middle of the night, and seemed to proceed on a diagonal, in a soft crescendo of sporadic taps, often for whole hours at a time.

Perhaps the man from the small walled square also made do without . . . But that list of all kinds of *without*, which was getting longer every day, made up his neighbors' meager lives as well: no one looked beyond *being* and *eating*. People counted the grains in their groats, while the same herring tail flailed from soup to soup, unable to reach nonexistence.

One day—this was toward spring, when sparkling blots of dampness had seeped out of the stone to meet the sun—Shterer's rangy, but big-boned figure and red raggedy beard appeared in one of the capital's vast double-elevation offices. Standing among the desks' contiguous corners, he stared at them as though they were some strange, many-legged, square-capped variety of mushroom produced by a random downpour. Then he approached a man sitting in front of a bare blotter. In his hands, Shterer held a sheet folded in four. The man behind the desk grabbed a two-eared instrument as though he meant to defend himself with it.

"Make it short."

Shterer began. "I am offering you a raid on the future. Ahead of time. My most exact formulas—"

"Um-hmm. Hello! Sorting? Get me comrade Zadyapa."

"Depending on the results of my reconnaissance in time, you may either occupy the approaches to the future or re—"

"Zadyapa, that you? Listen, here's the deal. On the doub— Who the hell's cutting us off? Hello!"

The speaker raised his eyes to the petitioner only to see a slowly retreating back.

In the vestibule Shterer again looked around. A grimy marble staircase. A guard with passes threaded on his bayonet. A group of exhausted and unshaven men on the landing with Colts pressed to their hips. A machine gun staring out of the entrance at the street.

Wait. Again he'd have to wait.

Gritting his teeth, Shterer retraced his steps down all those same submissive streets, jammed with millions of cartwheels and outsoles. The pages from a tear-off calendar—he could see them—were threading themselves, one after another, in a long and monotonous line, on a bayonet's trihedron.

In later years Shterer did not like to recall his seven-hundred-day march through the Hungry Steppe, as he dubbed this period. His biographer passes over it in silence, not counting several conjectures as to how Shterer again managed to avoid the grave. He seems to have worked for a time as a watchman at a warehouse on the edge of Moscow, conscientiously guarding an emptiness kept under lock and key. After that... but the important thing is that the idea stashed in his brain and the brain stashed in his cranium survived, and only the skin covering that cranium and idea became a bit wrinkled in places and closer to the bone.

7

This happened on one of those rare days in Moscow when the sky is like a round blue vault trimmed with a tracery of white clouds. The color of the sky, however, was of no more interest to one man ambling down the sidewalk than the dust and cobwebs on the square ceiling of the room he had just left. He walked along completely absorbed in his thoughts, now stopping abruptly with them, now continuing on his way after a jump-started syllogism. The problem was evidently a sticky one because his steps were slow and his outsoles devoted more time to the pavement than to the air. Some of the people he passed might well have smiled at this strange method of perambulation, but all the smiles had been snatched up by the clear blue-and-white day.

The light knock of a board against the man's knee happened to coincide with the logical wall that now checked the progress of his thought. His outsoles stopped instantly, though he didn't immediately notice either the board or the outrage: "Hey! Where do you think you're going?!" Since the exclamations wouldn't let him finish his thought, he must get away from them. He tried to take a step, but found he couldn't: the ground had caught hold of his outsole and wouldn't let go. Now Shterer looked down and saw that his right foot was buried up to the ankle in cooling asphalt. He pulled his foot harder—the foot emerged, encased in an absurd lump like an asphalt clodhopper.

Accompanied by the curses of workmen and the merry whistles of little boys drawn to the uproar, Shterer continued on his way, but the sense of his legs' lopsidedness mixed up the order of the premises and threw his thoughts off-balance. For all he knew, the ground under him might play other mean tricks. He now proceeded with his eyes fixed on the pavement. If not for this circumstance, the meeting of a pair of eyes and a new pair of square-toed, patent-leather ankle boots might never have taken place. The boots entered Shterer's field of vision gleaming busily with black lacquer, but an immediate association stripped away the lacquer to reveal gray felt. Shterer ran his eye from toe to head and saw round gold glasses on a round face: here was the attorney whose felt boots, treading gently, had passed sentence on his life's work the day he returned to Moscow three years ago. Whether the owner of the patent-leather boots recognized his former client is not known; we know only that the patent-leather boots—after nearly tripping over an old shoe tied up with twine and caked with a hideous clod of asphalt—jerked back their toes and hustled off.

Shterer, however, did not need greetings. He needed only to decode a fact or, rather, to integrate a series of facts: felt boots—three years to replace them—and now...this not yet petrified asphalt lump, a sort of errant ankle boot that kept reminding him of his misadventure. Shterer instantly extended the integrated series: if under one's feet one had not felt but leather, as before, then under that leather there must be not mud and pits but smooth asphalt; but if that were so, then that meant that not only on the sidewalks but above the sidewalks at a height, perhaps, even of people's heads, if not inside their heads . . . Shterer raised his eyes and, for the first time in years, looked intently and cautiously around him.

A milliner and a watchmaker had divided the tinplate sign above a mended shop window. At a crossroad, in a rusty cauldron under caracoling smoke, a new sidewalk was boiling. A street photographer was fastening a backdrop of blue-and-white mountains to a tired acacia. A disk bisected by an arrow proclaimed in black letters: STRENGTH IS THE BEAUTY OF MAN. From out of a stone recess on the pavement, books piled high were again presenting their spines to the world. It seemed as though, from under the scabs, now here, now there, the city's new epidermis was beginning to emerge.

On returning to his room on Zachatevsky, Shterer found the sheet folded in four. Its letters had already faded, and the text too struck him as not sufficiently clear or convincing. He decided to rewrite it. By the following day he had finished both the plan and the estimate, a dry script of terms and numbers. Again Shterer took them up the marble staircase to the double-elevation hall filled with desks. Only now, a noiseless lift overtook the steps, while the desks had been rearranged in a neat, trilinear U and weighted down with mounds of folders. Through a door, typewriters chirred like crickets in the grass. To sign the registry, there was a long line.

Shterer stood in back of the last back. The back wore black, tinged with the green of years, and a collar edged with faded piping. A second later Shterer also noticed some shabby braid since the collar had turned around to face him.

"Be here forever!" the collar sighed, straining a smile through a silver mustache. "This is my sixth time—I want to patent my Economic Soldering Iron. What do you have?"

"A timecutter," Shterer cut it short.

"I'm not sure I understand."

"*You* don't have to."

The line inched forward.

"Time—timebreaker—icebreaker—timegrinder—meat grinder," the greenish collar muttered, and suddenly Shterer again saw, a foot from his eyes, the silver mustache, by now minus the half-hidden smile. "What is it then? A transit across the times? Or..."

Shterer did not reply. The greenish man glanced under the overhang of his brow.

"So tell me, your machine, if that's what you call it, can it go into reverse?"

"Yes."

"How very intriguing... Assuming it's not a... not a..." His eyes came right up to Shterer's. "Listen, let's step over there. An unwanted ear might, you know, and..."

Shterer did not budge.

"How much do you need? Name the sum. You won't get anything here in any case, and even if you do, then... or do you have a lot of time to spare?"

This last argument had its effect. Standing on the landing with the unexpected patron, Shterer unfolded his sheet of paper. The greenish man's eyes had managed to skim only halfway down the page when Shterer took it back and went off down the stairs. But the faded piping followed close behind.

"I don't understand everything, but... I can tell it makes sense. I'm a railway engineer, you see. All I know about are tracks and crossties. Your transtemporal routes, as you are pleased to call them, are beyond my poor grasp. But if not by intellect, then by intuition. I want to introduce you to Pavel Elpidiforovich. Let him be the judge, and if this isn't all a hoax, then... You know, the shape of your forehead is quite extraordinary. I noticed it right away."

Four days later something like an improvised conference took place. The railway engineer led Shterer up a backstairs and into a long, narrow room. Shterer's palm met six handshakes. He couldn't immediately make out the faces, particularly as the room was filled with a conspiratorial twilight. A man seated on the windowsill, his back seeming to lean up against the yellow sunset, spoke first.

"You, Mr. Shterer, have communicated only part of the idea; we have collected only part of the sum. But if you can prove the soundness of your design in its entirety, if you can reveal to us— that is, to me—all the unknowns, then we too, in our turn—"

Shterer raised his gaze to the dark oval throwing out these words: "For me to prove the soundness of my ideas would be far easier than for you to prove that you won't steal them. I suggest we start with the more difficult task."

"Gentlemen, gentlemen, please," fussed the faded piping, now completely dissolved in the gloaming, "don't let's knock heads right off the bat. Pavel Elpidiforovich, allow me. The first shareholders, so to speak, of this joint-stock company have gathered here in good faith . . . faith in you, let's put it that way. Inasmuch as we respect the right of the inventor to his trade secrets, we are prepared to buy the outline, so to speak, of your enterprise. There's no telling what may happen. Your Excellency, be so kind as to turn on the light, and let us discuss the estimate."

The lampshade cast a green glow. The facial oval above the windowsill, the corner of its mouth twitching, spoke again.

"We need a reasonably inexpensive construction that can seat two or three and take us back to, well, say—"

"Well, to at least 1861, or ten years before that, and stop. Or can't it take us that far? It'll crack, will it?" growled a voice by the wall.

Shterer turned toward the sound: two merry pupils leaping like awls out of the bags under a pair of watery eyes; on the red, tightly collared face, the marks of a dull but determined razor.

"Don't interrupt, General"—the man on the windowsill wanted to go on.

"You're hiring me as a cabby," Shterer admonished.

For a minute there was silence.

Then the railway engineer, his eyes fixed on the furrow in Shterer's brow, spent a hundred words trying to smooth it over. Without much success. To questions about the estimate Shterer responded with dry numbers: a two-person timecutter would increase the cost by 50 percent. With that, a shrill voice began to trill.

"I shan't give you a kopeck more. I've already given you everything: my table silver, my lace, my pendant, my diamond earrings. Not a carat more. Fine, set me down in the past, but what am I to wear there: my own skin?"

"Let a peasant woman into heaven and she'll take her cow with her. Please understand, madam, you have only to go back ten years, and they will return to you all your—"

"And once you're there," the voice of the railway engineer plowed into the general's bass, "you may sell your property, send the money abroad and yourself after it. And from there, through the 'Matins,' you know, and the 'Timeses,' you shall be able to watch all this supermegarevolution calmly through binoculars; as Lucretius said: ''Tis sweet, when tempests lash the tossing main, Another's peril from the shore to see.'"

The obstreperous stockholder was eventually persuaded.

"Well, all right. But only on one condition: that I go first."

"Why?"

"Very simple: my past gives me the right—"

"Well, if that's how it is," a bald man with eyes hidden behind blue lenses stirred in the corner, "if that's how it's going to be, my past is more past."

This remark clashed with another. But now Shterer pushed his chair back and stood up. The argument stopped. Shterer went out into the front hall and fumbled in the darkness for the door. But the railway engineer was already bustling about beside him, taking his elbow, and whispering words of apology in his ear. They descended the narrow stairs together. There were more questions than steps. Answers did not follow. And only on the last step, his hand in the grip of two damp palms, did Shterer finally say, "Makes no difference."

The palms released his hand.

Finding himself on the evening pavement, Shterer heaved a deep, deep sigh and threw his head back: thousands of squinting emerald pupils were peering intently at the earth.

8

The life inscribed in the square on Zachatevsky and the lives around that square never crossed paths. The one thing the neighbors noticed was the metamorphosis of the sound of footsteps inside the square into other, quieter, more muffled noises; if one added to this the sporadic visits of a man, his neck in piping and packages under both elbows, who usually ducked quickly inside the square, then that was all that residents of the apartment on the fourth floor could shake out of their memories, even given the strongest jolts to those memories.

Then again, their memories weren't up to much: in their wrangles with questionnaires, they were constantly having to pigeonhole their lives—no simple task—from 1905 to 1914, from 1914 to 1917, from 1917 to ———, and again from and to; they were always having to quickly forget one past and learn another, while memorizing the present according to the latest editions of the papers.

Meanwhile, here in their midst was he, preparing to launch a machine whose first thrust would overturn all pigeonholes before and after; the past and the future would become two sidewalks of the same street along which people could stroll on either side—future or past—as they liked.

Nothing could stop Shterer's work now. The construction itself, filtered so many times through his mind, had assumed such a logical final form that its realization required significantly less effort than when design and matter first met. The idea, separated for so long from its realization, fairly leapt from Shterer's fingers into the network of electronic orbits, switching atomic circuits to blaze a secret trail from century to century. Materials were in short supply. But the sly faded piping managed to obtain everything by some unknown means. Shterer refused to let anyone see his work until it was finished. Obedient to the inventor's every word, the piping never took more than two steps inside the square, and that on tiptoe. "Now, now, just let me look you in the eye; blessed fire, how terrifying; now, now, I'm off, I'm off, I wouldn't even for a second..."—and flapping his hands like a bird preparing for flight, he would vanish out the gently closed door. But one day the piping lost count of his steps and seconds. He leaned toward Shterer, who had come grudgingly away from his work, and whispered, "Things are not well with Ivan Elpidiforovich. They're looking for him. He's got to get out of the present. Could he possibly go— even though it's not finished? The man's life is at stake. Well, and then—that thread will lead to others. Don't you see?" This time the piping didn't need to ask Shterer to look him in the eye; Shterer glanced up of his own accord. The piping, shrinking away, pushed the door open with his back and disappeared. The door closed noiselessly behind him. Instantly forgetting his guest's face and words, Shterer went calmly on with his work.

Many days went by after that and not a single word intruded upon the soft, muffled, glassy stirrings of the construction now coming to life. Shterer checked and rechecked the regulators and listened closely to the pulse of his idling machine. That whole day raindrops tapped at the panes, toward evening a many-colored rainbow straddled the roofs, and come night it turned cold; the windows, which had fallen silent, remained closed.

In the occupant of the quadrature next to Shterer's, the dampness had triggered a toothache that was now describing agonizing spirals under the crown. Breathing into his pillow, the occupant first counted the footsteps through the wall and swallowed his sour saliva. Finally the footsteps stopped. The pain continued to spiral. Then suddenly through the wall he felt a short, dry gust of wind: a light but resonant blast and a stipple of receding pin-pricks—as though a hundred compasses, sliding across the panes on their sharp points, had rushed toward their radiuses pell-mell. Then everything was still, except in his temples where a distinct clink-clink echoed softly in his brain. The pain vanished. The occupant pulled the bedclothes up about his head, and a minute later his brain cells released him to sleep.

Next morning the square room was strangely quiet. Around noon the doorbell rang: one long and two short. The square room, to which this combination of rings pertained, did not answer. Again: one long and two short. Pause. And again: a droning dash and a colon. The square room remained silent. A neighbor, his cheek bound up in a bandana, slipped his feet into sloppy slippers, shuffled to the front door, and took off the chain: the politely nodding piping, he recognized; but the cumbrous figure in an officer's greatcoat, his face hidden by a stand-up collar, puzzled him somewhat. The neighbor dawdled in the hall, eyeing the visitors. The two passed through the poorly lit vestibule and stopped at Shterer's door: first the piping knocked vigorously with the knuckle of his forefinger—the room remained silent; to the foreknuckle's knock, the middle knuckle now added its muscle; a second's wait—and the other man's fist suddenly pounded on the door; the door hummed, but still no one came. The piping bent down to the keyhole, jerked back, and whispered, "It's locked from the inside, so..."—and, softly scratching at the door, quietly-quietly, as if to blow his voice in through the crack: "Maximilian Fyodorovich, it's only us, you know, as we agreed..."

The door continued to block the entrance. But then two other doors opened a crack. Inquisitive noses peeped out, and someone said the word "police." The piping's companion pulled his collar up to his eyes and turned his square toes to leave. But the piping lingered by the keyhole, fumbling about the blank panel. Five minutes hadn't gone by before the lock crashed to the floor and the door recoiled, exposing the square room to a dozen eyes.

Along the left wall was a bare mattress on bare floorboards; in the right-hand corner, a bundle of books weighted down with a box from which protruded the necks of empty vials; and by the window, an unpainted desk etched with the motley blotches of various solutions. In addition to the blotches, there was something else on the desk that immediately drew all dozen pupils: a candlestick, a blinding yellow flame winking from its round metal socket. Again the onlookers scanned the emptiness—the person who had lit the candle was not there. The neighbor with the bound-up jaw touched the key sticking out of the broken cylinder: the person who had locked himself in had vanished without trace. A policeman licked the end of his pencil and set about his report, but how to begin he did not know. Just then the yellow flame winked one last time and went out.

The meeting of passengers on the trip that never came to pass was brief and ineffectual. They looked like people past whom the twinkling windows of an express train had flashed, plunging from darkness to darkness. The faded piping seemed utterly crushed; the greenish tinge had crept from his coat up into his face, while his mustache twitched fitfully: "Who would have known—who would—"

"You," the general's collar bristled, "came up with a plaything—'an inventor,' 'a genius'! Milking people for money and making off—that's an old invention."

"I want my diamonds back!"

"Of course you do. But you'll have to catch the rogue red-handed. Go to the police and—"

"No, thank you! I don't hang about police stations. You go—but see they don't..."

The conversation petered out. True, there were many more words of bitter recrimination, but they had no driving force.

Needless to say, the empty square on Zachatevsky soon lost its emptiness. The unintelligible candlestick was still warm when someone's bed, legs screeching against the floor, shoved into the room, and a shelf, holding on with nails, climbed the wall. Moscow, that gigantic flattened human hive, had instantly squeezed itself into those empty square feet in the person of a soft-stepping, clean-shaven man with a bent back and a briefcase permanently attached to one elbow.

The new tenant, having exchanged a writ for a square, took little interest in his abode. From morning till late at night his briefcase steered him from meeting to meeting, from folder to folder, from this numbered file to that; come evening the briefcase bulged while the briefcase carrier felt flattened and, having trudged up to the fourth floor, sought support from the four legs of his bed. His time was so exactly divided between his absence while present in various offices and his absent presence in the room (if one may so call his deep, completely disconnecting sleep) that he didn't immediately notice an insignificant but strange phenomenon requiring a certain silence and keenness of hearing. This phenomenon was discovered by the new tenant the night of November 7: that day the briefcase had—oddly enough—let the tenant go off by himself. He returned at dusk and lay down with his hands behind his head. Through the thin walls all was quiet— the holiday had lured people out to clubs and theaters. The tenant, eyes half shut, could still see the floating stream of banners, the swaying of the thousand-body crowds—then suddenly he became aware of a faint, exceedingly faint, but distinct and rhythmic sound. At first he sensed the sound only as a resonance tripping along the edge of the noisy day still in his brain, a stipple of perforations along an unwound reel, but then, gathering objectivity, the sound became sharper and clearer, and the tenant, raising himself up on his elbows, could place it: the glassy, mechanical sounds piercing the air were coming from somewhere in the middle of the dusk that had filled the room cube, either above the desk or a few feet to the right. The tenant sat up and made to take a step toward the phenomenon but just then the front door banged, neighbors' feet clumped down the hall, and the fragile, barely audible sound was driven out. Yet the tenant was somehow disturbed by this seeming trifle; he decided to lie in wait for the trifle and recheck his perception. That night, when the apartment had quieted and around the square the silence had closed in, the tenant peeled his ear off the pillow and began to listen: at first the noise of the bed in his ears prevented him from catching the sound, but then by slow degrees through the blood subsiding in his temples came the rat-tat-tat of a faint but distinct ticking. The tenant didn't sleep the whole night or the next. Then he went to the doctor. A black stethoscope ausculated his heart and breathing; the edge of the doctor's palm checked his knee reflex; and the patient was asked to recall the illnesses of his father, grandfather, and great-grandfather. Wrapping its fingers around a pen, the palm prescribed a bromide, formed a handshake, and brushed off the banknote.

The bromide did not do away with the phenomenon. The punctate, needlelike sound would invariably wait for the silence only to reemerge with the same monotonic, automatic precision. The tenant began to avoid encounters with this silence meter. Two or three nights in a row he found excuses to stay with a colleague. Finally, unable to invent any more, he told this man about the silence meter, as he called it. His colleague first raised his eyebrows then distended his mouth.

"Oh, I see, you're a mystic. Perhaps you'd like to play a little whistic? For shame: panicking over a tiny worm like that."

"What do you mean?"

"Just that: there's a very peaceable little worm that bores into walls and cabinets and desks and taps: rat-tat-tat. A meticulous timber worm, only I don't remember the Latin name. In France they call it "fate": *destin*, or something like that. Well, this little worm, this *destin*, has given you a fright. Plain as day."

The overnight guest from Zachatevsky wasn't convinced: he asked his colleague again, requested specifics. Next morning, rummaging in entomological reference books, he found what he was looking for, read it, reread it, and suddenly felt that he had been released from the mental vise.

That evening he calmly entered the square of his room and slept a dreamless sleep, undisturbed by either the silence or its meter.

9

The daily turning of the tide, the sun-shot ebb and flow quietly added something each time and took something away. The bank of burial mounds by the Kremlin wall grew gradually longer. Five-domed churches behind high gates vanished with the ebb tides, and cobbles grew over the ground where they had stood. Trucks stopped guzzling alcohol and exhaling drunken fumes. Above the canted roofs radio sound began to weave its wire web; round-mouthed loudspeakers drew thousands of greedy ears. Motor buses, overstraining their springs, bounced from pit to pothole. Behind the old Peter Palace there stretched—like a stone ellipsis—a gigantic stadium for forty thousand eyes. Forty Martyrs' Lane was renamed Dynamo Street. On Novoblagoslovennaya Street the stacks of Moscow's first vodka distillery began smoking. Meanwhile, the theatergoer's nose would occasionally detect, amid the smell of sweat and cheap eau-de-cologne, a whiff of imported Chypre. The resident of the square on Zachatevsky now inserted the crook of his back into an ordinary jacket, rather than the service kind. The motley blotches on his desk had disappeared under a tablecloth, made his property by three blows of an auctioneer's gavel. His briefcase, now very worn though not particularly old, continued to direct his endless outgoings and incomings, from the four legs of his bed to the four legs of his office desk and back again. His key went from lock to pocket and back into the lock. Then one day there yawned before the key not a lock and not a pocket but, shall we say, an abyss. One might, of course, having slipped one's key into the abyss, turn it twice from left to right. The resident did just that, but...we mustn't violate the logic of *chronos* or, as it's generally known, chronological order.

The resident arrived at the door to his room, as usual, after eleven at night. The corridor was dark since the apartment was already asleep, but the resident, who knew this dark by heart, had no need of light. A half step from his doorway he stopped, shifted his briefcase from right arm to left, and dug in his pocket for the key. Just then he clearly heard: someone's soft but distinct footsteps moving on a diagonal in his room. The footsteps were uneven and intermittent. Upon reaching a corner, they would stop and after a two- or three-second pause start up again. A thief? He must wake the apartment. But what if this was that old illness, *destin*, a proliferating hallucination that only he could hear? Besides, a thief wouldn't pace from corner to corner like a pendulum. And also: if it were a thief, the door would have been forced. Hand pursued thought to the door. Closed. Therefore . . . the resident stood there in the dark, feeling his heart's agonizing jolts. The hallucination intensified, causing the pseudo-footsteps to multiply. A tingling in his fingers reminded him of the key. He must open the door, throw it wide to the ostensibility, and prove his nerves false. A sudden movement—and his briefcase slid out from under his elbow and flopped heavily on the floor. The steps stopped short. For a minute he listened to the silence. Not a sound. "It's over." His heartbeat slackened. Almost calmly he felt about for the keyhole and twice turned the steel. The door's soft creak met a short but loud shriek: opposite the threshold, hunching tall shoulders, black against the night-blued window, stood a man.

From all walls came the clicks of switches. A dozen bare feet stumbled to the rescue. But in the now-illuminated square, in the calm attitude of what cannot be switched off, stood a man: his clothes were half turned to dust, his long thin face fringed with a fiery shock of red hair, while across his enormous forehead, as if to cross it out, a cicatrix shone blue with phosphoric glints. A convulsively coiling spiral, like a mercury worm, was caught in his hair. He flicked at it—and the spiral disintegrated like cinder. The bare heels of the apartment's inmates, ripped so abruptly from their beds and dreams, shifted from floorboard to floorboard in puzzlement. Surveying them, the man with the crossed-out forehead said, "How far is it to the eighteenth? I need . . ."

Again he glanced around, and understood: very far. He fell silent. But now the others, who till then had struggled in vain to wake up, all began talking at once. Morning hadn't yet risen over the towers of the Krestov Gate when the entrance door slammed after the intruder, and Shterer, his shoulders hunched against the cold black air, set off down the stone meander of a deserted Zachatevsky Lane.

The space through which his muscles now hacked seemed dense and difficult. The air, which felt strange after so many days away, was viscous and resistant. Not a leaf was stirring on the trees along the boulevard to which Shterer, weak from the effort, now trudged; the air was all of a motionless wind with a speed equal to zero and a force of impact increasing to infinity. Returned from spans of time to the length of a boulevard, he felt like a swimmer who, forever cleaving the agitated and salutary surface of the open sea, has been suddenly cast into the square confines— stagnant beneath the green duckweed—of a freshwater pond.

The very first bench caused his knees to bend. Shterer sat down, wiping away sweat. He didn't immediately notice that the other end of the bench was not empty. But from the not-empty end he had been noticed long since. The woman, who had been up all night between two walls with darkened windows, had a professional interest in nighttime passers. The approaching male shape with its oddly jerky and unsteady gait might, who knew, swap the remains of the night for rubles. He staggered once, then again—so much the better: drunks were more apt to stop.

For a minute the woman said nothing, swinging the leg thrown over her knee. The man seated at the other end of the bench did not move closer and did not speak. The woman now turned toward him and asked, "Taking a walk?"

There was no reply. Worse than that: there was no smell of

wine. Her practiced eye traced the tall figure of a strange man staring into the darkness. No doubt about it: not a kopeck in his pocket. The woman pulled her skirt down over her flaunted knee and inquired through a yawn: "From out of town?"

The figure nodded. The woman whistled.

"And what's brought you here? What's your business: wiping benches with your backside? What do you want from Moscow? The good old days?"

The figure turned toward the question.

"Yes." And after a second's pause: "The good old years. Since I didn't understand, I'll have to go through them again and again until..."

The man's voice and intonation were exceedingly serious and intent. The woman peered at him uneasily: could be a lunatic.

A slight wind came up. In an effort to redirect the conversation, she said, "The night's nearly gone."

The man, his outline becoming gradually clearer in the half-light, leaned lower to the ground.

"I know a night about which you could never say that."

This bore little resemblance to an offer to go to bed. To boot, the man chuckled and turned away. The woman stood up, shook out her skirt, and walked off. At fifty paces she glanced back: the tall angular outline, brightened by the first glimmers, was still sitting on the bench, shoulders hunched over the ground. For some reason she thought of her very last guest her very last night who would appear, fall on top of her, and crush her into the ground.

Meanwhile the dawn, risen like red leaven somewhere behind the heaps of stone houses, swashed over the roofs, coloring the black air red. Shterer remained inert. Beyond the boulevard railing, an empty two-wheeled cart rumbled by, avoiding dustbins. In among the trees a twig broom began scratching at the ground. Milk cans dully clanging against one another loped past. Somewhere in the distance a tramcar ground around a bend in the tracks. A pair of drunkards performing a complicated four-legged exercise tripped over each other's feet as they zigzagged down the boulevard. Some people were hurrying home to sleep, others were still struggling awake. The figure pitched forward on the bench, his bare brow braving the breakers of thought, delayed no one's steps for long. And it's too bad, incidentally, that among the passersby—and among the living—there could no longer be a certain writer who specialized in ghosts, who in recent years had loved to spend his dawns on the sandy orbits of Moscow's boulevards: an encounter with Shterer's sleepless figure might have caused him to substantially revise his story about Eleazar. Little by little the city was being unlatched and unlocked. Now one person, now another hurrying down the boulevard paths would glance at Shterer's bench. A nursemaid with two diminutive charges, out for their morning portion of oxygen, skirted Shterer's shadow intending to sit down next to him, but then the spokes of her eyes met in his petrified figure and she dragged the children on. In the grip of her thin knobby fingers, one child squeaked, "Strange man."

A young Gypsy, swaying hips swathed in grimy silk, trod on the motionless shadow blackening the sand and, thumping a dog-eared deck of cards on her palm, began: "Good citizen, shall I tell you your fortune? You'll be happy. You'll be rich. A princess of hearts loves you. In the big house. And you'll go abroad."

Then her eyes met the eyes of the man with the motionless shadow. Her nostrils flared in fright, the pupils under the black cambers of her eyebrows flashed, like sparks in the wind. Hiding the deck in her sleeve, she hastened silently away, swirling the silks twisting and untwisting about her lithe legs.

The day was going past faster and faster. Automobile horns sawed and bored through the air. The vociferous names of newspapers dodged between boulevard tree trunks. The disjointed shadows of harried passersby hurried down the sandy path, skimming over the motionless black outline. A coin tried to press itself on the petrified figure but, taking fright, leapt back into its pocket. Next to a bench across the way, the elbows and brushes of a bootblack began to dance. The dust rushed about in myriads of gray specks, seeking refuge on shiny surfaces, on panes of glass, and in respiration sacs.

Then suddenly Shterer heard his name. It sounded again and again, forcing both him and his shadow to stir. Before his wide-open eyes, he saw three-fifths of a hand outstretched. The hand was so insistent that Shterer, purely reflexively, made a reciprocal gesture and shook the three-fingered palm.

"Don't you recognize me? No, of course you don't! Now me—I may have lost a few fingers, if you'd care to see, but not my memory. Come on, come on, four beds over, in camp, we were prisoners. Or've you forgotten that too?"

Shterer stared and continued not to remember. The man, having tucked his claw under a heavy corded book pressed to his left side, was vigorously bending and unbending his other hand.

"I picked you out back then too: brainy sort, not like us. Seemed like a German, and a cut above. Hard for us to judge, of course, 'cause we had the sense of one flea between us, and that flea was no go-getter. But even without smarts, a man's got instincts—and the brainpower coming out of you, out of those eyes of yours, trip over it and you'd never get up."

In the absence of a rejoinder, the speaker became flustered and tugged at the visor of his cap with his claw. But the cap, instead of tipping goodbye, slipped from his left temple to his right, then from his right to his left.

"I'm Zhuzhelev. Prov Zhuzhelev. Those rags of yours, I see you've...Put plain, you're barely dressed. Well, and besides, a man's got to have a place to lay his head. Even a violin, you know, lives in a case. C'mon."

And before the sun had bowled through its zenith, Shterer was settled in something like a residence. The energetic Zhuzhelev, who turned out to be the yardkeeper for a house on Krutitsky Val, wasn't long in finding space. Under the staircase, covered with a crooked line of stone steps, a tiny windowless closet was triangularizing; the stove wood lived there under lock and key. Zhuzhelev's eight fingers evicted the logs and installed Shterer. In place of the birch blocks that had crammed the triangle, a patched hay mattress now lined its base, a nearsighted lamp hung from the hypotenuse, while at the junction of the catheti a short-legged stool doubled as a desk.

"Your very own case," Zhuzhelev grinned, smoothing out his mustache and his smile with his claw. "Get too big for your britches in here, and the walls'll cut you down to size."

Now it only remained to settle the new tenant's name in the corded registry book. The House Committee first grumbled then applied the necessary stamp.

Exhausted after his long journey, Shterer stretched out on the hay mattress and listened through the swelling diaphragm of sleep to people's shoes playing the steps overhead with ascending and descending passages and extended arpeggios. Among the dozen pair of shoes banging up and down the stone keys, his wakeful ear may have picked out the abrupt staccato of a man running up to his room on the top floor: this was Joseph Stynsky, whose meeting with Shterer would prove, as we shall see presently, momentous for them both.

10

Joseph Stynsky's pen was distinguished for its exceptionally restless nature: now it fussed about inside a short satirical sketch, now it became bogged down in the dilatory meanings and periods of a socioeconomic tract; having plunged into the inkwell, it never dried with an unformed phrase; it knew the art of sliding but not slipping; it saluted every new fact and idea with a flourish. Stynsky's two gray eyes, with their asymmetrical set and odd narrow slant, were masters of both shadow and light. One day there was a demand for light, next day shadow had gone up in value, and

Stynsky, having shifted his theme by a halftone, would transpose it from major to minor. On his shelf next to amusing little leather-bound books from Paris stood a gaunt volume of Husserl's and *The Poverty of Philosophy* by Marx. Stynsky, in short, had a way with words. According to both his well- and ill-wishers, he possessed undeniable literary talent and could have, perhaps, if not for... But for two years now his pen, caught fast on that annoying *if not for*, had found itself outside first-rank shop-window literature, unfit for the plump journal and the personal per-page fee. For all its fluency, it had slipped, strangely enough, on a seemingly harmless article called "The Revolution's Hammer and the Auctioneer's Gavel." Written on commission, the piece argued that as soon as the revolution's glass-shattering, metal-forging hammer stops banging, the staccato, businesslike banging of auction gavels begins, dealing the final blow to what little remains of the old world—in picture frames, under the lids of carved boxes, behind wardrobe doors—now knocked out of all its cozy retreats. The commissioning editor accepted the hammer-and-gavel article but, as luck would have it, held on to it longer than usual; by the time the piece appeared, it was out of step and at odds with the times, and after that Stynsky simply couldn't get his rhythm back. Disqualification leads, as we know, to a disquantification of income. Stynsky was eventually reduced to living on "Great Men" —a cheap series of pamphlets that could dispense with any genius in ten or twenty pages. He soon got the knack, and the "greats" poured from his pen, turning into banknotes. Stynsky did not overrate this work. "The one lively thing about it," he said, "is the lively sense of slapdash." But in moments of bitterness he was far more outspoken: "Damn it! These great dead men repel me, let the flies have them; what I wouldn't give for one living one; would-be greats are everywhere, but true greats, it seems, are nowhere to be found." With that he would tackle another pamphlet, which usually began: "This was in the era when commercial capital..." or "Capital, which felt confined on the continent of Europe, would have discovered America sooner or later. It was the Venetian navigator Co..." or "Socrates, the son of a midwife, belonged to the petit-bourgeois intelligentsia of Ancient Athens..."

Before meeting the under-stairs tenant, Stynsky had chanced on an entry in the registry book that caught his eye first because of the strange handwriting, then because of another strangeness: to the right of the angular "Shterer, Maximilian," the filled-in blanks read: "34—single"; *Arrived from where*: "the Future." True, someone's painstaking but clumsy hand (Stynsky immediately guessed whose) had capitalized the "f" and inserted "town of." Result: "the town of Future." Stynsky, who had borrowed the corded book to register a guest from the provinces, returned it to Zhuzhelev and cautiously, so as not to cause any ripples, threw out a question.

"By the way, Prov, the town of Future, what district is that in? I can't seem to remember."

Zhuzhelev's eyes stared through a grin.

"May not be a town, may be something else. That's just, you know, so the police don't pick holes. Besides, if a person—'cause of this or that—has only got his mind left, you shouldn't bother him with questions: there used to be wood, now there's a person. The wood you can move, but the person..."

Having learned about one of the nouns in that strange entry, Stynsky determined to demystify the other. That same day and the next morning, as he was passing through the front hall, he inspected the closed panels—like crooked halves of a hinged icon—of the under-stairs door. They were motionless, and through their yellow-painted boards: not a sound. In the evenings, when, as Stynsky used to say, wolves should profit from the fact that people can't tell them from dogs, he usually went out on errands of the heart (again Stynsky's expression). As he was skimming down the banister, a merry effusion whistling from his lips and a flower bobbing in his buttonhole, he suddenly heard a noise in the under-stairs triangle. He leaned over the banister to look: the panels of the crooked diptych flew open and a tall, broad-shouldered figure sprang out, just like a jack-in-the-box, and straightened up. Stynsky leaned lower still, trying to pierce the dusk with his eyes, and the slippery stem of his flower, leaning too, tumbled out of his buttonhole and down into the stairwell.

"Beg your pardon. Don't bend down, I'll get it."

But the man from the diptych had no intention of bending down. The first thing Stynsky heard when he got to the bottom of the stairs was the crunch of his overly curious flower underfoot: in the gloom and in his haste, he had trod on it himself. The face of the new denizen was not three feet from his eyes; it so stunned Stynsky that his hand couldn't immediately find his hat or his tongue speech.

"Very glad to meet you. Joseph Stynsky, hound. Not clear? Hound: that's what we writers call ourselves for short at *Izvestia*. Instead of 'citizen writer Tilnyak' or 'esteemed master Silinsky,' it's just 'hey, hound'—and they all come running, imagine that, hound after hound, right here to me: on Thursdays I host the whole literary pack. You, I see, haven't been in Moscow for quite some time; it's changed, hasn't it?"

"Yes, not since 1957. It has changed, if you like: yes."

This reply was so strange that Stynsky reeled back a step.

"Excuse me, but the year now is only..."

The conversation continued for another twenty minutes, without quitting the bottom of the stairs. In parting, as he clasped Shterer's hand eagerly in his, Stynsky said, "See you Thursday. No. No. Without fail. This has turned my brain upside down, damn it. I'll come and get you myself, nill-I-will-I, ha! ha! The hounds will all fall on you!"

Late to his rendezvous, a rumpled Stynsky said not a word in reply to "I was beginning to think you wouldn't..." His "object"—this time a yellow-haired abstractionist poet—had long ago planned her dress, remarks, half-closed eyes and kisses. But the kisses somehow never came to pass, and rather than half close her eyes she felt compelled to keep them wide open. For Stynsky, whose name had never had any negative associations among women, was anxiously absent. Holding on to himself by his buttonhole, he tugged nervously at his jacket as though he would hurl himself forward or up into the air.

"I seem to have met—it scares me even to say it—well, yes, the sort of man about whom I dash off pamphlets. It can't describe it, can't put it into words. Now I know what it means to find oneself in the palm of Gulliver's hand: if he clenches his fist—that's the end. He looked like a moonlight flitter, but—"

"Now listen, my not-dear man, if you have come to see a woman good enough to grant you a tête-à-tête—"

"Tête-à-tête: that's just it! This was the first genuine tête-à-tête of my life—head to head, thought to thought. In all these kissing trysts, the tête-à-tête is usually a million miles away."

"Not only ungrateful, he's playing hard to please. Move closer."

"In the twilight I was able to make out his words, but not his face. It seemed pale, but even so it put me in mind of—"

"Now put your arm around my waist."

"Around your waist? There. Even so it put me in mind of the legend about Dante's face, burned by the sun and by the flames in the circles of Hell. No, men like this are not to be pitied, there's no reason to pity them: they wouldn't notice your pity in any case, I swear on my pamphlets and per-line pittance! I'll let the hounds loose and ...we'll quarter him. We'll jump up on tiptoe, yes, and for once he'll have to bend down."

II

As of Wednesday Zhuzhelev had strict instructions to watch Shterer's lair. Stynsky's blood ran cold at the thought that his Thursday evening's pièce de resistance might somehow resist.

At nine o'clock the next evening the pack was beginning to

assemble. The large, top-floor room with whitewashed walls had thrown open not only its door but its two tall windows, their hospitable casements wide to the lambent stipplings of Moscow lights. Within half an hour blue-gray smoke was swaying overhead as someone's catchy epigram swirled from ear to ear. Behind the guests' backs, flat along the wall, under glass, hung stresses and leaps in pencil and charcoal. In a corner, between huddled heads, the latest political joke went punning and tumbling. Among Moscow's "Izvestians" scattered about on straight-legged benches and stools one might spot: a fashionable poet with a lyrical incandescence in his cold-blooded breast; a learned linguist who never opened his mouth—people called him "a mute in twenty-six languages"; a famous film director whose ever-gesticulating thoughts made him look like a six-armed Vishnu; a long-faced novelist with legs squeezed into gaiters, cheeks that twitched, and a habit of saying "as I was saying"; the fleshy, gray-fringed brow of a venerable critic; the abstractionist's deep décolleté; the round, carefully combed-over bald spot—like an eye on the back of his head—of a publisher; the crook of a nervous hand sticking out of a cartoonist's cuff. The teaspoons had done twirling in their glasses. The poet rose and, fingering the bow above his cold-blooded breast, lisped, "Since I have been asked to read, ah—"

Striding to the middle of the room, Stynsky gestured with impatience, redirecting his guests' eyes to the man whose tall, motionless back was inscribed in one of the windows' dark oblongs.

"Beg your pardon. Today we shall devote our attention to a man who has done away with the word 'today.' Dear hounds, citizen Shterer, inventor of the timecutter, will now tell us what he can tell us about his first journey through time."

In response to his name, Shterer turned to face the meeting; he continued to stand where he was, gripping the edge of the windowsill; yellow-and-blue city lights peered over his shoulder. Everyone fell silent. Pause. In someone's empty glass, a plaintive teaspoon rang out with a nickel-plated whine. Shterer began.

"The crudest diagram of my time-cleaving construction would

require a technical knowledge that I cannot assume here, among you. What I am about to present will resemble a genuine presentation no more than (to quote Spinoza)...an ordinary dog resembles the Dog Star. Science, which used to separate time from space, has now joined them together in a single space-time. My mission, in essence, was to proceed along the hyphen still separating time from space, to cross the bridge thrown over the abyss from one millennium to the next. If Riemann and Minkowski looked for a so-called world point at the intersection of four coordinates—$x + y + z + t$—then I have aimed to recoordinate those coordinates as follows: $x + t + y + z$. In climbing the stairs to this room, for instance, you injected space with a step-by-step quality, a gradualness—that is, a characteristic of time. Now if we go the other way, since in giving characteristics of space to the concept of time, we..."

In the corner under the charcoal flourishes, someone's ear leaned in to a whisper; notes began skittering from hand to hand. Calmly turning his head from shoulder to shoulder, Shterer surveyed his audience.

"You don't follow me, do you? I'll try to put it more simply. Time is not a chain of seconds driven from cog to cog by a clock weight; time, I would say, is a wind of seconds buffeting things as it whirls them away, one after another, into nothingness. I hypothesized that the speed of this wind *varies*. One may argue against this. I was the first to begin arguing with myself (thinking is just that—an argument with oneself), but how does one measure the time of time's elapsing? To do this, one must see *another* time, one must complicate Riemann's four-symbol formula with a fifth symbol: t. Have I lost you again?"

This time the question dissolved in silence. The notes lay still.

"But how do we treat...or rather, how do we move about in this unabating wind of durations? It's completely clear how: like weather vanes. Wherever this wind swings us, our consciousnesses follow. Our perception of time is linear, whereas time itself is radial. But I'll try to avoid terms; I'll try to circumvent all the angles and crossbars in the formulas. We are traveling along time, along the wind of seconds, but then one can also sail with a fore-and-aft rig across the diameter of t, by the shortest and most direct route, thus bypassing the bend in t-dimensions. How can I make this clearer?"

Searching for an analogy, Shterer's eyes ran around the walls and, coming full circle, turned around to the open window. Suddenly his hand was reaching out, like the glass panes, into the night. Here and there someone sat up, two or three stools moved closer to the gesture.

"Down there, among the lights," said Shterer, quickening his verbal stride, "is the river we all know winding through the city; we also know that somewhere, a certain number of miles away, that serpentine flows into another serpentine, which flows into the sea. But if we were to take the river by both ends (I refer to the tributary) and stretch it out into a straight course, it would reach to the sea all by itself and flow not into narrow bounds but into boundlessness. I mean to say that the course of time, like the course of a river, is winding, but if we pull it straight, we may transpose point A to point B, that is, we may jump from today to tomorrow.

"I won't go into how I first built my machine in my head, over the course of many years; and it would be useless to describe how I extracted it from there, from under my forehead, and took it in hand. It wasn't easy, of course. My machine resisted objectification. It was a long struggle. I can't put into ten minutes a process that took twenty years. To do that I would have to have recourse to my machine, but it crashed into . . . but about that later. Shipwrecks are possible even in the ocean of durations. But sooner or later I will again attempt to throw 'later' into 'sooner' and 'sooner' into 'later.'"

For a minute the words broke off. The novelist waggled his gaiters and leaned toward his neighbor.

"His frontal bone is like a lantern's shutter, don't you think? Open it—and your eyes will burn."

The novelist's neighbor wanted to reply, but Shterer had finished with his pause.

"Lobachevsky was the first to note that the line A–B is at the same time B–A, that is to say, it is a geometric ray that may be drawn from B to A, as well as from A to B. Therefore, one may draw not just one straight line through two points and, therefore . . . But it's time I told you about time, as Stynsky promised.

"I planned to take off one summer night. The window in my room was open, like the one now at my back: it would become a window in the train hurtling me from era to era. Even before launch, I understood the disadvantage of one of my spatial coordinates, but I had no choice. The horizon was almost entirely cut off by a firewall; off to the left one could see a short strip of street and a dirty façade studded with three rows of holes, and several roofs beyond—that was all. My setting off on a night train, so to speak, was no accident: darkness and dreams would shield my launch from prying eyes and the interference of unbidden ears in whatever acoustic phenomena might accompany the switch from air to ether. As a precaution I turned out the light and used a candle: it could be put out with a puff of breath, whereas the light switch was six or seven paces from my machine.

"I was under contract at the time. I had sold—I won't hide it from you—several trips to the past. I needed to jump back five or six years to check on the timecutter's operation and control mechanisms then 'deliver' the machine that same day. I planned to return in the morning. But at the last minute, just before inserting myself into the apparatus, I wavered. The materials I had used to build the timecutter were inferior, where was one to find better in Russia? To catapult my untested formula straight into the past, against the current of time, against the wind of seconds—that might damage it, or even . . . I wanted to be fair to people, but I didn't want to be unfair to my machine. After a moment's hesitation, I turned the indicator from widdershins to deasil and closed the circuit. You need to know that the most important part of my apparatus is a funnel woven out of gossamer spirals the color of air. You have only to squeeze your temples into that hat-like funnel—with the exhaust vent up—and make contact, and . . . Our brain, as we know, consists of liquid drops; my funnel decants these—or, rather, the thinking dissolved in them—from space to time . . . This isn't so easy to do: the complex of sensations hidden inside three cerebral membranes plus a bone case—I had to tear off all that swaddling in pure t and raise the frontal bone like the shutter of a lantern and let out the light." The gaiters squeezed each other more tightly. "I switched on the electron vortex—and time began to inhale me brain-first; my brain, coming unscrewed through the spiro-funnel, pulled my body by its nerve threads; excruciatingly crushed and flattened, my body didn't want to pass through the funnel; a little more pressure, it seemed, and the strained nerve fibers would snap, dropping the ballast suspended from my brain. I didn't let the contacts and regulators out of my streaming fingers; then suddenly—I could see myself . . . or, rather, I couldn't see myself. Out the square window something phantasmagorical was happening: a gigantic candlewick, burning low, seemed to keep blazing up and dying down, throwing the window now into light, now into darkness. In my room something was happening as well: something vertical kept looming, a shape my height, it would advance then retreat, scattering smatterings of fitful footsteps.

"I had apparently blasted off at top speed, my machine vibrating soundlessly around me; in my left hand I could feel a shuddering lever invisibilized by time and pushed to full throttle. I pulled it toward me and the picture through the glass became clearer: the blinding flashes turned into the sun—I saw it, the sun—it shot up like a yellow rocket from behind the huddled roofs then down a sparkling arc aflame with scarlet bursts of sunset, disappearing behind the firewall. Before its reflection on my night-cloaked retina could dissolve, it was again whizzing up from behind those same roofs like a yellow rocket to its zenith, striking its phosphorous-yellow head against the darkness so as to flare, again and again, with new days brief as the burning of a match. Almost at once a clanking sound in my machine began stabbing the air. I'd made a mistake, of course, in going right to full speed. I'd have to watch out: I pulled the lever a little farther back—the sun slowed its flight; now it looked like a tennis ball that east and west were hitting back and forth over my firewall, as over a net. Absorbed in this strange spectacle, I forgot about the one in my room. Not until the timecutter's speed had leveled off did I finally look back at the convulsive drumming by the floorboards. It was a funny and slightly pitiful sight. Although the door to my room was a plain, ordinary, single-panel door, it now gave the impression of a swinging door at a chaotic, slot-sized entrance. At any rate, there was a person, or persons, or no, a man with a briefcase under his elbow who simply could not extricate himself from the door's batting panels—he would tumble out and then, as though he'd forgotten something, dash back inside, tear all his clothes off and dive under the covers only to remember something else, jump into his clothes, and vanish out the door only to come racing back in again. And all of this against competing flashes of sun and electric light. The bizarre, breakneck pace of this poor man's days struck me, I repeat, as faintly amusing, the very sensation of my machine's reckless velocity was enlarging my heart. I again pushed the speed lever a little forward—and something odd happened: the sun, about to bolt up from behind the roofs like a ball off a taut tennis racket, suddenly rushed back (the west was returning the ball), and everything, as though it had hit a wall beyond the horizon, stopped and froze. The reel of seconds threading through my machine had jammed at a certain instant, a certain fraction of a second—it wouldn't go forward, it wouldn't go back. Somewhere below the horizon, the sun's orbit had intersected with eternity. Ugh, 'eternity,' what a horrible word for those who have seen it not in books, but in...The air was a cindery gray, the way it sometimes is before dawn. The lines of a roof and the crooked outcrop of a street were etched in immobility, as in a steel engraving. The machine was silent. The undawning dawn, stuck between night and day, would not budge. Only now could I discern all the details in the sorry urban landscape pressed to my dusty window: on the front of an engraved building, above a stone ripple of cobbles, hung the end of a blue sign edged in gold; over the blue, in white: '. . . RY,' the rest was cut off by the next house; hiding in the cavern of an archway was the petrified shape of its shadow on the pavement; above the cavern, sticking out of a clamp, was a red flag; the now-clotted wind had pulled up the flag's red calico hem, and the cloth, as though traced in air with a galvanoplastic agent, had coagulated above the street; beside a curbstone, a dog's hind leg was cocked—eternity's spasm had suspended it. Having seen all there was to see of the street, I now turned to my room. What I saw there made me . . . No, that's not true. To shudder one would need at least one-tenth of a second, and time, having turned to stone, had taken everything, right down to the smallest fraction of the smallest instant. So then, opposite me on the bed, fingers dug into the flimsy mattress, eyes round with terror, sat a man.

"I was looking at what seemed to be a waxwork of horror; the stereoscopic paralysis of that dead world was seeping into me. How long this lasted, I cannot say: I was, you must realize, outside all lengthitudes. My thoughts, which through force of inertia had continued to slip through the wax, were slowly congealing and coming to a stop, like clouds in a calm. My strength failing, I made the sort of superhuman effort that happens only in nightmares: I jogged one lever, just reached another and the timecutter, grinding up the sand of seconds, propelled itself off the shoal. I proceeded slowly, with the brakes on. The days, blurred as the spokes of a fast-spinning wheel, now became separately visible. The future was mine to observe. My window gave on the end of the 1930s."

"Well, and what did you see out your window?!" a female voice, vibrating with curiosity, cut in.

Shterer smiled with some embarrassment.

"I'm afraid my time machine distracted me from time itself. I feel very badly that I can't . . . But a stoker by an overheated firebox has no time for the landscapes whooshing over the window of his locomotive. I too had not a minute for time: ten years away from the present on a malfunctioning machine, forced to remedy defects in flight, I couldn't very well—"

"So then," the attentive gaiters tucked abruptly under their stool, "so then, eyes, in your opinion, are black eyes for sharp eyes. But if your eyes weren't flecked, forgive me, with even one fact, if you managed to see nothing in the future but a level field, a racecourse for your machine, if you've nothing to propose to my colleagues here, then I don't understand exactly—"

Shterer raked a hand across his brow.

"Level? Wait a minute, I seem to recall something after all. I do."

The ring of silence closed in again around his words.

"Now this, for example, happened just when nothing was happening. That is, during one of the pauses in my machine's operation. I won't return to the sensation, which I've already tried to convey. I'll describe only the fact. This time the thread of seconds broke in broad daylight. A sunbeam that had banged into a post at a speed of 186,000 miles dropped down to zero. The motes in the beam did not stir; it was as though the air were infested with golden flies. Beneath the static beam lay an old newspaper (whoever had left it was gone): a copy of *Izvestia* dated July 11, 1951. That one instant stretching to infinity impressed everything on my brain, in spite of me—from the headline to the last letter on the page sprawled opposite my eye, and if you like—"

"Cut!" Stynsky's sharp shriek blocked the words' way. "Can't you see you're among writers? That paper cost a lot more than five kopecks. Now let's go on. The machine restarted: the dust motes began dancing in the sunbeam. We're listening."

"But allow—"

"Why won't you give him—"

"Just when—"

Stools shifted with indignation. In the corner someone whispered, "We know why."

Stynsky turned a little pale.

"You don't know a thing, my hounds, and not a single 'just when' will you get. Now, my dear guests, sit! Shterer will continue."

"If this...is to be with cuts, then there isn't much more to tell. Since this was only a test flight, I needed to turn back. But my machine was so shaky I feared a sharp turn could cause it to crash. Consequently, I continued to yield to the time current carrying me farther and farther into the future. So absorbed was I in righting my rickety machine that I didn't immediately notice that the space out the window was shrinking. At one point a casual glance of mine ran into a towering wall of stone and glass (while I'd been looking the other way, evidently, a gigantic new edifice had crushed the three-story building with the '...RY' and the cavern under the flag). Another time (I'd picked up the pace) the brick curtain of a firewall vanished into the past only to reveal a...but that's immaterial. Now that I had left the present far behind, I began to sense the incompleteness, the flatness and impalpability of this anticipated time through whose millisecond pores, in pursuit of the future, I was now making my way higher and higher. My artificially grown future, like a plant forced upward ahead of the natural cycle, was painfully thin, withered, and wan. Everything, absolutely everything—the red flag, for instance, that I think I mentioned earlier was gradually turning from red to—"

"To?"

"To?" Two or three stools edged soundlessly closer.

"No, not that," Shterer brushed the question aside, "the flag hadn't faded, but like everything else it was being gradually becindered together with the seconds by a grayness, by the colorless residue of the unreal. A strange anguish sucked at my heart. And although I knew that that bygone year, the one you have yet to see out, was twenty lengths behind, I could still feel it coming after me: the tramp of seconds upon seconds. I increased my speed—the gray reel of days chafed against my eyes; I closed them and, gritting my teeth, tore blindly on with the levers thrown forward. I can't say exactly how long this lasted, but when I opened my eyes again, I saw something so ... *so* ..."

Shterer's voice stuttered to a stop. His hands gripped the edge of the windowsill. Even the tic on the novelist's face did not twitch.

"Now both my machine and my story make a sharp, one-hundred-and-eighty-degree turn. After that unexpected blow to my pupils, I was no longer afraid of being capsized by the side-swipes of durations. A crash? So be it. And if you can believe it, chance was on my side—the turn succeeded, and I went against the wind of seconds. My progress was slow, the sun rolled like a yellow disk from west to east, the familiar roadside of days stretched from *Futurum** to *Perfectum*.† Now I knew just where I was going. An error had undoubtedly been committed: not in the construction but in the constructor, in me. Time is not only sinusoidal, sinuous, it can expand and narrow its course by turns. I hadn't taken this into account; in experimenting with t values, I had proved a poor observer. Behind me was a blank, a chain of three or four years gone completely out of my head. One can't get used to life if behind one is not-life, a gap in existence. Those destitute years stained with blood and rage when crops and forests perished while a forest of flags rose in revolt—they appeared to me as a hungry steppe, I walked through them as through a wasteland, not realizing that ... that in a certain present there is more of the future than in the future itself. People tear off their days like the pages from a tear-off calendar, only to sweep them out with the rubbish. Not even to their gods do they give power over the past. But my durations were the leaves of a single book: my timecutter was far more sophisticated than a knife for cutting pages, for un-sealing unread leaves—it could return me to pages I hadn't understood and lie like a bookmark between any two while I reread and reconsidered the reconstructed past. Even in the field of crude

*Future (*Lat.*).
†Here: Past (*Lat.*).

spatial technology, we're already close to achieving the speed of the Earth's rotation—by doubling the propeller's motive power, one might attempt to come level with the sun slipping below the horizon. That was what I wanted: to throw the levers to full speed and head straight for the gap, to overtake what had gone before and so re-prepare my after. I was going more slowly. But coming at me was time itself, the real, astronomic, conventional time toward which the hands of our clocks all point, as the arrows of compasses point toward the pole. Our speeds banged into each other, we knocked heads, my time machine and time itself; the bright brilliance in a thousand suns blinded my eyes and a soundless jolt ripped the contacts out of my hands. I was standing in the middle of my room, newly visible to me even in the semidarkness. The dusk was not moving; but inside it the city stirred dully. My machine had perished midway. The burns on my fingers and across my frontal bone: these are the only traces it has left in space.

"How strange, only recently I was forcing the stars to race through the night like a blue swarm of fireflies, and now here I am with you, again on this absurd and sleepy raft that can float only downstream and only with the current, and which we call: the present. But I can't accept this. Even if my machine is wrecked, my brain is not. Sooner or later I'll finish the journey I began."

Shterer broke off and, turning away from his audience, stared at the reflection of lights in the windowpane. From somewhere in the distance came the hoarse whistle of a night train. Behind him, stools began to fidget. Voices, hushed at first, grew a bit louder. A lighted match wandered this way and that. Cheeks inhaled meditative smoke. Two or three hooks on the coatrack now stood bare. Suddenly the linguist, extending an obliging flame, broke his twenty-six-language silence.

"One question . . . May I?"

Shterer glanced over his shoulder and nodded: he was listening. The novelist, having inserted his right arm into the sleeve of his coat, let drop his left, and waited. Two or three people paused by the door.

"My question is this: there's a certain discrepancy—or so at least it seems to me—between the duration of your sojourn in ... well, in ahead-of-time time, let's say, and the quantity of ordinary, vulgar time that elapsed while you ... I realize that t and t speak different languages, but even so, how did you manage it?"

"Absolutely right." In his bewilderment Shterer took a step toward the gauntlet of words. "How did I manage it? That question has tormented me for days. Needless to say, measuring t inside t isn't easy. My calculations make me think that I may *not* have managed it, that my meeting with real time may never have occurred (my machine could have been destroyed by a less serious obstacle), and that I am among ghosts, forgive me, engendered by ghostly durations. I have tried to express myself as simply as possible and ... as politely, and I was pleased just now with my hypothesis about t banging into t. But if you ... if this hypothesis doesn't satisfy you, then we may suppose that my machine never managed to reach reality, that it crashed into the shadow cast ahead by t time and ... My sense of the people now surrounding me is that they are people without a *now*, people whose present has been left behind, people with projected wills, with words resembling the ticking of clocks wound long before, with lives faint as the impression under the tenth sheet of carbon. Then again, a third hypothesis is also possible: I, Maximilian Shterer, am a madman who's denied even in a straitjacket, and everything I've told you is nonsense, gibberish. I sincerely advise you to embrace this last point of view: the most profitable, solid, and comforting of the three. Thank you, it's been an honor."

Shterer walked past heads as they turned to watch him go. The two or three people by the door remained transfixed. The novelist, grappling air, kept missing his slithery left coat sleeve, while his tic kept tugging at his lip trying to shake out a word.

"Yes, quite the philosopher," the poet whistled and surveyed the others in the hope that before going someone would remember his unread verses. No one did.

The film director rumpled his hair with a six-armed gesture.

"I should have shot it all and made a movie!"

The novelist finally caught his sleeve.

"So roll the camera. Only all this timecutter blather is just a bluff. So much Shtererism..."

Feeling suddenly liberated, the two or three by the door issued out after the yellow gaiters.

"As for me," the linguist leaned toward Stynsky, "I feel as though Shterer had inscribed a new convolution in my brain."

Stynsky smiled wearily.

"Someday a historian, in describing the times we live in now, will say, 'It was a period when creeping about everywhere, attaching itself to this name and that, was a blind and slippery "ism."' In fact, that's probably how I'd begin a biography of Shterer were I to..."

12

Next morning a walking stick rapped at the door of the under-stairs triangle.

"Who is it?"

"Get up. We're going out to sell those cuts."

"I don't understand."

"Nevertheless, we're going."

A minute later the two men had left the house. Stynsky hooked Shterer's elbow with the crook of his stick and laughingly dragged the inventor after him, as a bear ward would a bear.

"All machines are made with money, isn't that so? Thus it follows... follow me. Having a mind, my dear Shterer, is not enough: you must also have a mind mindful of dealing mindfully with that mind, a driving belt for one's ideas. So allow me to be the tugboat that tows the towering steamship. I've already called a publisher. He heard you yesterday—the combed-over bald spot, remember? Memoirs are all the rage now. Crown princes, revolutionaries, mistresses, ex–prime ministers, cooperators, emperors, they're all earning pin money with their reminiscences. Starting tomorrow, you're writing a book. I've already thought of a title: *Memories of the Future*. Sounds like a best seller. How much do you need for your machine? Oho! But if the book goes through four or five printings...then you can go back on the road. The publisher has the editorial board in his pocket; but stealing under his bald spot won't be enough, you've got to go further—to the cashier."

That same day the preliminary negotiations were successfully concluded. The editors, for all their doubts, were intrigued. And in a pinch, if it didn't turn out to be history, it could always go to fiction, *se non e vero*...* An Underwood tapped out the contract. An advance? Certainly.

On the way back Stynsky, merrily waving his hat at the greetings of acquaintances, exhorted his companion.

"Now then, Shtererton, it's down to shirkless work. From inkwell to paper and back and nowhere else. If you're not comfortable under the stairs, you can write in my room. You don't mind? Well, as you like."

Shterer's pen now set out along the blue rule, repeating his journey in words. With his back to the wall and the lines propped up on his knees, the builder of the timecutter remembered his future: he refused to let a single second hide as he gathered his days like the wildflowers along a roadside; in his ears the roar of his late machine alternated with the pounding of his pulse, while caught in the crease between his brows was a stubborn thought.

Coming down the zigzag stairs, Stynsky always silenced his steps over Shterer's closet. Sometimes—once or twice a week—he would hang over the banister and knock on the diptych with his stick.

"Hello, this is 1928 speaking. Where are you?"

"In 1943," the muffled reply might be.

"Oho! And is your ink power still strong? Will your pen bear the brunt or will it crack? Now don't grumble, I'm going."

---

*Se non e vero, e ben travato: Even if it's not true, it makes a good story (*Ital.*).

Sometimes Stynsky didn't limit himself to a knock at the door and would lure Shterer out for a walk to learn about, as he put it, "the future's home front, namely, the present day." They would climb the steep incline of Krutitsky Lane past the ancient, stone-baluster-surmounted Assumption Wall to the airy gate tower raising its age-old ceramic scales shimmering with sea-green glazes and enamels over the racket of Moscow. Above the coils of the gate's bronze, the way was barred by tin: Quarantine Station. And the two would turn around.

"But really," Stynsky smiled as they were returning home one day, "our present is a chaotic castoff, the topmost layer of paper pasted to an advertising pillar, women painting their lips, men prettifying what comes from theirs—and all this like something out of an old book with its pages stuck together."

Sometimes Stynsky would take Shterer on more extended walks and excursions so as to acquaint him with what he called the "archaeology of news." Meek and hunched, Shterer would appear in his cicerone's wake at crowded literary and scholarly gatherings, listen to speeches at meetings, peer beneath the rising curtain at the theater, and judging by his eyes, at which Stynsky often looked on the sly, it was impossible to tell whether the minute hand's endless minuet reminded him of his years in the future or not. Shterer's presence didn't cause problems if one didn't count minor coincidences—like the one at a lecture on the impending world war: as he was summing up, the lecturer had the bad luck to lock pupils with Shterer: he mixed up his pages, lost the thread, and couldn't think what to say next. There were two or three other lesser episodes, but as a rule the people jostling around the refreshment counters and cloakroom half-door were too busy swallowing bubbles of lemonade, recounting silver change, negotiating women's sharp elbows, and clutching coat checks to notice the tall man calmly striding past behind their backs.

True, certain members of the literary world had yet to forget the story of the timecutter that had cut into the regular readings at Stynsky's: rumors about the contract for *Memories* about what

hadn't yet happened infuriated some while intriguing others...
how much, so to speak, did the future cost and mightn't they
come too? Occasionally someone tried to question Stynsky as the
person closest to the work going on in the under-stairs closet, but
Stynsky had become a man of fewer and fewer words, his answers, if any, were peevish, terse, and enigmatic. Acquaintances
agreed that the character of their Thursday-evening host had
changed, and not for the better. The Thursdays themselves began
to skip then stopped altogether. The merry master of the hounds,
the convivial organizer of the "Izvestians" now took to avoiding
literary people and gossip.

Once during their usual walk up to the Krutitsky Tower—this
was on a silvery gray September evening—Shterer said, "Now I
understand why that *future* which is now *past* looked so dead to
me and shrouded: I had merely obtained the difference between
my existence and my nonexistence; I mean to say: a dead man
strapped to a saddle may be borne up a steep slope, but...that of
course is the silliest coincidence and if not for it, you understand..."

Upon reaching the tower's ancient enamels glittering in the
gray air, the two men stopped and peered through the gate's
bronze lattices at the melancholy cobbles in the quarantine yard.
Lingering a minute, Shterer added, "Tomorrow I'll finish writing
the last page."

They walked home in silence.

A few days later the manuscript remembering the future arrived on the publisher's desk. The author was told to "inquire in a
week's time." But before two days had gone by a telephone call
found and summoned Shterer. Shterer appeared at the appointed
hour. The bald spot, bent over the familiar notebook, leapt nervously up to greet him.

"Listen here, what is this?! Have you given any thought to
what you've written?"

"I had hoped other people might do that: my concern is the
facts."

"Facts, facts! Who's seen them, these facts of yours? Where, I ask you, is the witness who will come forward and corroborate them?"

"He's coming. Or don't you hear him? I mean the actual future. But if you suspect—"

Shterer's hand reached for the notebook. The publisher pressed the pages to the desk with his palms.

"No, no. The writing on the wall won't be brushed aside. This is an exceptional case. Please understand: I can pay for this most astonishing manuscript with two sleepless nights, but for the sake of its null-and-void-making lines to risk all this," the publisher poked the piles of notebooks and folders heaped either side of his desk, "that is more difficult, and moreover, while your snail, or whatever you call it, is making its way..."

The publisher moved closer to Shterer.

"Or perhaps you'd agree to amend certain things and omit others? What do you say?"

Shterer smiled.

"You're suggesting that I mix up my signal flags and signal instead that the line is clear."

The bald circle blazed up like glass stained scarlet.

"I know perfectly well that I can't alter the reflection in the mirror. I know better still that if I strike that reflection, I'll—"

"Break the mirror."

"Worse: I'll leave myself open not to the mirror but to *what it reflects*. Time must be taken by storm and forced to retreat...into the future. That's right. You see, I've mastered your style. Oh, that I know. But best of all I know—this is not about reflections but about a stamped impression—that narrow rectangle with the ten letters inside: DO NOT PRINT."

The conversation broke off between "yes" and "no." The manuscript remained in an editorial folder tied tight. But texts are capable of diffusion; certain paragraphs and pages of *Memories* seeped through the cardboard folder and, multiplying and modifying, began to whirl from hand to hand and mind to mind. The pages hid in coat pockets and stole into briefcases, squeezing between official records and reports; they unfolded their folded-in-four bodies so as to slide into circles of lamplight; their lettered residue settled in the convolutions of brains, turned up in private discussions between public lectures, became twisted into jokes and circumlocutions.

One windy morning, fall raindrops pelting their faces, Stynsky and the taciturn linguist bumped shoulders at a crossroad. Through the droning air, Stynsky managed to catch these wind-blown words: "Birth of a legend."

Staring at the linguist's crimped mouth, Stynsky said, "So be it. What's banished from sight will find its way to the brain through the skull's seams. So be it!"

The linguist clearly wished to reply, but the whistling wind had stopped up his mouth and the words would not form. Bowed down by the buffets, the two struggled on, clutching the brims of their hats. The wind blinded them with dust that stung like salt, it beat on the kettledrums of roofs, screamed in the organ pipes of downspouts, and broke the strings of telegraph zithers, driving the score of dread chaos to a desperate *dis**; a little longer, it seemed, and torn-off heads would go flying after their torn-off hats; longer still, and the Earth, blown out of orbit like a leaf that has lost its branch, would go gliding from sun to sun.

A dark-blue motorcar eased around the arc of Krutitsky Val over the first snow. The ribbed wake of its tires, embroidering the white cover, stopped at the front entrance just as Zhuzhelev, brandishing his broom like a scythe, was clearing the sidewalk bricks of the first winter sowing. The air was glassily dead. Flags were smoothing out their folds like red laundry hung out to dry. The chauffeur beckoned to the yardkeeper and asked; then, turning toward the glass partition, he gave a respectful salute: this is the house. The car door swung open; Zhuzhelev sprang back just in

*D sharp (*Ger.*).

time to let pass the calm, forcible stride of the man ascending the front steps. His face, reflected hundreds of times in posters placarded on kiosks, was instantly recognizable. Overcoming his panic, Zhuzhelev rushed to open the front door. But the visitor had already swept inside. Zhuzhelev spied his slightly stooping back by the panels of Shterer's cage. Then the panels opened and the tall back disappeared inside. Zhuzhelev raced up to the fourth floor to alert Stynsky; but there was no answer. He scratched his head with his claw and, trying to disentangle his tangled feelings of pride and fear, went back down to the vestibule. The two voices behind the under-stairs diptych were exchanging words so muffled as to be indistinguishable. Retreating to the double front doors, Zhuzhelev stood in the attitude of a guard standing by a banner. Anyone who came running down the stairs or shoving in at the front door was stopped by a peremptory whisper: "Shh-h! Tiptoe! If you can't be quiet, go around the back"—and then the soft (soft as a rustling) name. At the sound of it, residents' heels jerked up on tiptoe automatically so as to trip around the back.

The conversation, cramped by the blank panels, was still in progress. The tall visitor's voice had fallen silent—now only Shterer was talking. Peering through the glass prisms of the vestibule, Zhuzhelev could see the fine soot of dusk gathering about the motionless figure of the chauffeur, a glimmer of light clamped between his teeth. Then from behind, through the panels, there was a long pause. Zhuzhelev straightened up, expecting an exit. But the silence grew longer like a tapering thread. The visitor's voice, slightly hoarse and even lower, finally burst forth on a questioning note. There was no reply. Suddenly the diptych flew open and the visitor swept out. Zhuzhelev quickly pulled open the door, and the tall guest passed out to his automobile without even looking: his face was indiscernible in the obscurity, but his shoulders seemed slightly more stooped, his tread heavier and slower. Inside the automobile a light flashed, and then, motor softly rumbling, the car lurched off. Zhuzhelev wiped the sweat from his face and, trying not to make a sound, crept up to the newly closed panels and the silence. Having stood for a minute debating, he decided that after that visitor from on high, he, a simple man, had better not.

Around midnight it began to snow. The soft hush of snow-flakes swathed the lightly powdered cobbles with fresh white festoons. The steady cascades of snow were rushing, while the streets were still deserted and dreams hadn't yet turned into lives, to prepare a winter's porcelain-fragile landscape. And the one post-midnight wheel track, sinking down into the drifts, was carefully covered over by flatteringly soft, soft snow.

Stynsky, who had come in very late and woken just before noon, saw with pleasure the swags of snow settled on the window frames, as on roosts. Throwing on his clothes, he went to look out: the roofs fell away like snowy mountains, the trees had donned white blossoms, and even the clouds' fantastic shapes suspended above the city seemed to have been fashioned from snow. "I'd like to hear the crunch of snow," thought Stynsky. Without waiting for the next thought, he put on his coat and dodged down the stairs' familiar zigzags. Over the shuttered triangle he stopped, as always, and called out: "Hello, Shterer."

No one called back.

Stynsky descended another three or four steps, leaned over the banister and raised his voice: "Hello, Shterer, now don't play possum with me. We're off."

There was no answer.

Stynsky dashed to the bottom of the steps, stopped by the panels, and knocked: his knock sounded dull and disjointed. And not a sound in reply. Then he opened the panels wide: the entire under-stairs closet, right up to the ceiling, was stacked with sticks of stovewood; pressed snugly together, their flat ends protruded from the throat of the cage like a tight damp gag.

Stynsky started back with dilating pupils: dark spots slid through his field of vision; he seemed to be seeing flat flakes of falling black snow.

The disappearance of Maximilian Shterer did not go unremarked. The whispers became whirrs. Silence itself was afraid of keeping silent too loudly. Then again, neither Stynsky, nor the reticent-in-twenty-six-languages linguist, nor the publisher, who had promptly removed the manuscript of *Memories of the Future* from the Central Publishing archives, was surprised: the manuscript had predicted precisely this outcome—in the nearest term.

Some days the room on Krutitsky Val found all three of them poring over Shterer's surviving papers. Stynsky, recalling phrases thrown out in passing by the timecutter's creator, had managed to trace the whereabouts of some of his old notebooks and writings from the prelaunch period, but couldn't bring himself to entrust these to the eyes of experts. Rearranging and ordering the faded sheets, the friends rejoiced when, among the inscrutable hieroglyphics of doubly indecipherable formulas, they came upon clear—as glades in a forest—words.

So it was this evening. The three—among the icy December stars plastered to the panes, with the door closed and the metal eyelid lowered over the keyhole—were silently intent, each on his own paper pile. It was after midnight. Suddenly the linguist raised his head.

"I've just found this phrase leaning against a formula: 'Crossing time here is dangerous!' And yet he crossed time and—"

"Indeed," muttered the publisher, adjusting his horn-rimmed spectacles, "and have you seen this evening's paper? On the button, on the nose—"

Stynsky interrupted: "I shall use this as the epigraph for my biography of Shterer." And, looking away, he declaimed: "'Take me to the land of those who understand.'"

"'Who perish,'" the linguist corrected him.

"It's the same thing."

And the three went on with their work.

1929

NOTES

INTRODUCTION

vii *"I live in such a distant future..."*: Sigizmund Krzhizhanovsky, *Collected Works* (CW) in five volumes in Russian (St. Petersburg: Symposium, 2001–2010), Vol. V, 1st Notebook.

"Before it had all seemed so simple...": CW, Vol. IV, p. 383.

"The translation was rough and inexact...": CW, Vol. IV, p. 384.

viii *"I'm enough of a poet not to pen verses"*: CW, Vol. V, 2nd Notebook.

"The Runaway Fingers" (1922): In *Seven Stories*, Sigizmund Krzhizhanovsky (Moscow: GLAS/New Russian Writing, 2006).

"People who had been to Moscow scared you": Krzhizhanovsky, "Autobiography of a Corpse" (1925), in *Seven Stories*.

ix *Ludmila Severtsova, wife of the noted evolutionist:* Aleksei Severtsov (1866–1936).

"The crowdedness in Moscow is dreadful": Kornei Chukovsky, *Sobranie sochinenii v pyatnadtsati tomakh*, Vol. 12 (Moscow: Terra, 2006), p. 84.

"I've discovered a new way of successfully stretching out my legs...": Letter to Anna Bovshek (12 August 1924).

"Shtempel: Moskva": CW, Vol. I, pp. 511–549.

x *"the timid peals of church bells..."*: CW, Vol. I, p. 540.

"I have lunch every day...": Letter to Anna Bovshek (25 July 1925).

"The toes of my new shoes have a proud and perky look...": Letter to Anna Bovshek (17 July 1925).

"I am a crossed-out person": CW, Vol. V, 2nd Notebook.

"Strany, kotorykh nyet": CW, Vol. IV, pp. 129–150.

"Swift, as a true artist...": CW, Vol. IV, p. 137.

xi *"the flavor and personality of his writing is all his own"*: Review of *Seven Stories*, John Bayley, *The Spectator* (8 April 2006).

xi *Krzhizhanovsky first read Kafka only in 1939:* Krzhizhanovsky has to
have read Kafka in the original. Not only did he know German
but the first Russian-language publication of Kafka—*Metamorphosis* translated by Solomon Apt in *Inostrannaya literatura*—did
not appear until 1964.

xii *"I have a platform ticket to literature ":* CW, Vol. V, 3rd Notebook.

xiii *Poetika zaglavii:* CW, Vol. IV, pp. 7–42.

"pell-mell and in haste, like the hats on their heads": CW, Vol. IV,
p. 24.

articles on laconism... Shaw and Shakespeare: CW, Vol. IV, pp. 679–
680, 684–686, 110–128, 387–415, 473–568, 153–384 (respectively).

"The answer is plain": CW, Vol. IV, p. 174.

"In revolutions, events attain a speed...": CW, Vol. IV, p. 236.

xiv *"Perhaps it's all for the best...":* CW, Vol. I, p. 548.

QUADRATURIN

6 *mf: Mezzo forte.*

fff: Fortississimo.

8 *House Committee:* "The little tyrants of [Soviet] Russia are the house
committees in these crowded dwelling houses...The committee
decides about the disposal of the rooms, settles conflicts, which
are bitter and numerous, determines rates—which are fixed upon
the class of the person who pays and not upon the space itself, so
that a foreigner or a concessionaire or a trader pays manyfold
what a factory worker is charged for similar quarters—collects
rent, water and gas bills, and sees to repairs." Dorothy Thompson,
The New Russia (New York: Henry Holt, 1928), pp. 19–20.

10 *Remeasuring Commission:* Created by the Soviet authorities in the
early 1920s, this commission remeasured rooms in order to determine who had "excess" living space. One person was entitled to
no more than nine square meters (ninety-seven square feet). In
this respect, Sutulin had technically nothing to fear.

THE BOOKMARK

16 *Spinoza:* Dutch Jewish philosopher (1632–1677) whose famous *Ethics* holds that "he who clearly and distinctly understands himself and his emotions, loves God."

   Vita nuova: A short work (ca. 1293) by Dante composed of thirty-one sonnets and connecting prose commentaries.

18 *they had equipped the inside of its pointed crown:* A permanent radio station was installed at the top of the Eiffel Tower in 1906.

20 *Lake Constance:* Occupying an old glacier basin, the lake borders Switzerland, Germany, and Austria, and has an average depth of three hundred feet.

23 *a fashionable Boston religion:* A reference to Christian Science.

24 *one of Metner's Fairy Tales:* Nikolai Metner (1879–1951), the Russian composer, wrote many genre pieces for pianoforte, including a series called *34 Fairy Tales*.

25 *February—July—October:* From the February Revolution of 1917 through the Bolshevik putsch in July to the Bolshevik coup in October, when the Bolsheviks seized power.

29 *that translation of Woodward's* Bunk: William E. Woodward (1874–1950), American advertising man turned novelist. In his best-selling *Bunk* (1923), he coined the verb "to debunk," meaning "to take the bunk out of things." The Russian translation (*Vzdor*) appeared in 1927.

33 *Fire the hearts of men with the Word:* The last line of Pushkin's poem "The Prophet" (1826) about the role and purpose of the poet.

35 *Holberg:* Ludvig Holberg (1648–1754) is claimed by both Norway and Denmark as a founder of their literatures. His satirical *The Journey of Niels Klim to the World Underground* appeared in 1741, the Russian translation in 1762.

37 *those wild bees described by Fabre:* Jean Henri Fabre (1823–1915), a French entomologist, demonstrated the importance of instinct in insects.

38 *"How can they be brothers when one is three hundred years older?":* Roger Bacon (ca. 1214–1294), English philosopher, scientist, and

Franciscan, and Francis Bacon (1561–1626), English philosopher, essayist, and statesman.

49 *Arabat Spit:* In the Crimea, a long and very narrow sandbar running north to south between the Sea of Azov and the Gniloye ("rotten" or "decayed") Sea.

Genichesk: A town at the northern end of the Arabat Spit.

SOMEONE ELSE'S THEME

57 *Leskov:* Nikolai Leskov (1831–1895), a Russian novelist and short-story writer known for his use of colloquial expressions and folk etymologies; an early master of *Skaz*, the device of telling a story through a particular character in his own idiom.

59 *foot wrapping:* Strips of cloth wrapped around the feet for warmth.

chastushka: A two- or four-line ironic or satirical folk verse sung with or without accompaniment.

60 *Hennequin:* Emile Hennequin (1858–1888), a French literary critic; author of *La Critique scientifique* in which he calls for an impartial approach to works of art based on an aesthetic, a psychology, and sociology.

61 *Feuerbach:* Ludwig Feurbach (1804–1872), a German philosopher and moralist who influenced Marx; he maintained that the Creator is man's projection of his own human nature.

Danilov: Aleksei Mikhailovich Danilov, a Moscow law student. He killed and robbed a retired captain (who was also a moneylender) and his maid on 12 January 1866; two weeks later (30 January) the first chapters of Dostoevsky's *Crime and Punishment* (about a student who murders and robs an old woman pawnbroker and her half sister) appeared in the journal *Russky vestnik*.

Turgenev's Rudin, Lezhnev, Bazarov, and Pigasov: In the novel *Rudin* (1855), Rudin is the intellectual but ineffective protagonist and Lezhnev a rich local landowner with no imagination; in *Fathers and Sons* (1862), Bazarov is a nihilist and Pigasov a misanthropic philistine.

62 *Ferdyshchenko:* A base and unscrupulous party guest in Dostoevsky's *The Idiot* (1868).

Molchalin: The conniving secretary who lives in his patron's house while making love to his patron's daughter in Griboyedov's *Woe from Wit* (1822–1824).

65 *my eyes on Gogol's bronze back:* A statue of Nikolai Gogol, seated and brooding at the head of Prechistensky Boulevard, facing Arbat Square. A symbolist projection of Gogol's angst, the statue was eventually banished by Stalin and replaced with the positive, Soviet-style Gogol who stands there today.

67 *Les Adieux:* Piano Sonata No. 26 in E-flat major, opus 81a (1809–1810), by Beethoven; it has three movements: *Das Lebewohl* (*Les Adieux*—The Farewell), *Abwesenheit* (*L'Absence*—The Absence), and *Das Wiedersehen* (*Le Retour*—The Return).

68 *Stuart Mill:* John Stuart Mill (1806–1873), an English philosopher and political economist. In the introduction to his *System of Logic* (1843), Mill notes that "in the case of anything which can be called a science, the definition we set out with is seldom that which a more extensive knowledge of the subject shows to be most appropriate."

69 *Double beds are double graves:* Until shortly before his death, Krzhizhanovsky insisted on living apart from his longtime companion, Anna Bovshek. He maintained that life in one apartment, with the inevitable trivial concerns and unpalatable conditions, would destroy the enchantment of their relationship, kill the poetry of feeling.

72 *"Nothing in excess":* Said by Solon (ca. 640–558 BC), the Greek statesman and gnomic poet.

73 *notes published by a famous French sculptor:* Auguste Rodin (1840–1917), whose conversations with Paul Gsell about art were brought out by Éditions Grasset in 1911.

74 *Altenburg:* Peter Altenburg (1859–1919), a Viennese poet and impressionist writer; master of short, aphoristic stories drawn from passing events in everyday life.

77 *the four laws of thought:* The basis of rational thinking according to

Schopenhauer: 1) everything that is, exists; 2) nothing can simultaneously be and not be; 3) each and every thing either is or is not; 4) of every thing that is, it can be found why it is.

77 *"evening sacrifice":* See Psalm 141:1–2.

78 *The ax laid unto the root is a sorrow to haymakers:* See Matthew 3:10.
The parable about the wise virgins: See Matthew 25:1–13.

79 *Bartholomew's Day:* A wave of Catholic mob violence against Huguenots in Paris and the provinces (1572); the century's worst religious massacre.

the so-called insulted and injured: A reference to the title of Dostoevsky's 1861 novel.

81 *paralogism:* A fallacious or illogical argument or deduction.

THE BRANCH LINE

89 *harking back to Stephenson's time:* George Stephenson (1781–1848), an English engineer and inventor of the first steam locomotive (1814).

90 *Urania ripheus:* Diurnal sunset moth (originally mistaken for a butterfly) endemic to Madagascar; black with iridescent red, blue, and green markings.

92 *To sleep—to die:* An inversion of "To die, to sleep" in Hamlet's soliloquy.

"For the power of the poets": Recalls the last verse of a song that was famous in Soviet Russia during the Civil War:

> *Bravely into battle we'll go for the power of the Soviets*
> *And as one we shall gladly die in this struggle to best.*

In addition, this phrase half rhymes in Russian with the famous Bolshevik slogan "All power to the Soviets!"

93 *Thomas More:* English statesman and humanist (1478–1535); author of *Utopia* (1516), a political romance about an imaginary island nation in the New World living under a communistic democracy.

The head with the Head, I mean: More's principled refusal to accept King Henry VIII as head of the Church of England led to More's beheading for treason.

95 *Plato's famous cave:* A well-known analogy in *The Republic* in which prisoners chained in a fire-lit cave mistake their shadows on the wall for reality.

99 *the slow discharge of Crookes tubes:* Sir William Crookes (1832–1919), an English chemist and physicist, studied the phenomena produced by the discharge of electricity through evacuated glass cones or Crookes tubes, cathode-ray tubes that would lead to the invention of the television tube.

100 *Pascal:* Blaise Pascal (1623–1662), a French mathematician, scientist, and religious philosopher. For his discussion of dreams versus reality, see his *Pensées*, Section VI, number 386.

RED SNOW

111 *"Pravda, Pravda, Pravda!":* This phrase—that of a paper boy calling out the name of the Soviet daily *Pravda*—can also be understood to mean: "It's true, it's true, it's true!"—that is, it's true there isn't a soul in Moscow.

112 *a street photographer:* In a 1925 essay, Krzhizhanovsky called the canvas backdrops used by Moscow street photographers "the *last romanticism* remaining in the constructivist and efficient 'present day.' Only here can one still find fantastical castles, half-ruined towers, colonnades, and flights of marble steps overgrown with ivy and moss. Only here can one still see the garish stains of non-existent plants, blue spires of mountains and round blotches of weedy ponds with the inevitable white swans swaying among the reeds." CW, Vol. I, p. 562.

113 *"They sent me a questionnaire":* "Originally, the [Soviet] questionnaire was intended to cull people according to class, the crucial question being the one about social origin. For most of those with bad origins (noblemen, former bureaucrats, merchants, clerics), the doors to the new society slammed automatically shut. They could not find jobs or enter universities; they were deprived of ration cards and of the right to vote. During the 1920s and '30s

they were called *lishentsy* [disfranchised persons]." Andrei Sinyavsky, *Soviet Civilization* (New York: Arcade, 1990), p. 144.

113 *The Atheist: Bezbozhnik*, a satirical antireligious newspaper (1922–
1941) that used crude cartoons and caricatures to lampoon all religious belief as a sign of ignorance and superstition.

116 *twice-crowing cocks:* See Mark 14:30.

117 *the roar of a primus:* In *The New Russia* (p. 19), Dorothy Thompson
recalls the "subdued roar" of the primus, "the one-burner oil
stove, which more than any institution in modern Moscow as-
serts the eternity of the individualist ... On it one can cook one's
own *kasha*, boil one's own soup, in one's own sauce pan, and
while swearing allegiance to communism be one's own master in
the communal kitchen."

120 *In each of the square's four corners was a symbol—A, E, I, O:* The
square sign over the porch is a "square of opposition," a classical
diagram in Aristotelian logic showing how the four types of
premises in a syllogism relate logically to one another. A is diagonally opposite O, and E is diagonally opposite I. The diagonal
lines A–O and E–I are labeled contradictory (*contradictio*): A and
O premises are contradictory as are E and I premises. Premises are
contradictory when the truth of one implies the falsity of the
other, and vice versa.

A, E, I, O: These four vowels stand for the four types of premises in
a syllogism, which differ in quantity or quality:

1) A: All S are P—universal affirmative—All men are mortal.

2) E: All S are not P—universal negative—All men are not equal
No men are equal.

3) I: Some S are P—particular affirmative—Some men are wealthy.

4) O: Some S are not P—particular negative—Some men are not
wise.

it's for ... hmm ... logic: More specifically, this line is for deductive
syllogisms. First systematized by Aristotle, deductive syllogisms
are logical arguments consisting of a major premise, a minor
premise, and a conclusion. All three of the premises in a syllogism
consist of a subject and a predicate. For example:

Major premise: All men are mortal.

Minor premise: Socrates is a man.

Conclusion: Socrates is mortal.

or:

Major premise: All M are P.

Minor premise: All S are M.

Conclusion: All S are P.

middle terms: In a syllogism, the middle term (M) is the term that the two premises have in common; it serves as a bridge and falls away in the conclusion when the other two terms are brought together. Therefore, M never ends up in "S are P."

121 *'Barbara'...'Baroco'...'Bramantip'...'Bocardo':* Mnemonic names for four of the nineteen valid forms of syllogisms. The vowels in the names—A, E, I, O—show the types of premises in each syllogism: Barbara = AAA, Baroco = AOO, etc.

universal affirmative...particular negative: See note above on *A, E, I, O.*

"Next you'll be saying 'five or six,' like that landowner Chatsky home from Europe": At the end of act III in Griboyedov's *Woe from Wit* (1825), Chatsky admonishes Russian society for embracing "the little French man from Bordeaux" simply because he is French while rejecting the native son who has "five or six" ideas of his own.

THE THIRTEENTH CATEGORY OF REASON

125 *all twelve Kantian categories of reason:* In his *Critique of Pure Reason* (1781), the German philosopher Immanuel Kant distinguishes twelve pure concepts ("categories") of understanding divided into four classes: Unity, Plurality, Totality (Quantity); Reality, Negation, Limitation (Quality); Substance, Cause, Community (Relation); and Possibility, Existence, Necessity (Modality).

127 *recallist:* (Or *otzovist* from *otozvat'* "to recall.") Otzovists were members of a short-lived (1908–1909) radical faction within the Bolshevik Party. Rejecting all participation in Russia's legal institutions,

they demanded that their party's representatives in the State Duma be recalled.

130 *Antireligious Commission:* A secret commission created by the politburo in 1922 to undermine the Russian Orthodox Church and dismantle religion in the minds of believers. It would spawn *Bezbozhnik* (*The Atheist*, 1922), a newspaper whose readership would help launch the Union of Atheists (1925), a broad-based volunteer organization to fight religion and promote atheism with slogans like "Through Atheism to Communism!" The irate tenants of apartment 39 are evidently referring to the Union of Atheists, not the actual Antireligious Commission.

132 *Leonardo was right...:* In his posthumously published *Treatise on Painting*, the fifteenth-century Italian master remarks: "It would not be too much of an effort to pause sometimes to look into these stains on walls, the ashes from the fire, the clouds, the mud, or other similar places. If these are well contemplated, you will find fantastic inventions that awaken the genius of the painter to new inventions, such as compositions of battles, animals, and men, as well as diverse composition of landscapes, and monstrous things, as devils and the like..."

MEMORIES OF THE FUTURE

138 *Dal's:* Vladimir Dal (1801–1872), a Russian lexicographer of Danish descent whose classic compendium of Russian proverbs contains more than 30,000 entries.

A Russified German colonist: In the 1760s some 30,000 Germans settled along the Volga River at the suggestion of Russia's German-born empress Catherine the Great; she invited her compatriots to farm the Russian steppe while preserving their language, culture, and traditions.

the year 1905: The first Russian Revolution began in January 1905 with labor strikes in St. Petersburg and the Bloody Sunday massacre of a thousand peaceful demonstrators near the Winter Palace;

the peasant uprisings that followed were especially acute along the Volga.

139 *Rupert's drops:* Glass teardrops tapering to a needlelike end formed by dripping molten glass into a vat of cold water. The compression of the water-cooled outside coupled with the still-warm inside produces a body that can withstand the blow of a hammer, whereas the wispy end, if broken, will cause the drop, as Samuel Pepys noted in his *Diary* (13 January 1662), "to break all to dust." These glass mysteries were brought to England in the 1640s by Prince Rupert of the Rhine.

140 *Gomel:* A city in Byelorussia whose population in the nineteenth century was more than half Jewish.

141 *a cipher jumping from atom to atom:* "Modern laboratories of psycho-technology are working on measuring the so-called *duration of the present*: it turns out that 'the present,' that atom of time indivisible in minds, divides into parts and changes its value when in a psychotechnological gage . . ." From Krzhizhanovsky's 1925 essay "Kollektsia secund" (A Collection of Seconds), CW, Vol. I, p. 569.

The Time Machine: A pioneering science-fiction story (1895) by H. G. Wells. An amateur inventor travels 30 million years into the future where he discovers the dark and deserted Earth to be all but dead.

144 *Schopenhauerism:* The extreme pessimism of German philosopher Arthur Schopenhauer (1788–1860), who saw man as doomed to live at the suffering effect of his selfish desires.

145 *Spencer:* Herbert Spencer (1820–1903), an English philosopher and social scientist whose works include *Principles of Psychology* (1855).

150 *Pythagorean:* Pythagoras (6th century BC), a Greek philosopher and mathematician.

The genius who settled relations between the hypotenuse and the catheti: Pythagoras, whose theorem in Euclidean geometry states that in a right triangle, when c is the hypotenuse (the longest side) and a and b are the catheti (the other two sides), then: $a^2 + b^2 = c^2$.

Leibniz: Gottfried Wilhelm Leibniz (1646–1716), a German philosopher, mathematician, and logician. His treatise *Monadology* (1714) holds that the divine order of the universe is reflected in each of its irreducible parts, or monads, subjects that contain all their successive predicates.

152 *Kozikha:* A section of Moscow in and around Bolshoi Kozikhinsky Lane and Maly Kozikhinsky Lane, not far from Patriarch's Ponds.

155 *the syllogism's major and minor premises:* See notes on syllogisms for "Red Snow."

Khapilovka: A small river in northeastern Moscow; the Yauza's largest tributary.

160 *Roland ... Roncesvalles:* Trapped in a pass (Roncesvalles) in the Pyrenees by an army of Muslims, the dying Roland strikes his magic sword repeatedly against the rock. He wants to break it to keep it from falling into pagan hands, but the sword will not break. (*La Chanson de Roland,* stanzas 171–173.)

162 *"Raum und Zeit":* "Space and Time," a lecture delivered by Hermann Minkowski (see note for p. 195) in Cologne in 1908. "Hitherto, natural phenomena had been thought to occur in a space of three dimensions and to flow uniformly through time. Minkowski maintained that the separation of time and space is a false conception; that time itself is a dimension, comparable to length, breadth, and height; and that therefore the true conception of reality was constituted by a space-time continuum possessing these four dimensions." J.W. Carter and P.H. Muir, editors, *Printing and the Mind of Man,* (London: Cassell, 1967) p. 241.

167 *Moscow's Bryansk Station:* Now the Kiev Station.

168 *the events of October:* A euphemism for the Bolshevik coup in October 1917 that brought Lenin to power.

169 *House Committee:* See note on same for "Quadraturin."

two Zachatevsky lanes: In all, Moscow has three Zachatevsky lanes (1st, 2nd, and 3rd), old roads which grew up around the sixteenth-century Zachatevsky Convent.

173 *A street photographer:* See note on same for "Red Snow."

175 *to at least 1861, or ten years before that:* In other words, ten years before serfdom in Russia was abolished.

176 *Lucretius:* Full name Titus Lucretius Carus (ca. 98–55 BC), a Roman

poet whose *De rerum natura* (*On the Nature of Things*), a philosophical epic in six books, champions atomism as opposed to divine providence. The quoted verse (translated by G.S.) is from the opening of Book II.

177 *in their wrangles with questionnaires:* Soviet citizens had to fill out detailed questionnaires concerning their past (that is, their life before the 1917 Revolution) when applying for a new job, to a university, for membership in the Communist Party, etc. To avoid incriminating themselves, applicants often invented new pasts, which they then had to remember for the next questionnaire.

178 *Ivan Elpidiforovich:* Apparently Pavel Elpidiforovich's brother (Elpidiforovich is the patronymic derived from the very uncommon name Elpidifor).

181 *November 7:* The New Style anniversary of the October Revolution.

183 *Chypre:* A French perfume created by François Coty in 1917, based on a blend of bergamot, amber resins, and oak moss from Cyprus.

187 *Eleazar:* A story with a biblical theme by Leonid Andreyev (1871–1919). Eleazar (the Hebrew form of the Greek name Lazarus) is the brother of Mary and Martha, whom Jesus raised from the dead. In Andreyev's version, Eleazar returns to life in body but not in soul; his dead eyes suck the life out of everyone and everything around him. Andreyev also wrote a story called "Prizraki" (Ghosts).

190 *Husserl:* Edmund Husserl (1859–1938), a German philosopher known as the father of phenomenonology, a science describing consciousness and its intentionality.

The Poverty of Philosophy: Written in 1847 by the German socialist Karl Marx as a rebuttal of *The Philosophy of Poverty* by the French socialist Pierre-Joseph Proudhon.

192 *Izvestia:* Daily newspaper and official mouthpiece of the Soviet government.

193 *moonlight flitter:* A person who disappears in the night with all his belongings to avoid paying rent.

195 *Riemann:* Bernhard Riemann (1826–1866), a German mathematician who developed a non-Euclidean geometry dealing with curved spaces in two, three, or more dimensions.

195 *Minkowski:* Hermann Minkowski (1864–1909), a German mathematician who introduced the idea of a four-dimensional continuum called "space-time." A point in space-time is located by means of three space coordinates (x, y, and z) and a time coordinate (t).

197 *Lobachevsky:* Nikolai Lobachevsky (1792–1856), a Russian mathematician; founder of non-Euclidean geometry.

widdershins: In a direction contrary to the apparent course of the sun; counterclockwise.

deasil: Clockwise.

208 *the airy gate tower:* Krutitsky Teremok (tower), a seventeenth-century addition to a thirteenth-century ensemble originally used as an archbishop's residence. The tower and holy gates are faced with some 2,000 multicolored enamel tiles.

214 *"Take me to the land of those who understand":* In Russian, this line of Shterer's nearly rhymes with a line from Nikolai Nekrasov's poem "Knight for an Hour" (1862): "Take me to the land of those who perish" (*Uvedi menya v stan pogibayushikh*). Shterer substituted *ponimayushikh* ("of those who understand") for *pogibayushikh* ("of those who perish").

OTHER NEW YORK REVIEW CLASSICS*

TITLES IN SERIES

*For a complete list of titles, visit www.nyrb.com or write to:
Catalog Requests, NYRB, 435 Hudson Street, New York, NY 10014*

ANDREY PLATONOV Soul and Other Stories
J.F. POWERS Morte d'Urban
J.F. POWERS The Stories of J.F. Powers
J.F. POWERS Wheat That Springeth Green
CHRISTOPHER PRIEST Inverted World
RAYMOND QUENEAU We Always Treat Women Too Well
RAYMOND QUENEAU Witch Grass
RAYMOND RADIGUET Count d'Orgel's Ball
JEAN RENOIR Renoir, My Father
GREGOR VON REZZORI Memoirs of an Anti-Semite
GREGOR VON REZZORI The Snows of Yesteryear: Portraits for an Autobiography
TIM ROBINSON Stones of Aran: Labyrinth
TIM ROBINSON Stones of Aran: Pilgrimage
FR. ROLFE Hadrian the Seventh
WILLIAM ROUGHEAD Classic Crimes
CONSTANCE ROURKE American Humor: A Study of the National Character
TAYEB SALIH Season of Migration to the North
GERSHOM SCHOLEM Walter Benjamin: The Story of a Friendship
DANIEL PAUL SCHREBER Memoirs of My Nervous Illness
JAMES SCHUYLER Alfred and Guinevere
JAMES SCHUYLER What's for Dinner?
LEONARDO SCIASCIA The Day of the Owl
LEONARDO SCIASCIA Equal Danger
LEONARDO SCIASCIA The Moro Affair
LEONARDO SCIASCIA To Each His Own
LEONARDO SCIASCIA The Wine-Dark Sea
VICTOR SEGALEN René Leys
PHILIPE-PAUL DE SÉGUR Defeat: Napoleon's Russian Campaign
VICTOR SERGE The Case of Comrade Tulayev
VICTOR SERGE Unforgiving Years
SHCHEDRIN The Golovlyov Family
GEORGES SIMENON Dirty Snow
GEORGES SIMENON The Engagement
GEORGES SIMENON The Man Who Watched Trains Go By
GEORGES SIMENON Monsieur Monde Vanishes
GEORGES SIMENON Red Lights
GEORGES SIMENON The Strangers in the House
GEORGES SIMENON Three Bedrooms in Manhattan
GEORGES SIMENON Tropic Moon
GEORGES SIMENON The Widow
CHARLES SIMIC Dime-Store Alchemy: The Art of Joseph Cornell
MAY SINCLAIR Mary Olivier: A Life
TESS SLESINGER The Unpossessed: A Novel of the Thirties
VLADIMIR SOROKIN Ice
VLADIMIR SOROKIN The Queue
CHRISTINA STEAD Letty Fox: Her Luck
GEORGE R. STEWART Names on the Land
STENDHAL The Life of Henry Brulard
ADALBERT STIFTER Rock Crystal
THEODOR STORM The Rider on the White Horse
HOWARD STURGIS Belchamber
ITALO SVEVO As a Man Grows Older